The Pond Scum Gang

Gregory Saur

Also by Gregory Saur

Finding Innocence, Book One: Strange Old World

Finding Innocence, Book II: Strange New People

Finding Innocence, Book the Third: Strange Happenings

Royal Pains and Angels in the Outhouse: One Big Little League Story That Goes a Bit Foul

Otherworld: Orcish Delight (as G. D. Saur)

Stuck in the Past (with Jack Irish)

Panterror! The Epic Babysitting Adventures of Rachel Pugsley

Soccer Star

The Pond Scum Gang

Gregory Saur

A Saur & Saur Publishing Project

Pond Scum Gang

Copyright © 2016 by Gregory Saur.
All rights reserved. No part of this book may be reproduced, stored in a retrieval system or
transmitted in any form or by any means without the prior written permission of the
publisher, except by a kind reviewer who may quote brief passages in a good review to be
printed in a newspaper, magazine, or journal. Please do not treat books or any person like
pond scum.

This is a work of fiction. All characters and events from this novel are fictitious and
are not meant to bear any resemblance to any real or imagined persons, living or
dead. Thank you for your cooperation.

First Paperback Printing
October 2019

Printed in the United States of America

ISBN-13 (pb): 978-1949317121

Cover art by R. S.
Copyright © 2016 by Saur & Saur

To Amanda, for having the courage and grace to bear with the beasts all those years ago.

And ...

Thank you, Richard Church, for starting the journey so many years ago...

May the adventure never die.

Acknowledgments

Many wonderful people had a hand in allowing me to create this story. Firstly, this is a work of fiction. I did grow up in Yorktown, Virginia, and have had a great many adventures in the woods around battlefields from the Revolutionary War and Civil War periods. That said, this story is about an entirely fictional battlefield that exists only in my imagination. The National Park Service has been and is nothing but brilliant. Its work and support for Yorktown and other parks is exceptional and laudable. I particularly want to thank all the Park Rangers who gave their time to speak to and answer questions from a particular nosy brat from 1990 to the present. Secondly, a big thank you goes to all my editors and readers for their support and patience. Special thanks to Ce-ce Cox of Outside-Eyes Editing & Proofreading for her patience and talent. Also to Diana Cox for her skill and sharp eyes. And finally, thank you to my family—especially my younger sister, for her love and patience in dealing with my writing habit. May it continue.

Two students forward, in the front of the class, Lisa barely moved her blond curls as she sidled closer to the teacher's side.

"Mr. Freeman, we're safe, right?" Her large grayish eyes quivered slightly and her hands tugged at Mr. Freeman's sleeves. "The dogs won't come around here ... right?"

"Oh, of course!" came the confident reply. "As long as we stay on this path and away from the woods, we're perfectly safe! The Park Service warned about the dogs, but they mostly come out at night. Maybe if we were chickens we would be in danger." The teacher laughed at his own joke.

"Uh-oh, that's you, Danny!" quipped Derek, digging in another elbow. Derek was taller than most in the fifth grade and his elbow always went high on Danny, getting the upper ribs.

"I'm not a chicken. Besides, you're a boy, too," Danny muttered as he rubbed his pudgy side. "So there. Girls are smarter than you too."

Danny had a round head and a round body—so much so that his nickname in the second grade had been roly-poly. While pudgy, he had boyish good looks that he carried well. Light-colored skin had tanned nicely and he had short brown curls covering the top of his head, with round, light blue eyes and a button nose. These eyes took in a lot, but he let little escape. Often his feelings were well bottled, but when they did come out, it was like he spilled the entire bottle. Derek liked to call him emotional, but mostly Danny controlled his feelings. When he did get angry, it never lasted for long and he never held grudges. Despite this, Danny liked being a follower and could be counted on to go with the group. While never with the popular crowd, he was at least well liked.

"You're wrong, Danny boy." Derek stretched to his full height and grinned down at his friend. With a long neck and lightly tanned skin, Derek looked grown-up compared to Danny. "I'm practically a man."

From behind them, a girl with roughly cut bangs and shaggy hair the color of burlap snorted.

Instantly Derek's handsome face curled into an ugly sneer. "Quiet, Beast!" he shot behind him. "The wild dogs are probably part of your family! They're out here looking for you, you know."

Even though he spoke through his teeth, he was clearly heard. Corey and some of the other boys in the class laughed. Even so, Mr. Freeman never looked back. Not one of the three chaperones even glanced at Derek. One, Lisa's mom, kept looking back behind her, in almost desperate hope.

Ducking in shame, the girl known to the entire fifth grade as the Beast hid behind the shaggy hair that hung in her eyes and made no reply. It was with a resigned slump that she lowered her shoulders and followed the path.

Derek's eyes slid by her and fell back to Danny. "Well, at least you're smarter than *some* girls."

Corey chuckled. "She's not a girl. She's a beast."

Nearby, Corey's best friend Jonathan laughed raucously like he hadn't heard that five hundred times.

Danny gave a tight grin but said nothing.

It was the end-of-the-year field trip—the one promised way back in September as a sort of celebration for surviving the standardized testing season. And tempers were getting as short as some of the students. Set up by Mr. Freeman, it featured a walking tour of the famous Revolutionary War battlefield just outside the school grounds. At the same time, it also served as a goodbye to fifth grade and goodbye to a popular teacher. In just a couple of (long) weeks, the school year would draw to a close and give way to the two sweetest words in the language of children. Summer vacation. That seemed like a long time coming.

To get to the battlefield from Knox Elementary, the fifth-grade classes had to walk across a side road and then cut through a thin strip of woods before reaching a wide-open field. Almost 250 years before, an army of British soldiers had surrendered to Washington's army in that very field.

Surrounded by trees, the wide grassy area was just a small section of the miles and miles of the National Park. All around this field were leftover trenches once occupied by Washington's men. Stretching for miles in some areas, they faced other trenches built all around a small town with its back to a river. These trenches were once used by the British soldiers. Dotting the trenches on both sides were historical cannons and signs describing the events.

14

The other fifth-grade classes had declined this part of the tour. It was a hot, muggy day in subtropical southeastern Virginia. The humidity had risen with the sun and promised to hang around. The trip that had started early in the morning, just after the 9:05 bell, had now moved an hour past noon. Lunch had ended and so had many of the good moods. Only Mr. Freeman kept a bright, cheery attitude.

In the morning, the fifth graders had walked through the field and followed a road to the main battlefield. The whole time, Mr. Freeman acted like a kid in a toy store. He wanted to stop at every cannon and at each sign to not only read but to teach in great detail just exactly what happened at that particular spot. To the other teachers, and many fifth graders, it was hot, sweaty torture.

After hours of walking through and around the battlements, they eventually had come to a small museum run by the National Park Service. Located just outside the town in the middle of the British line of defenses, the museum not only had a gift shop but also air-conditioning. The other teachers, all female, older, and plumper than Mr. Freeman, had staged a mini-mutiny and declared that their classes would remain at the museum until departure time.

When hearing this rebellion near the end of lunch, Mr. Freeman was undeterred. Tight-lipped and with fists clenched, he'd turned his back on his colleagues and took his students from the air-conditioned museum. Crossing a road and marching like a general to battle, he'd led his class to the American line of trenches. At the time, none of his students complained. Mr. Freeman had promised extra time at the gift shop on their return and an ice cream party the next day.

"Does everyone see how these trenches were made?" he called out loudly, gesturing to the large wall of dirt on their left. "If you boys were in the army back then, you would have made these with just shovels and your hands."

"It's so hot," wheezed Danny. "I would let the other guys do it."

Derek stepped on the back of Danny's shoe, causing it to slide off his heel and flatten underneath.

"Flat tire!" Derek crowed. "If you were in the army you would be cleaning my boots. I would be an officer."

Danny grunted. "Oh, yeah. I would spit shine your boots—on the inside." Bending down to fix his shoe, he reached over and yanked at Derek's shoelaces.

Derek nearly tripped into the back of the student in front of him.

The girl known as the Beast laughed.

"Shut your face, Beast," Derek snarled. "If you were in the army you would be shot for food!"

"Quiet back there!" barked Mr. Freeman. As he turned to his class, his words were obeyed.

Possessing an inexhaustible supply of energy, Mr. Freeman rarely lost his temper. Usually he just needed to sweep his sharp eyes over his class and he gathered instant attention. At this moment, his usually smiling mouth tilted toward a frown.

"We're all on the same side, remember," he told his students gravely. As he did so, his large hand brushed aside a lock of his sandy hair, darkened by sweat. (Lisa fluttered her eyelashes.) "Let's act like a good army and support each other. Right?"

"Yes, sir!" called Corey.

Derek promptly saluted. His dad served as an officer in the Air Force and he made sure everyone knew it. Derek didn't actively play sports. He tried baseball, but it never caught on. Soccer, he claimed, was for sissies, and he would play football the following fall.

Still, he was considered a better athlete than most and almost always got to be a team captain at recess. He carried a few extra pounds, but carried it well. His chest puffed out and his stomach sucked in, he had the look of a rooster in a barnyard. One day he too would be an officer. This was something else he let everyone know.

Mr. Freeman grinned. "That's the spirit! Forward, men ... and, uh, women. Let's march!"

Lisa and the other girls giggled. They looked ready to follow their teacher anywhere. Even the boys bit their tongues and stood up straighter.

Many of the earthen walls of the trenches were hidden by the thick trees that covered much of the National Park. Only the front lines were exposed to the sunshine and these were mostly covered in tall grass. A narrow path ran between the trenches and woods and was once perhaps used by American troops to stage the final assault that broke the British spirit and led to victory. At least this is what Mr. Freeman told his class. They were walking in the footsteps of history.

"More like footprints of sweat," Danny had moaned.

"Okay," announced the teacher. "Everyone, stop right here."

Danny breathed a huge sigh of relief. "Finally," he groaned. "My feet hurt … and these bugs are everywhere!"

"Not near me," Derek said, running a hand through his hair. A mane of dark brownish-blond hair ran to the back of his neck. Cut short on the front and the sides, it was spiked in the middle. Danny liked to tease him that he had a mullet. On this particular morning, his hair smelled distinctively of bug spray.

Other kids were slapping at the bugs, but few voiced their displeasure. Nobody wanted to be seen as a complainer in front of Mr. Freeman.

Derek smirked and stood tall. Immediately a large black horsefly buzzed in his face and caused him to slap wildly while dancing back.

"Gather around, kids!" Mr. Freeman's command rang through the tall grass and caused the entire group to crowd forward and form a semicircle around their teacher. "Remember, stay away from the woods. Not only are there wild dogs loose out there, but also ticks and other bugs."

"What other bugs?" mumbled a chaperone, a large woman with tight-fitting jeans. She waved a disgusted hand in her face. "Every bug on the planet is following us."

"That's because we have the Beast," Corey cracked. "They're following her."

"She should shower once in a while," said Jonathan rudely.

Both boys were on the hefty side, but athletic. Jonathan was a star football player, while Corey shined in soccer. They were popular and knew it. Even the girls giggled.

"Where's the little spaz?" Corey suddenly asked. "He could eat all the bugs."

Immediately the last chaperone jumped and looked back again. All the chaperones were moms and looked flushed, tired, and miserable. This one looked not only miserable but almost frightened ... and a little guilty.

"Okay, troops, listen up!" Mr. Freeman barked. He stood like a flagpole in the midst of a disorganized militia. "Everyone here?"

The last chaperone jerked uncomfortably and quickly searched the back trail again. She did not like what she did not see.

"Present and all accounted for, sir!" Derek snapped a crisp salute and stood his straightest.

"Good!" snapped the teacher. "You boys and girls are enjoying this trip so far?"

"YES!" chorused twenty-one high-pitched voices, led by Derek.

Mr. Freeman flushed with pleasure at the response. "Great!" he said. "Are we going to show the other classes all the fun they're missing?"

"YES!" cried the obedient chorus.

"Excellent!" Mr. Freeman beamed a bright smile and put his hands on his hips. "Then let me tell you about this fence behind me ..."

Chapter 2

The "little spaz" had a name.

Thad Utley leaned impatiently against the tall pine tree. Tilting over the deep ravine, it looked ready to plummet into the stream below at any moment. A hurricane the summer before had loosened the soil around the roots. Nearly defying the laws of physics, the tree provided a good place for a body to rest … until the day when it would lose to gravity.

Thad wasn't trying to rest. He desperately was trying to control his temper.

The object of his sour disposition crouched beneath him at the stream. This was the little spaz.

Why did he have to be partnered with *him?* Thad thought for the millionth time since the pairings were first made in the classroom that morning.

"Hurry up," he yelled without looking down. "They're probably way ahead of us now!"

"Are you guys finished yet?" called Donald Bass.

Thad sighed again. "No, not yet!" he called back. He couldn't believe Mr. Freeman would lose track of not one or two students, but three!

"Don't move, Thad. I'm coming to you."

"Sure, okay." Thad pushed himself from the tree and nearly stumbled into the ravine. "Join the party," he mumbled, slapping at a mosquito.

In a few moments, Donald nervously emerged from a crowd of bushes and gulped.

Donald was a tall, thin boy with lean muscle and a short flattop haircut. His face was a little thin, but still handsome with a wide nose, narrow lips, and bright white teeth. His rich dark brown skin nearly blended in with the trees. With long legs and a short torso, he ran and played basketball with the grace of a gazelle.

However, once away from civilization, when surrounded by trees, he moved like a victim in a horror movie. His soft brown eyes widened in horror as he took in all the trees around him. Every few moments, he slapped a bug.

"What are you guys doing?" he demanded, searching the trees for a wild animal.

"I'm doing nothing! It's that dumb spaz down there holding everything up!"

Donald grunted. He had a high pleasant voice that was now tinged with fear. He clearly preferred to do his nature walks on video game screens in the comfort of his house.

Thad never said a word about Donald's fear of the outdoors and never would. Donald Bass was his current best friend ... soon to be his former best friend. Just one week into summer vacation, Donald would be moving to California. When that happened, Thad's life would utterly stink. Thad would lose his best friend. Gone.

They'd first met at a summer camp when they were both in the third grade. Instantly bonding, they became even closer when Donald's family moved into Thad's neighborhood the previous summer. Unfortunately, Donald's father moved a lot since he had trouble finding work. Former military, Donald's dad was going back to be near his parents, who happened to live on the other side of the country.

Thad kicked at a pinecone. Why couldn't some other kid have to move—a kid like the little spaz?

Once Donald left, Thad would be left with just Danny and Derek as his friends. Danny lived across the street from him and was almost as close a friend as Donald. Derek, however, lived a few streets over and tended to take charge whenever he was around.

20

Thad suspected Derek kept their friendship only because nobody else put up with his bossiness. For the past week the boys had been meeting after school to come up with plans to say a last goodbye to Donald. They wanted one final adventure, but so far had come up with nothing. The biggest obstacle, Thad didn't want to admit, was Donald's absolute fear of anything to do with nature. Camping—Thad's suggestion—was certainly ruled out.

Donald's voice broke into his thoughts. "Hey, Thad," he said worriedly, "maybe you should go and see what he's doing."

Thad scowled. "He's supposed to be using the bathroom, so I'm not real sure it's a good idea to look."

Donald grimaced. "Jak?" he called. "Jak, what are you doing?"

"There's fish down here!" cried a high, excited voice. "I almost caught one! You should come down and see!"

Thad slapped a hand over his eyes. "Why me?" he groaned. He knew why. It was for the simple reason that no other kid, besides Donald, would ever tolerate being near the little spaz. Once Donald had partnered with Lisa and the little spaz stood all alone with nobody even looking at him, Mr. Freeman had told Thad to pair up.

His actual name was Jak Tranner. Almost every other kid in the fifth grade was eleven years old and acted older. Jak had just turned ten and acted half that ... but with a keen, devious mind. So far Thad had only discovered two things Jak liked doing: playing soccer and getting into trouble. He was very good at doing both.

Moving to the edge of the leaf-covered ravine, Thad looked down. "Jak, it's been over five minutes! You're going to get us in trouble!"

A small boy crouching at the water looked up. Dirt smudged his face and his jeans were covered in mud. The rumor was that Jak had been adopted from Romania and had gypsy blood. Few doubted.

While he had chestnut brown hair, his eyes were a dark, dark brown and nearly black. Narrow and slightly slanted as if Asian, they almost always glinted with mischief. Thad heard more than one teacher, when thinking no students were around, refer to him as part evil and definitely possessed—and advise others not to be fooled by his appearance. His nose was slightly upturned and his mouth had dimples when he smiled. His hair hung just over his eyes and ended just above his neck. Unruly tufts of sideburns nearly covered his two small ears. Scrawny and short, his legs were thin but lined with muscle, and he ran like a deer.

This helped him a lot, because his angelic looks were the opposite of his behavior. Constantly trying to skip class, he had no problem with walking out whenever bored with an assignment, or just not showing up in the morning.

During the times he was in class, it was even worse. Tapping his pencil, pretending to snore loudly, dropping his books, throwing pieces of paper, and pulling off dried gum from the bottoms of desks to put on the chairs of other students were just some of his classroom shenanigans.

Whenever the class lost recess time or was lectured for poor behavior by another teacher, it was always his fault. When he first arrived as a new student in September, the girls and teachers thought he was cute.

By October the girls thought him an annoying pest and the teachers a curse from the school board. This was because, despite all his trouble, his father, real or not, was an instructional specialist working for the county's school board. This meant Jak had to be tolerated ... which was virtually impossible.

And Jak seemed to know he was safe. No matter what the teachers did, no matter how loud or long they yelled at him, Jak just took it with a grimace. Or worse, he would smile. When Jak smiled, his eyes, full of intelligence, peered at you and through you, locating and pinpointing your weakest point. His lips would curve dangerously, much like the Grinch before stealing Christmas, and he would know. Then he would wait.

He would wait until a time when he could exploit whatever weakness he'd found. Most of it would be done in such a way he wouldn't get into any trouble.

For instance, Mr. Freeman loved a quiet classroom during work time. Once, still fairly early in the year, he'd called Jak to the front and gave a long, pointed lecture about how Jak needed to stop distracting others and do his work quietly.

The entire class heard and clapped long and loud when the lecture had finished.

Jak had only listened with tight lips. When dismissed, he'd never said a word, but marched to his desk and sat down loudly. This had prompted a reprimand from Mr. Freeman and Jak crossed his arms crossly and sulked. After a moment of silence, he'd suddenly smiled and picked up his pencil to work.

After the class, Mr. Freeman had complimented him for doing a great job.

The next day, Jak had been the first to arrive and was sitting quietly. Later, during math class, Jak's least favorite class, Jak had continued his uncommonly good behavior. While the class had worked busily on a series of pre-algebra problems, Mr. Freeman smiled.

He'd just opened his mouth to tell how wonderful it was to hear great minds think when a sudden, loud beeping noise went off. Everyone but Jak had looked up with a start. Nobody could find the source. Mr. Freeman ended up searching his desk for three minutes before finding a small timer stuffed in the bottom of his drawer.

"Must have accidentally set itself," he'd mumbled, puzzled.

He'd never used timers and deplored their use—having students work under the pressure of time wasn't learning to him. But then another timer abruptly went off—this one coming from his closet across the room.

Mr. Freeman's jaw clenched. "What the ..."

He'd eventually found it buried in a dark corner ... next to a pile of dead cockroaches. It was the second of many loud interruptions to come.

In total, by the end of math, fifteen well-hidden timers had gone off, each at a different time and each in a different part of the classroom. Many of them had dead or alive cockroaches nearby—including the timer stuffed in an eraser box crawling with legs.

By the end, Mr. Freeman had been red faced with silent fury. Through it all, Jak had never stopped working and had turned in his papers just after Mr. Freeman had called for a janitor to conduct a thorough search for timers and cockroaches.

The principal had been less than amused when he arrived, accompanying the puzzled janitor. By that time the classroom was in shambles. Girls and boys were shrieking over cockroaches and yelling whenever the next timer went off.

It had gotten to the point where silence was the worst—because at any moment another timer could go off. When it was all over, nobody could pin it on Jak, but every timer found did have a school board label stuck on the back.

If Jak had any friends after that incident, they were well hidden. At the same time, nobody went out of their way to bother him. At recess, he dominated in soccer, and besides, to get on his bad side meant waiting for something horrible to happen … at any moment.

Thad was very aware of all of this. He sat behind Jak in class and was a keen observer. Many times he'd seen Jak bring in a beetle or bug from recess and keep it in his desk. Jak was very comfortable with insect life and would find nothing wrong with touching dead or live cockroaches. Thad could have told Mr. Freeman this, but that would only bring Jak's wrath on him. Besides, he was no tattler, and sometimes Jak's antics could be a good thing—especially when it delayed a test nobody had studied for.

Only now, he desperately wished Mr. Freeman would send somebody to find them.

When they'd just reached the American line of trenches after lunch, Jak had sweetly told their chaperone, Mrs. Jefferies, that he needed to use the bathroom. They were near the back of the group and Jak had been having one of his good days—he'd actually behaved himself most of the morning. Resembling her daughter, considered one of the prettiest girls in the class, Mrs. Jefferies looked down at the nice-looking boy and bit a long red fingernail.

"Er, I think we're too far from the museum …"

"I really, really need to go."

Mr. Freeman had stopped the class next to a sign telling which American regiment had fought at this section of the battlefield.

"I tell you what … you're a boy, um, run behind a tree real fast. Wait, don't go alone. Take your partner. Where is he?"

Thad had groaned and tried to duck behind Donald.

"Don't worry, I'll go with you, too," Donald said when Jak, jumping up and down, pointed to Thad.

So the three had left their class and went into the woods ... just before Mr. Freeman warned of the wild dogs.

Wild dogs were not uncommon in that area. Many owners, perhaps cruelly or maybe stupidly, abandoned their pets, often in the woods of the park. In this way, dogs found other dogs and formed new families. They lived free in the wild. The woods were packed with raccoons, deer, groundhogs, squirrels, and other small animals to eat.

Mr. Freeman told the class earlier that the Park Service occasionally would send hunting parties into the woods to get rid of the dogs, but only if they caused trouble by bothering humans or pets.

"And don't worry," he said. "They use tranquilizer guns for this business."

Apparently this particular pack had recently run into a flock of chickens owned by the Park for historical teaching and ate a good portion of it.

Going off after Jak, Donald had paused at the edge of the trees and nervously said he would watch out for dogs.

Jak had already raced ahead, and Thad, muttering to himself, had struggled to keep up. This part of Virginia was full of ravines, and being close to the river, some of the ravines had streams that fed into creeks. Thad found Jak at the first ravine and had been waiting ever since.

Now, looking down at the boy, Thad struggled to keep his temper.

Jak grinned and wiped muddy hands on the front of his green T-shirt and then on the back of his jeans. "Are you coming down?"

"No!" exploded Thad. "You're coming up! The class already left us."

Jak shrugged, unconcerned. "Let's follow the stream and see where it leads."

"Jak, you have to come back, now!"

He gave Thad another grin. "But I haven't used the bathroom yet."

"But, but—" Spluttering, Thad threw up his hands as Jak started running, heading downstream. Not knowing what else to do, he followed.

Donald called after them, but was soon far back.

This, Thad decided, was the worst day of his life. His best friend was moving away soon and he was about to get lost in the woods with a little spaz. But maybe things would get better— maybe a wild dog would eat him.

Chapter 3

Mr. Freeman beamed as he leaned against the split-rail fence, which he'd just thoroughly explained to his class.

"Let's review. What is this fence made out of?"

"Wood!" cried Lisa.

"No nails," Derek hollered immediately after, looking at Lisa.

They'd reached an opening in the line of trenches where a narrow tour road snaked through, heading off into the woods. On either side of the road, a fence made of stacked rails up to Mr. Freeman's waist zigzagged alongside up to the tree line.

Danny rolled his eyes and groaned. "I'm dying of heat and we're talking about a stupid stick fence on a hot day in the hot sun."

"Yes!" Mr. Freeman said over Danny. "And what's so special about these fences?"

"They're not sweating like me," mumbled Danny.

"They're missing," Mrs. Jefferies said after clearing her throat.

"These babies," Mr. Freeman said, patting his hand on the top rail, "are so strong they can keep bulls and pigs out."

"Really?" asked Lisa doubtfully.

Derek moved beside her. "How?" he asked as he looked at Lisa's face and tried to wink.

"Really," intoned Mr. Freeman. He backed up and leaned against the fence. "On farms they built these fences horse high, bull strong, and pig tight."

"Big whoop," Corey said, wiping his face. "They should have built air-conditioning."

Jonathan cackled. "Hey," he said, "pig tight, huh? Sorry, Beast, but you can't get through that fence!"

The girl known as the Beast shuffled backwards, her eyes hidden in her hair. Taller than most girls her age, she had the gait and posture of a boy trying to pose as a gangster. Long limbed and deep voiced, she had little chance of fitting in with her classmates. Everything was made worse by being new in town and living in a trailer park. The last part actually began as a rumor back in November, but turned out to be true when one Sunday Jonathan saw her outside a run-down trailer when driving to church. He couldn't wait to tell the news on Monday morning.

What started first as small gossip had turned into full-fledged bullying as the year progressed. Corey came up with the name "Beast" at lunch early in October and it quickly caught on. Nobody spoke to her unless they were mocking her. Everyone dreaded having to sit by her or, worse, work with her on an assignment. For her part, she took it well, at least in public.

Ducking her head to hide behind her hair, she bit her tongue and refused to react. Most thought she was too dumb to even notice … After all, she never noticed her wardrobe, right? Her clothes were always old and smelled bad—sneakers, jeans, and a T-shirt with a slight stale stench. In the winter months she had worn a torn jacket. Her name was Mandy Purcell. Everyone, except teachers, called her the Beast.

The day only grew hotter, and on this day everybody wore sneakers, long jeans, and T-shirts. At least, on that part, the Beast managed to fit in. Long pants were mandatory for the trip to keep ticks away and to prevent scratches from thorns growing next to the path. They did nothing to provide comfort or to give a boost in morale.

"Um, they're missing," Mrs. Jefferies said again. She nervously ran a hand over her face, smearing makeup and sweat.

Mr. Freeman crossed his arms and got comfortable against the fence. "Think about it," he said to his class, ignoring the chaperones. "You lived on a farm, right? Back then, all your animals were free range, which meant they could go anywhere they wanted. The fences were built to keep the animals out, not in! Pretty neat, huh?"

Hair streaked with sweat and face red with heat, Danny stumbled from the standing group and went to the fence to take seat. Touching the rail with his hand caused him to yelp and jump back. "Not neat, concrete!" he said in amazement. "These fences aren't wood!"

His teacher frowned at him. "Ah, uh, they were wood back then, Danny."

"They're missing!" Mrs. Jefferies practically shrieked. She'd pushed her way to the front to face Mr. Freeman. Lisa looked at her in horror, her face red with embarrassment.

"Oh, no," chucked Mr. Freeman. "These fences aren't missing anything. They just used concrete to keep rot—"

"No, not the fences!" Mrs. Jefferies said in exasperation. "The children! They haven't come back!"

Mr. Freeman's face faltered as he stared at her. "Wh-what?" he stammered.

"Hey, where's Thad?" Danny suddenly asked. "And where's Donald?"

"The little spaz is gone too!" Corey said. He laughed. "Good riddance!"

Mr. Freeman's jaw twitched and his eyes went cold like chunks of ice. A paleness spread across his cheeks as if they were spread with butter. Then he squeezed both eyes shut. "I knew it was too quiet," he hissed. Louder he said, "Who else is gone?"

"Th-that's it," squeaked Mrs. Jefferies. After her outburst, she looked shrunken. Makeup smeared across her cheeks like a child's scribble and lipstick was smudged at the corners of her mouth like blood. Beads of sweat spotted her forehead. She looked like a deranged circus clown. "One of the little boys needed the bathroom," she added, "so I sent him with his partner, but that was ages ago!"

Mr. Freeman stared at her incredulously. "And you only told me now!" he demanded, his voice tight with anger.

Swallowing, Mrs. Jefferies glared back. "Well, you never stopped talking long enough to give me a chance!" she responded defensively.

Mr. Freeman blinked and seemed to notice everyone looking at him. All at once he waved his arms at his side so he resembled a giant bird trying to take flight. "Okay, okay!" he said loudly. "Everybody calm down!" He asked Mrs. Jefferies, "Did you by any chance send Jak to the bathroom?"

The poor woman nodded. "Um, yes, I think that's the boy's name."

Mr. Freeman couldn't hold in a groan. No longer cheerful or smiling, his face went as scarlet as the coats the British wore over 250 years before.

"I hope they found some dog-tight fences," Corey said loudly. "Those wild dogs are free range, right?"

Thad gulped deep breaths of air as he finally caught up to Jak. The younger boy stood frozen to a spot just inside a small clearing next to a large pond. Thad stopped when he saw the body of water. He never knew it existed before. This was where the stream ended. Mostly hidden by tall green plants, the pond seemed to be at least the size of their entire school. Shaped like a rough oval, the water stretched itself out in the middle of the woods like a large puddle. And it teemed with life. Insects buzzed, birds sang, and several ducks swam in the smooth, dark water. Thad also spotted a turtle sunning on a log sticking from the water.

Jak wasn't looking at the pond. His eyes were rooted on a small tree-covered hill to the left of the water.

"I saw her," he whispered.

Thad stared at him. "Huh?"

Blinking as if broken from a trance, Jak looked at Thad. "A dog," he said excitedly. "I saw a dog up there. Big and brown ... I think it wanted to be friends."

"What?"

Jak's eyes slanted as he grinned. "I bet she's still up there."

"No, wait!" Thad was talking to himself.

Jak already took off, running up the hill.

Thad was about ready to tackle the kid and drag him back by force. First he had to catch him.

Ordinarily, Thad would enjoy exploring unknown woods. Most of the time, he kept quiet. He preferred watching others instead of talking to them. Only with his friends did he open up. When not with his friends, he preferred to be alone.

At home, he liked to go into the woods near his house to explore. Being so close to the battlefield, he often pretended to be an American colonial battling the British army. When he let this secret out to his friends, Danny and Derek would sometimes join him, but Derek always had to be in charge. Thad liked it better alone when his imagination could take charge. However, on this particular day, at this particular moment, he would much, much rather have Derek suddenly appear and take over. He knew Mr. Freeman would expect him to control Jak, but that was like trying to control a housefly. What Jak needed was a good swat.

"Stop, Jak!" he finally yelled out.

Amazing, but the little pest actually listened. Jak stopped short and Thad bumped into his back, just over the top of the hill, and sent both of them sprawling to their stomachs.

"Finally," panted Thad, getting to his knees and wiping off rotting leaves and dirt. "Are you crazy?"

Jak crawled to his knees, his eyes wide. "Look!" he exclaimed. Moving to a sitting position, he pointed down the other side of the hill.

Expecting to see a fierce wild dog ready to pounce, Thad's eyes followed Jak's finger and he gasped. No dog, or even an animal, waited. Instead, on the other side of the hill, in the middle of the wild tangled woods, a paved street appeared as if out of nowhere.

Thad blinked and for a moment his curiosity replaced his anger. "What in the world ..."

"And look over there!" Jak's voice flushed with excitement.

Thad looked. The road was obviously old and not used. It looked to have been given to the forest and rejected. Cracks had broken through its surface, sprouting weeds and other plants. Still, it had to have been used not too long ago. Following the road with his eyes, he saw through the trees, some distance away, the top of a house. Blinking, he looked again and saw not just a house, but multiple buildings. In the middle of nowhere a paved road, like a river of concrete, flowed through the trees and led to a cluster of buildings.

"Wow," he breathed. "I bet nobody lived here in like fifty years." In his mind, a great plan was already forming. For years he and the guys had talked of making a secret club with a secret clubhouse.

"Should we go and look?" Jak asked hopefully. His dark eyes danced with all sorts of possibilities.

Thad immediately came back to reality. "What?" he said and then quickly added, "Uh, no. I mean, Jak, we need to get back before Mr. Freeman calls the National Guard."

Jak frowned, but then he shrugged. "Yeah, he probably would do that, wouldn't he?" He sounded proud of this fact.

"Hey, Thad!" yelped Donald's voice. "Where are you guys?" Then his voice went high like a girl's. "Eeee! Another spider!"

"Up here, Donald!" called Thad. "Just follow the stream and go up the hill on the left of the pond!"

Donald sounded terrified when he answered back, "Pond? What pond? Oh my gosh, there are more mosquitoes here than leaves! Go away, bugs!"

Jak smothered a giggle, causing Thad to shoot him a hard look. "You're going to get in so much trouble," he growled to the boy.

Jak shook his head. "No, I'm not," he said innocently. "I have permission to use the bathroom, remember?"

"That was a long time ago!" Thad said hotly. "By now everyone probably thinks we're lost!" Thad suddenly went cold. He gulped. "Speaking of which, I think we are lost."

Jak got up and went to a tree with his back to Thad. "We're not lost," he said cheerfully. "We have the stream, remember? We can just walk from the stream and we'll soon come out somewhere by the trenches."

Thad frowned and then made face when a new stream started watering the tree in front of Jak. "Come on," he protested. "You could at least go out of my sight!" Turning with disgust, he went back down the hill, nearly slipping at the steepness.

The worst part, Jak was right. The stream pretty much ran in a straight line. By putting their backs to the stream, all they had to do was walk in one direction and eventually they should reach the battlefield.

As Thad reached the bottom of the hill, Donald sprinted from a deer path next to the stream. He beat at his head with both hands. "There you are!" he cried. "What are you guys doing? I thought the bugs ate you up!"

Thad jerked his head behind him. "The little, I mean, Jak is up there watering the woods." He sighed. "By now we're probably labeled as missing persons."

"I just hope we don't get to be eaten persons. I can't wait to go to my nice house and play hours of video games." Donald slapped his arm. "At least in video games the bugs can't bite you!"

Thad brightened. "Speaking of houses, you got to see what we found up there!"

"What, a snake hole?"

"No, Donald, I'm serious. There's an old road back there and some houses! I mean it!" Donald stared at him like he was crazy. "Well, they're all falling apart, probably, but there are real houses in these woods!"

Donald didn't share Thad's enthusiasm. "Huh," he said. "Probably left over when the Park took over this place. Hey, there's Jak. Now let's get out of here!" He slapped at his arm again.

"Hey, wait! What do you mean the Park took over this place?"

Donald looked back at him. "Don't you remember the tour guide at the museum? He said the Park Service had to buy this land. Before they took over, there were neighborhoods all over. They tore down the houses and planted trees. I bet the houses you saw are too far away to care about." He shrugged. "They just left them there."

"Well, I think we could—"

Jak's high-pitched voice cut him off. "Look out below!" From on top of the hill, Jak spread out his arms and tried sliding down the hill like a surfer. At first he actually slid. Then, picking up speed, he hit a root and went flying.

"Watch out!" shouted Donald.

Thad only shook his head as Jak cried out as he went face forward. Landing with a thump, he rolled head over heels the rest of the way down. Coming to a stop, he went still.

"Oh, man!" Donald said anxiously as he rushed to his side. "Are you all right?"

Jak had his eyes closed and head slumped to the side as he lay on his back. Suddenly he sprang to a sitting position.

"Boo!" yelled Jak, causing Donald to jump back so fast that he fell on the seat of his jeans.

"Hey," Donald complained. "That's not funny!"

"That was fun," Jak said between fits of laughter. "You guys have to try it."

"The only thing I'm going to try is staying inside from now on," muttered Donald, getting to his feet. He leapt a foot, thinking a piece of dirt on his leg was a spider. "Come on, dude. Let's get out of here." Reaching down, he grabbed Jak's wrist and yanked him to his feet.

Taking deep breaths to keep calm, Thad watched it all without making an effort to help. Only Donald's presence kept him from totally losing it. That was one thing about Donald—he was the nicest person Thad had ever met. He was the only kid in the school that never called Jak the little spaz. Donald, though, would be friendly with a zombie coming to eat his brains.

Donald helped Jak brush rotting leaves from his shirt and hair. As he reached for a dark clump sticking to Jak's stomach, Thad rushed over and grabbed his arm.

"Don't touch that!" he warned. "That's deer stuff. There's a whole pile where he fell—or there was."

Donald yelped and jumped back. "Gross! Man, sorry, Jak."

Jak frowned and bit his lip. "Ah, man," he said. Then he grinned. "At least I didn't eat it."

Thad grunted with distaste. "That can be arranged. Maybe you should try washing it off in the pond before we go back."

Jak eyed Thad and then Donald suspiciously. "You guys won't leave me, will you?" he asked suspiciously.

Thad's face flushed with anger. "No, of course not!" he nearly shouted. "That's something you would do!" Ordinarily he would keep his mouth shut, but it was hot and he was sick and tired of Jak being stupid. That kid could, and probably should, have broken a bone sliding down like he did. Instead he got what he deserved—a bathroom break, courtesy of Bambi.

"Here, Jak," Donald said kindly. "I'll go with you." He patted Jak's shoulder. "I'll get a rock, or something to, um, scrub your shirt."

Lifting his eyes to the treetops, Thad followed his best friend and worst pest to the edge of the pond. He watched sourly as Jak pulled off his shirt and slapped it into the water.

"Careful," cried out Donald. "I don't want deer doo-doo in my eye!"

Laughing, Jak swished his shirt around, splashing more water.

Thad eyed the skinny brown back and resisted the urge to kick the back end into the water. He could see every bone in Jak's torso and wouldn't mind breaking more than a couple. Instead he said, "Jak, stop it."

Jak immediately stopped and proceeded to walk into the water with his shoes.

"Hey," he said, "I think it's pretty deep out here. We could go swimming!"

"Jak!" cried Donald. "There could be snakes in there!"

The sun-browned boy ignored him. "There are some rocks you could jump from! This is awesome!"

Thad groaned. "Jak, just get out of the water and put your shirt on," he said. "We're going back now, got it?"

Maybe the boy had finally tired, because he made no argument. Jumping back to shore, he waved his soaked shirt over his head before sliding the soggy mess over his brown chest. A dark smudge remained in the middle and it clung tightly to his ribs. Otherwise he looked okay for a boy with soaked sneakers.

Donald wiped his face and grimaced. "That's it. I'm never going outside in a million years."

Thad swallowed and looked once more toward the hill that hid the road and houses. Then he raced after Jak. The little spaz ran ahead of them and impatiently waited.

"Come on!" he called behind him. "I see a shortcut!"

"To our graves," Donald moaned. He hurried to follow, beating at his head.

Chapter 4

Mr. Freeman pulled the class to the side of the path and sat them in the circle. Just to make sure, he called roll twice.

They were in the sun and sweat poured from red faces. Nobody looked happy. Mr. Freeman looked ready to explode. Stalking back and forth, he kept pulling at his hair and casting desperate looks at the back trail.

"Should we call the police?" asked a large chaperone worriedly. "I mean, they could be lost in those woods."

"Nobody is calling the police!" Mr. Freeman nearly snapped. "Not yet. I mean, they could be back at the museum ..." His hands clenched into fists. "I can see that little ..."

"Should we go back and look?" Derek asked hopefully, tugging at Danny's sleeve. "We can go really fast."

"You're crazy," Danny mumbled. Still, he got up.

Immediately the teacher shook his head. "No, no, no, you guys stay right there! I'm not going to lose anybody else." His voice trailed off. "Oh, for crying out loud, what will the others say when I tell them I lost ..." He sighed and cast a dark look at Mrs. Jefferies.

"I, I thought they would be right back," mumbled Mrs. Jefferies. "I mean, they looked so trustworthy and promised not to go far." Suddenly she looked ready to burst into tears.

Mr. Freeman rubbed his head. "Oh, it's not your fault, believe me. That little cr—er, little guy lives for moments like this. He'll do anything to cause trouble."

"I'm so, so sorry," Mrs. Jefferies said as she wiped her eyes. Lisa had already started running tears and a group of girls were sitting around her, patting her head. Either the tears came from the fear of losing classmates or from the embarrassment of having a mother to blame for it.

"Maybe he had to go number two!" Corey called out. "He could be sitting out there looking for paper!"

"Quiet, all of you!" Mr. Freeman snapped. "Everyone just be quiet!"

Nearly everyone gulped. The class had never seen Mr. Freeman look so frazzled before—at least not since the infamous timer incident. His hair stuck up in all directions and huge sweat stains soaked his shirt in the armpits and neck area.

Taking a ragged breath, the teacher tried to stand still but quickly resumed pacing. A nervous wave of silence descended. In that silence they heard a faint voice.

"Last one there is a toad sandwich!" called a high-pitched boyish voice.

Mr. Freeman went very still.

"Slow down, Jak!" called another voice.

The light shining from Mrs. Jefferies's face could have lit up a city. "Oh, that's them!" she cried with relief.

"And I almost wished the dogs got him," growled Mr. Freeman softly. But the relief on his face sagged away his anger. Cupping his mouth with both hands, he called out loudly. "OVER HERE! WE'RE OVER HERE! JAK, DONALD, THAD!"

It took a few minutes of calling, but from the tour road, the three missing children came into the sunlight. Jak had dropped back and now hid behind Donald and Thad. All three had shirts soaked with sweat and scratches on their arms. Jak's poor shirt still clung to his ribs and featured a dark brown stain.

"Where were you?" thundered Mr. Freeman, crossing his arms. Seeing the boys return safely brought back his anger.

Gulping, Thad looked down. Jak, the coward, remained at his back. Gathering his courage, Thad looked up and saw all his classmates sitting in a hot mass glaring at him. Relief had quickly switched to anger.

"We're really sorry," Donald said earnestly. "Jak had to use the bathroom, and we got a little lost."

"Get out here, Jak," rumbled Mr. Freeman, ignoring Donald, "where I can see you." A purplish vein popped up on his neck and looked ready to explode.

"Aw, man," Jak mumbled. Squinting so his eyes resembled dark slits, he stepped forward. Doing so, he brushed Thad's arm. Thad was surprised to feel Jak trembling.

Mr. Freeman clamped both his hands under his armpits, probably to keep from running over and slapping Jak to kingdom come. His face sure looked like it wanted to. "Do you realize all the trouble you caused?" he hissed.

Jak squirmed and ducked his head. "Um, no," he muttered.

"Say no, sir!" barked Mr. Freeman.

Jak swallowed and managed to barely lift his head. "Um, no," he said softly. "Sir."

Mr. Freeman leaned in close to the boy so his nose was mere inches from Jak's head. "Do you mean to tell me," he said with sarcasm, "that you just had to use the bathroom?"

Looking miserable, Jak nodded.

Mr. Freeman peered intently at Jak. His voice dropped to almost a whisper. "What did you see? Did you find anything in the woods?"

Jak twisted up his mouth in confusion and blinked up at the teacher. "Um, no."

"Then what took you so long?" spluttered Mr. Freeman. His eyes blazed as he straightened up and stood over the boy. "And why are you coming out here instead of from behind us? Do you know, I ran back and forth from here to there three times already!"

"Hey!" called Corey. "Look at his shirt—I was right! He had to go number two and used his shirt to wipe!"

"Yeah," added Jonathan, "the smell was so bad they ran away and got lost."

Corey laughed. "Next time, Mr. Freeman, just follow your nose."

"Not funny!" barked the large chaperone. "That is disgusting! This whole thing is disgusting!"

Mrs. Jefferies just looked relieved everything turned out okay—at least nobody died or got really lost. "Maybe we should go on and ... finish the tour?" she asked tentatively.

The last chaperone, a small woman with short black hair and a pinched face, shook her head. "I wish I'd stayed at the museum," she moaned.

Through all the talking, Mr. Freeman's face went from red to white and then turned back to red. After several deep breaths, it turned a more natural color. He didn't look at the disturbance behind him. His smoldering eyes bore into Jak. "So you didn't see anything or do anything?" he asked. "Just saw trees, right?"

Jak nodded doubtfully.

"What about a pond?" Mr. Freeman asked softly. "If you went that far ..."

Jak never blinked. He squinted even more. "You mean there's a pond back there?" he asked innocently.

Mr. Freeman sighed. Looking briefly at Donald and then at Thad, he shook his head and said, "You two go join the rest of the class. Jak, you stay with me."

"Are you going to teach him potty training?" Corey asked.

"Disgusting," hissed the large chaperone. "Just look at that boy's shirt!"

"Let's just finish the tour," pleaded Mrs. Jefferies. She refused to look toward Jak.

The class groaned. "It's too hot," moaned a tired voice.

"That's it!" Mr. Freeman barked. "We go to the buses! Now, let's move!"

"But," Lisa protested, "we, we didn't take any buses. We walked!"

"Oh, great," groaned the last chaperone. "How many miles away is school?"

"Come on, Mom," said her son. "Remember all those stories you told me about when you were a kid? You used to walk to school for miles all the time!"

"Hush, Henry!" she snapped. "This isn't like that!"

Mr. Freeman said nothing. Breathing heavily, he took Jak by the arm. Then, turning on his heel, he yanked Jak sharply forward and started the long walk back. After a moment, everyone silently followed.

Jak looked back once and found Thad's eyes. He started to grin, but Mr. Freeman yanked him onward.

About halfway back, Corey tried to break the tension. "I wouldn't hold his arm there, not after what he did with it."

"No talking!" snapped Mr. Freeman, but he did move his grip to Jak's wrist.

"Utterly disgusting," wheezed the heavy chaperone.

The return trip was not nearly as glorious as the departure. Mr. Freeman trooped back to his colleagues like a wet dog, drowned in sweat, who had been told his master had been hit by a car.

Nobody in Mr. Freeman's class got any time at the gift shop and there would be no ice cream party. The other fifth-grade teachers smiled all the way back to the school.

"What did you see, Donald?" Danny asked later.

Donald gave Thad a helpless look. "Well, I didn't actually go to the top of the hill ..." he said truthfully.

"Aw, he didn't see anything!" Derek said scornfully. "Because there was nothing to see! Thad is just making up one of his stories again!"

Thad felt his face go red. "Am not! I did see the road and there were houses back there! I mean it, Derek."

Danny snorted. "Yeah, right." He giggled. "Maybe he got spacey from sniffing Jak."

It was Friday after school, the day after the field trip. The four boys were lounging in Thad's room. Danny and Derek were flopped across Thad's bed, looking down at where Donald and Thad sat on the carpet. An abandoned game of poker lay between them. A pile of Legos served as the chips. Derek had taught them the game the previous summer and so far none of them had figured out why it was supposed to be fun.

"Yeah, maybe Corey was right," chuckled Danny. "The little spaz went number two and the smell messed up your brain!"

Thad hit the makings of a royal flush in front of him. "Guys, come on!" he said. "Be real!"

It was the first time they had been alone since the now infamous trip, that had caused Mr. Freeman to call in his first absence all year and, from what the other teachers said, the first of his career.

Thad had wanted desperately to tell his friends what he'd seen in the woods earlier, but after the field trip everyone was too tired to meet. At lunch that day there were too many people to overhear. Thad wanted this to be a secret. Needless to say, he was more than disappointed when his long-awaited story about the houses was met with disbelief. Since Donald never saw anything, he really had no support.

"You got to believe me!" He reached back and yanked his cowlick in frustration. "You, you can even ask Jak! He saw them too!"

Derek laughed and punched Danny's shoulder. "Are you kidding me? That little spaz couldn't be trusted with a penny!"

"Ouch!" shouted Danny.

"Don't be such a wimp!" Derek punched Danny in the same spot. "One day you'll thank me for making you tough."

Danny rubbed his shoulder. "Not if my arm falls off!"

"Ah, your flab protects you." Derek reared back for another punch, but Danny's shoulder plowed into his face and knocked Derek off the bed and onto the floor.

"Oh, oops," Danny said, not sounding apologetic.

"Hey!" cried Derek, getting to his feet. "What was that for?"

"You'll thank me one day for making you tough," muttered Danny.

Giving a dirty look, Derek rubbed his arm before jumping back on the bed. He didn't punch Danny again.

Thad glared at them. "Will you guys stop messing around? My mom is going to yell at us!"

On cue, Thad's mom called from the first floor. "Thaddeus, is everyone okay up there?"

His face burning, Thad answered back. "Yes, Mom! We're fine!"

His mom didn't sound so sure. "Well," she said, "come down in a minute and I'll have milk and cookies." She sounded a little nervous.

Thad sighed. "Sure, Mom!" Danny and Derek were already off the bed and moving quickly to the door. "Wait, guys!" he begged. "Stop right there."

Derek grinned. "What, Thaddeus?"

Thad ignored the mockery. "Just listen to me for a second!"

Danny sighed when Derek stopped and grabbed his shoulder. "Hold on, Danny," Derek said. "This is Thaddeus's house, remember. Thaddeus is in charge."

Thad grimaced. "Just drop it and listen to me." Thad took a deep breath. "What if there are houses back there? I mean, those houses are abandoned and left for years."

"So what?" Derek asked. He eyed the door. Thad's mom made great cookies. She never used packaged ones from a store.

Thad rushed ahead before he lost his chance. "Remember, we wanted to form a gang with our own clubhouse? Well, this is our chance! I mean, we can claim those houses and they'll be ours!"

"Sure," snorted Derek. "If they're really there."

Thad stared at him. "They are," he said earnestly.

"The pond is real," Donald said helpfully. "Pretty big one, too."

Derek moved from the door and flopped back on the bed. Danny groaned and followed.

"Hmm," Derek said after a moment. "The pond at least sounds cool."

"What about the wild dogs?" Danny asked as he leaned against the bed. "They're out there."

Sensing victory, Thad rose to his knees. He never mentioned the part where Jak claimed to have seen a dog. It probably never really happened.

"There are no dogs around there," he said excitedly. "And besides, they only come out at night, remember?"

"I have a dog and she doesn't just come out at night," Danny said doubtfully. "That reminds me, I need to give her a walk soon."

Thad waved a hand dismissively. "Listen, guys, we can make an expedition. We'll go exploring, like we're real adventurers."

Derek's eyes brightened. "When?" he asked. He could already see himself taking charge and leading a famous expedition into the wild jungles battling wild beasts.

"We have school," Donald said with a frown. "And how will we get there?"

"Yeah," Danny said, nodding. "It would have to be before Donald leaves." He grinned at Donald and then at Derek. "It'll be the last time the three Ds go off together."

"D as in dumb for you," Derek said, but he bounced up on the bed excitedly. "My dad has a cool tent we can use. Maybe we can have a campout!"

Thad beamed. "That's a great idea! Donald, didn't you once tell me that there's an old trail nearby that leads to the battlefield?"

Donald didn't look happy, but he nodded. "Yeah, my mom grew up around here; she showed it to me. But people built houses near it and we'd have to go through some backyards."

"No problem!" Thad got to his feet. "We can go the first week of summer."

"I'll bring my dad's tent!" Derek gave Thad a high five. "It's big enough for all of us!"

Donald shook his head. "Well, um, I don't know. The trail is old and I've never been on it."

"It'll be a real adventure then," Derek cried. "We can be real explorers!"

Donald grunted. "Who should go?"

Everyone stopped and looked at him.

"What do you mean?" Thad asked. "Just us, of course."

"What about Jak? I mean, after all, he's the one who really found it."

After the field trip, Jak never did get in major trouble because the chaperone had given him permission to go in the woods. In fact, the principal didn't even question him for very long. Thad and Donald were called to the office just to verify that they all did in fact have permission to go into the woods alone. After that, Mr. Freeman had spent a long time in the office speaking to the principal. A sub had greeted the class that morning.

Thad blanched and Derek sat down with a thump on the bed. Danny shook his head vehemently.

"No way we let little spaz near us," Derek said vehemently. "He'd ruin everything."

"Besides," Thad added hastily. "Jak doesn't need friends. He doesn't even *want* friends."

Danny nodded. "If he goes, we're doomed."

"Just us, the four musketeers!" cried Derek, leaping from the bed.

Thad gave him another high five and together they tackled Danny on the bed.

"Uh, sure, okay." Donald didn't look very pleased, but the other boys were whooping and hollering and never noticed.

"Boys!" shouted Mrs. Utley. "No playing football up there. Come down and get your cookies. Now!"

Chapter 5

The rest of the weekend flew by as they spent much of the time making plans. Derek said he would be the leader because he had experience camping with his dad and, besides, he would have the tent. Not letting Derek's bossiness ruin his excitement, Thad said everyone would be in charge until then and they'd meet the first night of summer vacation with all the supplies they thought they'd need. Then, and only then, would they decide on a leader—if there needed to be one.

On Monday morning, it was the start of the second to last week of school. Two more weeks before their adventure ... it seemed like an eternity away.

When Thad arrived at his desk he was surprised to find a large white envelope there with his name written in a black scrawl. Looking up, he saw that many desks had a similar envelope. The only other person in the room was Mr. Freeman.

After a long weekend, the teacher had returned. Sitting behind his usually orderly desk, he was almost hidden by a forest of flowers. With the different colors, shapes, and sizes, his desk looked like it belonged with Alice in Wonderland.

Seeing Thad, Mr. Freeman gave a tight smile. "My first absence and people treat it like a funeral."

Ducking his head, Thad quickly took a seat and became very interested in the strange envelope.

"Mr. Utley, kindly put your book bag in the closet, please. I know June has just begun, but there are still rules in the classroom."

Embarrassed, Thad quickly went to comply. Other students started arriving and Danny joined Thad at the closet.

"Did you hear?" hissed Danny.

"Hear what?" Thad asked.

Danny looked around and then shook his head. "Just open your envelope. You'll see." He looked as if he was about to laugh or cry.

Thad was going to ask more when the Beast entered and headed his way. Arms flapping and head bobbing up and down, she glanced at Thad. "Hey."

Hastily, Danny moved to his seat, and with a small grunt, Thad followed.

"What's this?" demanded Corey when he got to his desk and found the envelope.

"Open it and see," Leslie Fisher said wickedly. "I saw them get passed out. Then I had to run out and throw up in the bathroom." Leslie was one of Lisa's close friends and the daughter of a teacher in the second grade. She was always one of the first to arrive at school and one of the last to leave. Thad felt sorry for her, but not too sorry. Leslie had the bad habit of getting in other people's business for her personal pleasure. "You'll love it!"

Frowning, Corey tore at the envelope and ripped free a single sheet of paper. As he read it, his frown turned into an evil grin. "Well, well ... I'll be ..."

"You'll be standing in detention if you don't sit down, Corey," Mr. Freeman snapped, pulling a particularly ugly purple flower off the corner of his desk. "Everyone find a seat and get up and grab a sheet of morning work. They're on the table next to my flower shop."

"How can we sit down and get up to grab a sheet at the same time?" Danny asked.

"Figure it out!" barked Mr. Freeman.

"Oh, okay ... I got it now."

Danny and Thad exchanged glances. Usually Mr. Freeman would laugh at his own expense. Today, however, he looked to be in a foul mood.

Donald came in the door and nodded at Thad. Even though he rode the same bus with Danny and Thad, he always arrived later to the classroom because he walked his little sister to her kindergarten class.

On a different day Thad would have called out to Donald. On this day, he sighed and grabbed the envelope. Tugging it open, he dumped out the contents. His eyes grew wide when he saw before him an invitation. Jakavos Tranner requested his presence on Friday for a belated tenth birthday party and sleepover into Saturday. Arrive after school. Cake would be provided.

Thad nearly fell off his seat. Looking up quickly, he saw the back of Jak's head leaning forward in concentration, but his pencil was not moving. Jak, the most disliked boy in the school, had invited all the other boys in his class to a party.

By math class it was very apparent who was attending. Corey started it. Just after Mr. Freeman, who still hadn't recovered his humor, passed out a thick review packet, Corey snatched up his invitation and walked carefully to the back of the room. Reaching Jak's desk, he stopped and looked down.

"This weekend I'm going to be busy." Then he ripped the invitation in half and turned to drop it in the trash can. Wiping his hands clean, he sauntered back to his desk.

Thad watched with an open mouth. Nobody in the class spoke, but everyone heard it. Then, a few minutes later, Jonathan stood with his invitation. Moving slowly to the trashcan next to Jak's desk, he did the same thing.

"I have fun plans this weekend. I'm not ruining them," he said after tossing the ripped shreds away.

"Serves him right for hurting Mr. Freeman," muttered Leslie a little too loudly.

"Quiet and work!" Mr. Freeman said warningly.

The boy named Henry went next. His mom had delivered a stinging lecture about staying away from kids like Jak. Too embarrassed to say anything, he crumpled up the invitation and dropped it in the can.

Thad kept his head down on his paper, but his mind was on his invitation underneath it. After a minute, he heard another chair squeak against the floor. Looking up, he saw Derek walking toward him.

"Sorry," Derek mumbled when passing Jak. He dropped the spurned invitation into the bucket. Not surprisingly, Danny went next. Only he walked on the other side of the classroom to avoid passing Jak.

"Jerks," the Beast muttered when Danny passed by on the way back to his seat. She sat in the back corner on the opposite side of the room and Danny went right by her desk. His face flushed a deep red.

Donald, who sat in the front row on the far right, looked back and met Thad's eyes. Donald shook his head sadly.

Thad gulped. He'd been fingering the invitation. Besides Donald and him, there was only one other boy in the class.

Kevin Boston was a dark-skinned boy with large bushy curls on top of a head built like a box. Square jawed, with facial lines shaped by a chisel, he looked much older than the others. This was because he was repeating the grade. He sat in the middle of the room and did nothing, like he usually did. Perpetually quiet, he mostly was ignored. His older brother starred as quarterback for the high school and was expected to lead the team to the state championship the following year. Kevin hadn't gone on the field trip last week. He never did anything but play sports. Football and basketball star, he only spoke to his teammates and totally ignored his classmates. His envelope was on the floor next to his desk with more than one footprint on it.

That meant it was just Donald and Thad left.

Abruptly, Donald pushed himself to his feet. Moving straight to Jak's desk, he went down the aisle opposite the trash can.

"Jak," he said quietly. "I'm sorry I can't make your party. It's because my family is packing up and I'll be staying with my grandparents. Sorry."

Jak, his head bent down low over his paper, gave a brief nod. His small shoulders seemed to slump even lower.

Mr. Freeman peeked through the flowers. "What's that talking over there? Everyone get to your seat!"

Thad ducked low in his desk. Gulping, he slid his invitation far inside his desk, into the deepest, darkest corner. For the first time, he felt truly sorry for Jak. The boy, for the first time, looked like a little lost kid in need of a friend.

Well, he asked for it. Thad shook his head and settled down to work. He pushed Jak's party far from his mind.

Nobody else seemed to forget. Fueled by Leslie, the drama that had unfolded in Mr. Freeman's class tore through the fifth grade. By lunch, everyone was talking about it.

Mr. Freeman's table was the first table on the left when entering the cafeteria. That meant every class walked by on their way to the food line. Perhaps it was on accident or maybe on purpose, but by the time Jak got through the line, every seat was taken except for the four closest to the end near the food line. He hadn't spoken a word all day. Carrying his tray of steamed vegetables and a ham sandwich, he walked by his classmates without a single look.

Sitting at the opposite end of the table, Thad watched as Jak took a seat near the edge.

"They need to leave him alone," Donald said quietly.

Derek snorted as he ripped open a ketchup packet. "He did it to himself. The little spaz got Mr. Freeman in trouble and is now paying for it."

"What do you mean?" Danny asked, licking the same red goo off his fingers. They had both chosen the cheeseburgers.

"Didn't you hear?" called Leslie from several seats over. "Mr. Freeman almost got fired because of what Jak did on the field trip."

"You mean go number two on the battlefield?" Corey asked. He had two ketchup packets and ripped one open.

"Well, whatever he did," Jonathan said from his seat, "he's going to regret it!"

"Or we will," Donald said too softly for anyone else to hear.

Another fifth-grade class entered and stopped by the table to wait their turn for the food line. Alone, Jak sat on the end and played with the bread of his sandwich.

That end of the table was reserved for the loners today—those without friends. Kevin took a seat two over from Jak and started chomping on a cheeseburger. Two more burgers sat on his tray with a pile of fruit between them.

A shadow fell over Jak.

"Hey, there's the little birthday boy," said Eric, a hulking boy in one of the other fifth-grade classes. With short curly hair, pale skin, rosy cheeks, and brown eyes the color of amber, he could have passed for a nice-looking boy. Instead, broad in the shoulders and well stocked with muscle, he thought of himself as tough and rough. Smacking large lips, he grinned goofily. Already his voice was deepening and fuzz sprouted under his large nose. "I heard you're turning a whole ten years old!"

"Yeah, all by himself," another boy next to Eric said, laughing. "Nobody else will go!"

"Shut up," Eric said lightly. "I'm talking to him. What presents are you asking for, little kid?" Eric grinned. "Tell me so I know which of my little sister's toys I can give you. Let me guess, you like ponies!"

"Isn't your sister smarter than you?" Jak asked without looking up.

Eric frowned. "What did you say?" he asked.

Jak kept his gaze on his tray. "I said, your sister adopted you from the zoo."

Now Eric flushed. "What was that?" he hissed dangerously.

"The zoo wanted to put you down because you were so ugly, but didn't want to waste a bullet," Jak said calmly.

"I'm going to waste you in a second!" growled Eric. "Take that back!"

"That's what your sister tried to do, but the zoo wouldn't take you back," Jak said. He tore a piece of bread from his sandwich and rolled it in his fingers. "They had to pay your sister to keep you."

Eric's rosy cheeks flamed and the flush spread across his entire face. He loomed over Jak. "You little piece of—" he began.

"Piece of what?" Jak asked innocently. "I heard what your sister feeds you, and if I'm that, you might eat me." Jak spoke softly and never once looked up.

Eric raised his bulky arms and thrust out his chest to no effect. This only made him angrier. Over twice Jak's size, any violence from him wouldn't end well. He'd only be labeled a bully and get into major trouble. Still, his classmates could hear every word Jak was saying. They all waited for him to react. If he backed away now, he would lose a lot of respect.

Taking a deep breath, he bent low next to Jak's ear. "I know what you are," he hissed loudly so everyone could hear. "You're a little scrawny piece of moldy toast. You're a retard. A stupid freak from the circus who belongs in the special class with seat belts!" He stood back up and turned to his friends. "That little brat isn't worth it."

Just then a loud splat exploded against Eric's cheek and a piece of slimy fruit stuck fast.

"Hey!" he roared. "What the—" Whirling, he raised a fist at Jak.

"Eric Minters!" shouted a powerful voice from the middle of the cafeteria. The entire table went silent as Ms. Bromsald stormed toward Eric. The cafeteria monitor and special education helper, Ms. Bromsald was a powerful figure. While just over five feet tall and past middle age, she had the personality and energy of a tiger. "What do you think you're doing?" she demanded.

Eric jerked his chin at Jak. "This little spaz—I mean, he threw this peach at me!" he said angrily. "Look at it, it's rotten! It's turning green!"

"Give me that!" ordered Ms. Bromsald. She snatched the offending piece of fruit and jutted out her jaw. "Now you go back to your class!"

Not everyone at Knox Elementary despised Jak. Ms. Bromsald and the other school assistants treated him like their son. This was probably because they knew him so well due to his constant wanderings. Also, they'd spent many in-school suspensions with him. Having his father on the school board, though, didn't hurt.

"But, but," Eric whined, "he, he hit me!"

Ms. Bromsald glared at the boy. "You're twice his size, and besides, he doesn't even have fruit on his tray, Eric!"

Jak now turned from his tray and stared at Eric. Jak's deep-set dark eyes narrowed into tiny slits. They did not smile. In front of him, Jak's tray held only the steamed vegetables and dry sandwich. There was not a single piece of fruit in arm's distance around him.

Eric could only open and close his mouth before gritting his teeth. "Stupid gypsy," he finally muttered.

Ms. Bromsald grunted. "The lunch line is now open. Go!"

Eric muttered something about waiting until recess and then followed his class with as much swagger as he could manage.

Jak shrugged and went back to picking at his bread.

A few seats over, Kevin calmly started on his second cheeseburger. A smashed piece of grape fell from his hand next to a pile of other tepid fruit.

"Oh, hi, Kevin," said Ms. Bromsald sweetly. "How's your sister doing in the high school? We miss her here. Tell her I said hi, okay?"

Kevin merely grunted.

Ms. Bromsald gave Jak's hair a pat. "Stay out of trouble, and stay away from Eric, you hear?"

The boy nodded. "Sure, Ms. Bromsald."

"That's my boy." Mussing up his hair, she departed with a final smile at Kevin.

The two boys never looked at each other, but the atmosphere turned pleasanter.

It quickly soured when the Beast arrived and plopped her tray across from Jak.

"Hey," she said. "Those boys—" She stopped talking.

Not looking at her, Jak had picked up his tray and silently moved seats. He did the same thing when the Beast tried to move to follow him.

Finally, Jak got up and took his lunch to the trashcan. Totally alone, the Beast slumped down in the last seat.

Chapter 6

Thad watched Jak leave with a frown. While his friends started discussing summer plans around him, he'd focused on the other end of the table. He probably had been the only person to see Kevin fling the fruit at Eric—it was done so quickly and smoothly that it was nearly impossible to notice. After a few more bites of his suddenly unappetizing lunch, he got up and followed after Jak.

"Where's he going?" wondered Danny, munching on his burger.

"When you got to go, you got to go," Derek replied, his mouth full. "That reminds me. We're sorry you got to go, man." This last part he directed to Donald.

Donald nearly dropped his sandwich. "Pardon?" he asked.

Derek shrugged. "You know, you got to go and all ..."

Donald raised an eyebrow. "I need to go? What are you saying?"

Face going red, Derek shoved a fry in his mouth. "You're moving, man!"

"Now?" Donald asked.

Derek struggled to swallow. "Huh?"

"I'm not going anywhere," Donald said coolly. "If you don't want to sit next to me, you move." Suddenly he grinned. "Just messing with you."

"Man, I can't wait to see you leave," Derek muttered, shoving in another fry.

"Well," said Donald, "you're the one who equated my moving to California with Thad having to go the bathroom."

"Yeah, well, it stinks," Danny said, causing Derek to snort while drinking milk—two white streams burst through his nose.

Knox Elementary was prepping for the end of the year. The walls, usually covered in student art and school announcements, were bare, and giant, overstuffed trash cans were in almost every hall.

Exiting the cafeteria, Thad couldn't help but feel a sense of joy at seeing all the trash cans. It was like the whole year of worry and grades was being trashed to give way to relaxation and the freedom of summer. Sidestepping a large gray barrel overflowing with student papers, he saw Jak slip into the library's back entrance located just down the hall from the cafeteria. He frowned. The back entrance was for teachers only—students always had to go around to the front.

What was he doing anyway? The impulse to follow Jak was fading fast. All he wanted to do was to apologize about not making the party and that was it. Suddenly unsure of what he should do next, he stopped just outside the back door. Mrs. Stein, the librarian, was usually nice to him but could be very cranky at times. Licking his lips, he decided to chance it when the door's knob suddenly started to turn.

Acting by instinct, Thad jerked back and retreated toward the cafeteria. The last thing he needed was for Jak to see him following him. The door banged against the wall. Panicking, he ducked low and jumped to the first hiding place he saw—behind a large gray can topped with crumpled paper. Propped up by wheels, the can hid his body completely. He hugged his knees tightly and pleaded for Jak to go the other way.

"So that's the story ..." rumbled a deep voice of a man. "I tell you, it was a complete disaster."

Thad's head jerked up so fast, it banged against the lid of the can. A ball of paper bounced down and rolled onto the floor.

It wasn't Jak exiting the library—it was Mr. Freeman! Extremely embarrassed, Thad ducked even lower. Another man was with Mr. Freeman and chuckled loudly. His voice sounded like a cannon's roar. Thankfully neither noticed the moving trash can and piece of paper.

"And that was the kid who caused it all, huh?" boomed the stranger's voice.

Thad heard Mr. Freeman sigh. "I tell you, Frank, summer vacations were invented for kids like that. Gives us teachers a chance to recover."

"Oh, come off it! That little thing? Come to the high school and then you'll really earn your paycheck. My guys would eat him for breakfast and then spit him back out because he's too small."

Mr. Freeman laughed. "You may think so, but trust me. These kids know how to jerk your chain, especially that one."

"No way. I'd have that kid under my thumb in less than five minutes."

"I would love to see it."

Thad dared not even breathe. The two men were standing just outside the library and seemed in no hurry to leave. Thankfully, the hall was otherwise clear.

The stranger called Frank grunted. "I would if I could, but I need to be getting back. Now, before I go, you've got the map. Do you have any other questions?"

"Ah, well, not really … not here, but I tell you, Frank, I think I'm in. After last week … I think I'm definitely in."

"Great! I'm glad to hear it. I knew you wouldn't let me down. Give me a call after school and we'll make some plans. We can meet for a drink."

"Okay, sure. I could probably use one."

Frank laughed loudly. "I hear you. Every teacher needs one at this time of the year."

Thad leaned to his right and peeked from behind the can. He saw a short, heavyset man, wearing a navy-blue warm-up suit, standing next to Mr. Freeman. Taller, skinnier, and wearing professional attire, Mr. Freeman looked out of place next to the small mountain of a man. Frank's hair was buzzed on the side and cropped closely on top. His back was turned so Thad never saw his face. Instead he saw three deep creases of flab on the back his neck. Frank reminded Thad of a giant, overweight bulldog. The two men shook hands and then Mr. Freeman said the words that finally allowed Thad's heart to start beating again.

"I have to collect my class from the cafeteria, but I'll walk you to the door. Anything to make lunch last longer. I have recess next."

"Hmmph," Frank snorted. "Must be tough."

"Maybe one day you'll understand, Frank. These kids aren't easy …"

Thad breathed a huge sigh of relief as the two teachers walked away and rounded the bend toward the main entrance. He was just about to stand when the cafeteria door burst open and the Beast stumbled out. She went still at seeing Thad.

"Hey, what are you doing?" she asked.

Thad gulped. He never had anything against the Beast but just followed everyone else's lead. While he did not participate in the name-calling, he was certainly guilty of taking pleasure at her expense by laughing at other people's jokes. Mostly he avoided contact with her.

"Uh, I, um, I …" he stammered, looking around wildly for some way to escape.

The Beast folded her arms in front of her. "Why are you sitting behind a trash can in the middle of the hallway?"

"Well …" Thad grabbed the fallen piece of paper and held it up. "I was looking for this, see? I, um, threw it away earlier and, uh, was looking for it. I kind of dropped it."

The Beast's eyebrows were hidden under her bangs, but they surely lifted in disbelief. She just stared at him without moving.

Thad felt his cheeks go warm as he pushed himself up. Quickly he decided his best defense was to attack. "What are *you* doing out here?" he demanded.

"I was going to the bathroom. All your friends are wondering where you are."

"Oh, well, uh, thanks …" Not knowing what else to do, he quickly brushed by her and practically ran back into the cafeteria. When an attack failed, full retreat was the best option.

Thad stumbled into the sunlight and immediately covered his eyes. He could block the light, but the wave of heat struck him like a slap in the face.

"Come on, Thad!" Danny cried, running ahead with Derek. "We need you at the field!"

He sighed. It was close to ninety degrees and humid. Perfect weather for a soccer game ... indoors.

Recess at Knox Elementary was a lot like the shape-shifter in X-Men. It varied day to day and was never predictable. At the start of the year Thad and his friends were lucky to get fifteen minutes. Now, near the end of the year, recess went as long as thirty minutes or more, depending on the mood of the teachers.

Keeping his eyes shaded, he looked at where Mr. Freeman stood with the other fifth-grade teachers under the single tree between the playground and athletic fields. They looked comfortable in the shade.

"You okay, Thad?"

Turning, Thad saw Donald standing against the school's wall in a sliver of shade caused by the sun's ascent.

"Yeah, I just wish it wasn't so hot."

Donald nodded at the teachers. "So who do you think will lose today?"

Shrugging, Thad brushed back his cowlick. "I don't know ..."

It was a game Donald and he made up the week before. They decided that none of the teachers wanted recess to end and would play a game of chicken. Standing in the cool shade, they would wait as long as possible until one of them cracked and blew a whistle to bring their kids in. The rest would reluctantly follow.

"I say Mr. Freeman," Donald said. "He's been in a bad mood all day."

"Yeah, maybe," Thad said with disinterest. He hadn't told Donald about what had happened in the hallway. He didn't even know what had happened himself. So much was going through his mind. What were the teachers talking about? He had a bad feeling it wasn't a good thing. And he'd yet to apologize to Jak. Thad sighed. He just wanted to go away and think by himself for a while.

"So, want to do soccer again?" Donald was more of a basketball player, but the school's only court was inside the gym—all the outdoor hoops were broken.

Thad shrugged. "I guess."

Since the weekend, it seemed as if neither knew what to say to the other. Thad kicked at a patch of dirt. Most of the grass was dying—trampled by thousands of feet. He knew what was wrong. Donald was leaving. They only had a little over two weeks and then it was over. In his mind, Donald was kind of already gone. Thad knew Donald did not want a camping trip as their last adventure. He hated the outdoors.

"Well," Donald said, "we better hurry before they pick teams."

Walking side by side, but definitely apart, Donald and Thad passed by the noisy playground, the single tree, and finally the baseball field—where a kickball game was already under way and was quickly turning into a large debate club. Derek had decided to leave Danny and join the "fun."

"That was foul!" screamed Jonathan from the pitcher's mound.

"Fair!" yelled Derek, trotting to first.

"Foul by a mile!" claimed Jonathan.

"Fair by a mile!" Derek shot back.

By the time Donald and Thad passed by, Jonathan and Derek were face to face kicking dirt at each other. Soccer was definitely more fun than that.

But when they arrived at the soccer field they were just in time to see a different storm brewing.

Soccer was never as popular as football and basketball in the classrooms, but at recess it managed to grow into the sport of choice for athletes and for those who wanted to be athletes. Anyone could do it; all it took was kicking a ball in one direction. It was also fun and there was always a winner and a loser. However, for a select few, it was much more than that. It was a chance to show off.

"Hey, Lisa, you're pretty good," Eric said, lunging awkwardly at Lisa, who dribbled toward him. He missed the ball by a foot.

Thad and Donald arrived as the game was still getting organized. In the meantime, Corey and Eric were "teaching" Lisa how to play.

"They're never going to stop," murmured Danny, moving to Thad's side. "They started before we got here and are just showing off."

"Showing off?" Thad asked dubiously. He watched where Corey and Eric were acting like idiots.

"I'll get her," Corey crowed, jumping in front of Lisa.

Laughing, Lisa tried to pivot, but kicked the ball forward, right into Corey's foot. Somehow the boy stumbled and sent the ball right back to Lisa.

"Drat!" he cried.

"I've never played before," squealed Lisa as she dribbled past Corey.

Danny snorted beside Thad and rolled his eyes. "They'd do anything to get Lisa to like them. They're pretending they can't play so she'll talk to them."

Thad grunted and couldn't disagree.

"You're a natural," Eric said to Lisa with fake admiration. He charged Lisa, but overran her and fell theatrically. "Ouch!"

Immediately Lisa stopped running and the ball rolled from her. "Oh, are you okay?" she asked in alarm.

"Of course," Eric said, grimacing. "You're just too quick for me! Turn and dribble back to Leslie and then we'll make teams. You're so good I think you can be team captain!"

Lisa smiled brightly. "Okay!" After getting the ball back to her feet, she awkwardly turned and started dribbling. They were at the center midfield line in the middle of the big circle. Other kids were just arriving and getting impatient.

"Come on, Lisa!" called Leslie. "Show those boys how girls play!" She jumped up and down like a cheerleader.

"What a bunch of chumps," Danny scoffed.

Thad frowned. All the other kids milled restlessly behind them. Eric and Corey were two of the best athletes in the school and nobody dared to ask them to stop so everyone else could play. Thad had to admit, he was a little jealous.

"Wow, she has skill," Corey said, wiping his hair as if it were sweaty.

Just then a brown blur tore from seemingly nowhere and stole the ball neatly from Lisa's feet.

"Hey!" cried Corey in surprise. "What are you doing?"

"Playing soccer," Jak said, moving the ball effortlessly from his right foot to his left. While his body seemed to stand still, his feet and the ball constantly moved. He wore dark gray running shorts and a European soccer T-shirt, a size too big, and looked every bit a soccer player.

"We were using that!" snarled Eric. He charged at Jak, but the smaller boy easily cut left and took the ball with him.

This time Eric tumbled to his knees for real as he tried to stop and turn at the same time. Dirt streaked his mostly white shirt and now his black shorts. He looked nothing like a soccer player.

"Wow," Lisa said. "He's pretty good."

Chapter 7

"He's nothing," Eric spat, quickly getting to his feet. "I just tripped in a hole." He stared dangerously at Jak. "Well, well, if it isn't the gypsy boy."

"Go eat a peach," Jak said disdainfully as he expertly flicked the ball back with his foot and kicked it up to his hands.

Eric's eyes bulged. "What did you say?" he said.

Ball on his hip, Jak smirked mischievously at Eric and replied, "You heard me."

Eric sneered down at the boy. "Sure, but I just couldn't see you, you're so short!"

Donald quickly pushed forward. "Come on, guys. Are we playing or what?"

"Yeah," said Danny. "We've been waiting forever. Let's pick teams."

Flashing with anger, Eric turned his wrath on Danny. "Shut it, fat boy. The only team that would pick you is the cupcake team."

Danny stared at him and said, "Yeah, well, at least I didn't trip in a hole on perfectly level ground!"

Eric started to shove his way to Danny.

Sensing trouble, Thad quickly moved to stand next to his friend. While he didn't want to fight, he knew Danny would do the same for him if he were ever in a pinch. Everyone else backed away so Eric stood alone facing the two.

"Guys," Lisa said nervously, "what's going on? Eric, aren't we going to play?"

All at once, Eric stopped and chuckled. "Ah, I'm just messing around. Okay, Lisa. You're one team captain and, uh, the fat boy can be the other."

Danny grunted. "My name is Danny and I'm not fat!"

Eric waved a hand dismissively. "Whatever. Lisa, you pick first."

The girl bit her lip. "Okay … I pick Jak."

Corey's and Eric's mouths dropped at the same time. Eric recovered first.

"Why him?" he demanded.

"Well," Lisa said reasonably, "he's the only one who could steal the ball from me. He must be good."

"Uh, oh, I pick Eric," Danny said, causing everyone's mouths to drop. "What?" he asked. "He's really good and I want to win!"

When the teams were finished, there were twelve on Lisa's team and ten on Danny's. Donald and Corey ended up with Eric and Danny while Thad went with Lisa and Jak. The only other notable pick, picked last of course, the Beast ended up with Lisa.

"Two girls make one boy," Eric muttered when Corey pointed out that Danny should get the last pick to make the teams even.

The game began slowly, but quickly picked up in action. Leslie passed the ball to Lisa to start it off and she immediately lost it to Eric.

"Still think I'm not good enough?" he yelled back as he streaked down the middle of the field.

After blowing by the first two defenders, he easily sidestepped an awkward tackle from the Beast playing sweeper.

"Get your smelly self away from me!" he yelled at her.

Then he was on goal.

Playing goalie, his least favorite position, Thad gulped. He silently prayed Eric wouldn't miss the goal and hit him instead. From experience, he knew Eric had a wicked right foot.

Eric slowed down pnd swept back his huge right leg. Thad flinched.

Then, just before Eric could strike, Jak flew in from behind with a perfect hook slide. Turning on his side, his right sneaker slid past a surprised Eric and hooked around the ball, bringing it away from Eric and to his feet. Popping back up, Jak started dribbling the other way. None of Eric's teammates had followed him on the attack, so Jak had open field ahead of him.

"Hey! Get him!" Eric tried to chase down the smaller boy, but was too slow. He pulled up in disgust as Jak kept the ball completely under his control and went past midfield.

"Way to go!" the Beast yelled.

"Pass it!" cried one of his teammates on the left.

"Just don't pass it to me!" Lisa squealed from the other side.

Jak didn't pay any attention to anyone. His head up and feet moving in a blur, he faked out Corey, cut between two other defenders and outran Donald. Three fullbacks and Danny stood between him and the goal.

Thad watched with amazement. He knew Jak was good at soccer, but not this good. All of a sudden, all his mischief and trouble had switched to pure skill and adrenaline. There was no fooling around now. Using step-overs, feints, and an array of other moves, Jak made most kids look silly. Even Kenny Darwood, considered the best soccer player in the school, watched in admiration.

On Danny's team, he trotted in from the left wing position to get a better look. He was just in time to see Jak step over the ball to the right and then the left before using the outside of his right foot to go right to get past the first fullback. Immediately after, he avoided the next defender with a sharp cut back left. Outrunning the third, he slid a low, hard shot past Danny, who barely moved.

"GOAL!" cried the Beast.

"Come on!" yelled Eric. "Let's go, guys! Can't anybody stop him?"

"You try it," wheezed Corey. "He's like a fly too fast to swat."

"I'll swat him," muttered Eric. "Give me the ball."

Kenny went over to Jak and lightly smacked his arm. "Nice moves, man," he said with true admiration. "You should play club soccer."

Breathing hard, Jak looked at him in surprise. "Uh, yeah," he said in surprise. "Thanks."

The tide turned soon after.

Corey nudged the ball to Eric and Eric immediately took the ball right at Jak. As Jak moved in for the tackle, Eric abandoned the ball and instead rushed at Jak, shoving him back.

Tumbling, Jak fell heavily to the seat of his shorts.

"Watch it!" he cried out.

Smirking, Eric went back to the ball and resumed dribbling.

Eyes turning into slits, Jak got to his feet and gave chase.

Watching from the goal, Thad sighed. Eric had been waiting. As Jak neared, Eric again left the ball and this time shoved Jak in the back. The smaller boy sprawled onto the ground, bouncing hard on his stomach.

Corey laughed. "Come on, over here!"

"You better be careful!" the Beast said, moving to block Eric. "You could hurt somebody!"

Grinning, Eric made to kick the ball hard at her. "Like this?" he said.

She flinched and jumped as Eric brought his foot down but started to dribble instead. He easily moved past the Beast. As two defenders cautiously closed, he slid a pass to the left wing to a wide-open Kenny. Dribbling twice, Kenny launched a well-placed kick in the top right corner of the net. Thad had no chance.

"GOAL!" roared Corey.

Eric gave a thumbs-up. "Nice shot, Ken!"

"Actually, I think you had the nice shots," Kenny told him. He trotted over and slapped Jak on the back as he passed by. "You'll get it back, kid."

Lisa clapped her hands. "Come on, guys! We can score again!"

"Sure," Leslie said dryly. "Maybe if we start wearing football pads."

Jak said nothing. Biting his lip, he stared at Eric.

Thad groaned from the goal. This was not going to end well.

For a time, the game settled into a rough back and forth match. No longer tentative, the players started playing hard and stiffened the lines.

Jak still displayed tremendous skill, but now the opposing team, aside from Kenny and Donald, just went after the player instead of the ball. He bit the dirt four more times and was stepped on once.

His teammates fared little better. Only Lisa and Leslie were not harmed by kicked shins or elbows in the side.

Eric, in particular, made sure to shove Jak whenever the smaller boy tried to challenge him with or without the ball. He was so focused on this that he grew sloppy. While he could get close to Thad in the goal, he usually lost his dribble or made a poor pass to the wings. The Beast and the other fullbacks cleared the ball away from danger without ever aiming and the ball kept coming back. It was better than being shoved and stepped on. The only other goal was from Kenny—he got loose on the wing, cut into the middle, and managed to fake out the Beast before firing a hard liner past Thad's outstretched hand.

With the score 2–1 and the action bogged down in the middle of the field, the Beast abruptly turned to Thad.

"Let me play goal," she said brusquely.

Thad looked at her. "What? No."

"Yes! We need you out there. Besides, I'm better at goal."

"I don't want to be fullback. It's too hot to run."

"Come on, Thad! Just do it for the team."

Thad jerked back. It was the first time the Beast had ever used his name. Didn't she understand that nobody liked her? For a moment, he couldn't help but feel a sort of admiration for her. In her shoes he would be lying under a tree wishing for death.

Corey booted a long shot and sent the ball bouncing to where Thad and the Beast stood.

"Get it!" cried Lisa. Despite being new to the game, she was quickly developing a taste for it. "Don't let it go in!"

"Fine," muttered Thad. "Be goalie!"

Charging forward, he got the ball and raced for the sidelines. Soccer was his favorite sport, but he mostly played by himself. His parents couldn't afford the fees for club, so he played on the local recreation team. This only lasted a few months and then only a few days a week. So in his free time at home he played by himself—

mostly dribbling between trees or around homemade obstacles. He loved the feeling of controlling the ball and rushing to attack.

Nobody expected Thad to dribble out of trouble. When he kept going, Eric finally made to cut him off, but as he approached, Thad slowed and then sped up, catching the opposing player by surprise.

Kenny next charged from the wing.

"Hey, pass it here!" cried a voice.

In the corner of his eye, Thad saw Jak run to the middle of the field, cutting into open space.

Eyes down, he booted the ball in that direction just before Kenny reached him.

"Now we got something!" squealed Lisa.

Then Jak was shoved down by Corey and the ball went back the other way.

Breathing heavily, Jak got to his knees and looked up at Thad. Dirt covered his arms, jersey, shorts, and legs. But what Thad saw were the tears were forming in the dark slanted eyes.

Swallowing, Thad approached him cautiously. "You're not bleeding, are you?" he asked tentatively.

"Bleeding mad," Jak said through gritted teeth. He lunged to his feet and brushed by Thad, racing after the ball.

Thad smoothed down his cowlick and watched as Corey passed the ball over to Kenny. Dribbling twice, the soccer star waited for a defender to converge before sending a centering pass into the open space towards Eric.

"Here's another goal," Thad groaned.

Donald had trotted near him and grunted. "Maybe not."

They watched as Eric settled the ball and lined up a shot. Giving a swift kick, he sent the ball rising straight for the left corner of the goal.

Turning to celebrate, he missed seeing the spectacular save.

Having watched Eric's feet, the Beast had guessed the shot and was already moving in that direction. Stretching out, she lunged just in time to get both hands on the ball. Crashing down, she kept it firmly pressed to her stomach.

"What the—" Eric turned and kicked at the grass in frustration.

"Robbed by the Beast!" Corey said, almost in wonder.

Seeing the save, Jak ran to the right side and waved a hand. "Hey, Mandy!" he called. "Over here!"

The Beast actually froze and let the ball drop from her fingers. It was the first time she'd ever heard her actual name spoken by a peer ... in forever.

"Get the ball!" shrieked Lisa.

Seeing the loose ball, Eric rushed forward. Mandy jumped as if slapped. Desperately, she tried to dive as the ball rolled from her.

"Not today, Beast," grunted Eric. He threw a hip check, knocking into her left shoulder and she went flying.

"GOAL!" he yelled as he blasted the ball into the empty net from point-blank range.

Corey crowed and rushed to celebrate with a chest bump.

Thad and Donald stared at each other in disbelief.

"Is this really soccer?" Donald asked. "It's more like hockey."

"It's your team," Thad said, frowning.

Donald shook his head. "Believe me. Not by choice."

Nobody checked on Mandy. Everyone watched in either embarrassment or, in some cases, secret enjoyment as she picked herself up and dusted off the dirt. On this day, like most days, she wore ragged jeans with a faded green T-shirt. At one time it had a generic football design, but that had washed out. Now it was covered in dirt.

"Come on, guys!" she yelled, clapping her hands. "Let's get it back!"

Thad swallowed. How could she get back up and act as if nothing happened? Didn't she know she was alone in this? She had no real teammates.

"You're the one who dropped the ball," one of the fullbacks muttered.

Mandy ducked her head and kicked at the hard-packed dirt in front of the goal. It was like kicking concrete. It felt like concrete when falling on it. And Thad knew that she knew.

Jak went still as he watched the ball being retrieved from the goal and moved up to the center. Thad saw him and gulped. The mischievous grin appeared beneath dark, flashing eyes.

Eric, Thad thought, was in trouble.

The next time Eric got the ball, he was immediately set on by Jak. Eric shielded the ball and tried to shove him away like always. This time, Jak ducked under the shove and moved in close. Reaching out, he grabbed a handful of Eric's shirt and pulled.

"Hey," yelped Eric. "What the heck, man!" He twisted away, pushing Jak down with a forearm. Falling, Jak grabbed the nearest thing, the back of Eric's shorts. As Jak went down, Eric's shorts followed.

With an elastic band, the black shorts easily slid to his knees before Eric even knew what had happened.

All at once he jerked to a stop. Looking down, he saw what everybody else saw. Bright red boxer shorts.

He turned to Jak with a mixture of anger and horror. "Why, hey, you-you—!"

In the distance, the whistle shrilled as Donald proved to be correct when Mr. Freeman waved in his class.

Immediately Jak leapt to his feet and raced in that direction like his shorts were on fire. Based on all the scrapes and bruises they hid, it may have felt that way too.

Corey fell to the ground laughing as Eric went to give chase and ended up waddling like an overgrown duck.

"You're dead, gypsy!" Eric screeched. His face flushed a deep crimson as he tried running faster while pulling up his shorts at the same time. He ended up planting his face into the hard, scratchy grass.

Everyone else, except for Lisa and Leslie, burst out laughing. The two girls covered their eyes and moaned about stupid boys.

"Eric!" shrieked his teacher. "That better not be what I think it is! Get over here!"

The game ended with the score 3–1 in favor of Danny's team, but Eric lost anyway. He'd lost face in a major way.

Chapter 8

After school, the bus ride home was spent reliving the "Underwear Game," as the fifth-grade class dubbed it.

"Oh, man," Danny gushed to Derek at the end, "you should have been there! My team won, but, oh man, you should have seen Eric's face!"

Next to him, Derek grimaced. "Did his pants really fall down?"

Donald chuckled from the seat across the aisle. He'd managed to get his little sister to sit near the back, so was able to join the fun. "You could say that, but they had help. I bet he wears a belt tomorrow."

"Jak is really okay," said Danny suddenly. "I mean, I'm sure it was an accident, but still … Eric needed somebody to stand up to him."

"You mean down to him, right?" Donald said.

Derek scoffed. "Don't tell me you're going to his party now."

"No way!" Danny said hurriedly. He shook his head with a look of disgust. "I just mean, can you imagine what he's like at home?"

Thad sat up suddenly. He'd been listening with half an ear while staring out the window next to Donald. "We're still not inviting him on the camping trip, right?"

"Camping trip?" Derek asked, sounding puzzled.

Thad stared over at him with an open mouth. "Don't tell me you already forgot—remember we planned it last weekend! We're going right after school ends!"

"Oh, uh, right. I remember." Derek did not sound convincing.

"I'm not real sure my parents will let me," Danny said. "Maybe if I get good grades I'll ask them."

"You mean, you didn't tell them yet?" Thad demanded, suddenly growing anxious. Was the trip over before it even began?

"Well, did you ask your parents?" Danny shot back.

Thad was forced to shake his head.

"Let's just wait and see," Donald said quickly. "We still have lots of time."

"In the meantime," Derek said, "tell me again how Eric lost his shorts."

Thad thumped his forehead against the window. He needed a plan to make this trip a reality. Fast.

Thad inadvertently got his chance that night at dinner. Thad's parents were two of the nicest people he knew, but that wasn't always a good thing.

His father, Mr. Utley, resembled his son with his dark hair and average height but was built more solidly. He wore glasses and a thick moustache that his mother called a hairy caterpillar. While he could be very serious, he often kept a smile on his square face, and laugh lines creased around his eyes and mouth. One thing Thad knew about his father: even though he rarely bragged, he was almost never wrong. He worked in a computer office doing government work and made frequent trips to Washington, D.C., and sometimes New York City.

Mrs. Utley stood only slightly shorter than his father and kept her thick, coffee-colored curls piled neatly on a nicely shaped head. Thad had inherited her oval face, long graceful fingers, and quiet disposition. While she didn't speak much outside the home, she had a watchful eye and did what needed to be done, often before anybody else knew about it. Constantly cheery, her idea of a rage was clapping her hands together and ordering Thad or his sister to their room. Both his parents were near their forties and still acted very much in love. Thad did his best not to mind.

Sitting at the dinner table, Thad listlessly stirred his macaroni and cheese with his fork.

He had an older sister, Candace, but she was a senior in high school and worked at the mall. Thad barely saw her most days.

"Thaddeus, we don't play with our food at the table," admonished his mother. Her eyes twinkled. She was the only person who called Thad by his given name. Working as a special education teacher at the high school, she always said a name was the first important thing about a person. Though often coming home exhausted, she always managed to have food ready and the table set soon after Thad arrived home from school. On this night, the top button was undone on her high-collared, cream-colored blouse. This meant she had an especially long day. "Tell us about your day."

"Yes, Thad," his father said from the head of the table as he wiped his mouth with a napkin. "How did it go, Tiger?"

Thad twisted his lips and shrugged. "Ah, it was okay."

"Great!" said his father jovially. "I had a long meeting with my boss today. I gave him a few proposals that I think he really listened to and—"

Thad's mother cleared her throat and interrupted. "Roger, I think Thad was trying to speak."

"No, I'm fine," Thad said quickly.

His mother smiled at him and said, "Oh. Well, in that case, it's my turn to talk."

"Of course, sweetie," Mr. Utley said. He put a hand over his wife's and smiled at her. "Tell us about your day."

"Well, let me skip all the horrid parts and tell you what happened after school," she said, still smiling at Thad. Suddenly Thad had a bad feeling. "I received a phone call this afternoon while you were napping."

"I wasn't napping," Thad said automatically. "I was doing homework." Mr. Freeman's foul mood had never left and at the end of the day he'd given the entire class a math review packet to be finished by Friday.

His mother's eyebrows lifted. "Well, when I peeked in your room, you were asleep. Regardless, the phone call was about you, Thaddeus."

Thad put down his fork and frowned. "Who from?" he asked.

"Oh," she said vaguely, "it was about this weekend."

Mr. Utley, up to this point more interested in his food, abruptly put his knife and fork down. "Don't forget, Susan," he reminded her, "that we have a dinner party with my boss on Saturday night. They're expecting us at seven."

Thad's mother smiled even wider. "Oh, I didn't forget. In fact, this phone call was about that too."

Thad groaned. "Oh, was it a babysitter?"

"Much better than that, Thaddeus," his mother said lightly. "Mrs. Tranner called me."

"Who?" Thad asked in genuine confusion.

"She's a mom of one of the boys in your class," explained Mrs. Utley. "You know, the boy who invited you to his sleepover this weekend?"

A look of horror passed over Thad's face. "Y-you mean ... No, Mom! No way!"

"Thad!" Mr. Utley frowned across the table. "Don't raise your voice, and listen to your mother."

"Thaddeus," Mrs. Utley said evenly. "I had a long talk with her and she sounds like a perfectly nice person."

"Maybe, but her son certainly isn't!" Thad said hotly.

Now his mother dropped her gaze and frowned. "Well, sorry. I'm afraid you will have to change your mind because I already said you were going."

"Mom, he's the kid who always gets into trouble! He's a menace to society!"

"Thaddeus!" Mrs. Utley looked at her son sharply. "Mrs. Tranner explained everything to me. She's worried that her son has no friends."

"No kidding!" Thad burst out. "He's, he's like the Beast!"

"The what?" his mother asked him.

Thad groaned and shook his head. "Never mind, Mom, but I can't go. I mean, nobody else is going."

Mrs. Utley sighed. "That's not a good reason not to go. Dear, talk to your son."

Clearing his throat, Mr. Utley took a sip of water and gently placed his cup down. "Thad, I know you don't want to go, but … sometimes we all need to do things we don't want to do."

"But, Dad, I don't need to do this!"

"Thad, don't interrupt," his father admonished. "The situation is this. Your mother and I will be gone all Saturday night. We don't particularly want to go, but it's for the benefit of my job and that benefits all of us."

"How is going to a dumb sleepover benefiting anybody?" Thad demanded to know.

"It will benefit that boy, Thaddeus," cut in Mrs. Utley.

"The only thing that would benefit him is therapy!" Thad said grimly.

His mother glared. "Thaddeus," she said severely, "don't ever say such a thing!"

Thad took a deep breath. "Okay … sorry, Mom." Inside, he trembled. How could he get out of this one? What would the others say when they found out? "Um, did she say she would call any other parents?"

His mother frowned and a dark cloud passed over her eyes. "Well, I don't think so. She would really like it if you came, though. It's going to be a birthday party and you can pick out a present tomorrow after school … maybe even pick one out for yourself too."

Mr. Utley coughed. "Now, Susan, let's not bribe the boy. Thad, do you really not want to go to this boy's party?"

Thad licked his lips and bit down his gut response. No way did he want to go. All his bad feelings about missing Jak's party were forgotten. However, he doubted his parents would let him off the hook so easily. Suddenly he got an idea. A brilliant idea. He had to control his urge to smile.

Crossing his arms, he looked both his parents in the eye. First his father and then his mother. "I'll go on one condition," he said firmly. "On the first week of summer vacation I get to go camping overnight with my friends."

A moment of silence passed. Mr. Utley carefully dabbed his moustache with his napkin. He slowly looked at Thad. "Who are your friends and where would you go camping?"

"Roger!" his wife cried in protest.

"Hold on, Susan. He's getting to be a big kid now. Let's hear him out."

Thad swallowed. This could be it. "Danny, Donald, and Derek … Um, we're going into the woods, you know, behind Derek's house."

His father nodded slowly. "That seems reasonable."

Mrs. Utley sniffed. "Who's bribing who?"

Mr. Utley grimaced and tapped two fingers on the table. "We'll discuss it," he finally said.

Thad sensed victory and wasn't ready to back down until he had it complete. "Come on, Dad!" he said. "Donald's moving right after—it'll be our final goodbye!"

Mr. Utley gave him a sharp look. "Wait a minute, Thad," he said. "One thing at a time. Let's talk about this weekend first."

"I'll only go if we can go camping."

"Thad," his father said carefully. "Camping is not that easy. But this weekend … your mother and I will be gone on Saturday. Candace will be working late. You need a place to go."

"Oh, yes," Mrs. Utley said hastily. "I told Mrs. Tranner I would let her know by Thursday." She exchanged a look with Thad's father.

Right then Thad knew two things. One, his parents had already discussed this matter before dinner. Two, he was going, no matter what.

"That reminds me, Thaddeus," his mother said, suddenly sounding slightly nervous, "the party was for a sleepover on Friday night. I talked with Mrs. Tranner and she agreed to have it on Saturday night. Now, they go to church on Sunday, so you'll have to pack some nice clothes." She forced a tentative laugh. "If you want to go, of course."

A deep rumble of anger rose from Thad's stomach. He watched as his mom hastily gulped water to hide her guilt. The decision had been made.

"Fine," he finally said, pushing his chair back. "Then I'm going camping this summer!"

He left the table before his parents could react. By the time his father called his name, he had already locked his door up in his room.

It took a lot of discussion, begging, and even a little crying, but in the end, Thad got his wish. He would be the sacrificial lamb and go to Jak's sleepover. In return, he would be allowed to go on a one-night camping trip with at least Derek and Danny. He hoped Donald would come, but wasn't too confident his best friend would agree, even if the whole thing was supposed to be his goodbye present.

The rest of the week went by all too quickly for Thad. No matter how much he dreaded its coming, Friday afternoon came. The next day would be the dreaded sleepover.

On the bus home, the boys were in their usual seats, except for Donald. His sister wanted him to sit up front with her. Always being nice, he complied and was stuck in the midst of kindergarteners and first graders.

Derek and Danny were bouncing up in their seats in a great mood.

"One more week!" sang Danny. "I can't wait for summer!"

"And no more homework! I can't believe Mr. Freeman forgot he gave us that stupid homework! I didn't even do the last two pages!"

Thad groaned from the next seat and slumped down in disgust. He'd done the entire packet. It was now ripped to tiny shreds, lying in the bottom of one of the trash cans back at school. He stared listlessly out the window. Jak had ignored him the whole week. Thad wondered if the guy even knew he was coming to his house the next day. Of course he didn't tell anybody about it, so was forced to suffer alone. Everyone else seemed to have forgotten about the party.

After the soccer game on Monday, the boys had stopped giving Jak grief. Still not accepted, he was at least tolerated. Speaking of soccer … that sport had been banned from recess.

Eric's teacher never found out what exactly had happened so decided the students should avoid organized (or disorganized) sports for the rest of the school year. It didn't matter; telling the story was more fun than playing soccer. Eric glared at everyone who mentioned it, but nobody cared. In fact, he'd tried to wear extra-loose shorts on Tuesday, just to show everyone he didn't mind having his boxers seen, but had ended up being sent to the office for a belt. In any case, he walked very carefully around Jak, but made sure to glare.

Now on the bus, Thad clenched his fists. Jak hadn't even acknowledged him the whole week—didn't even turn around to give a nod or anything.

"What's wrong, Thad?" Danny asked, breaking his train of thought. "Aren't you ready for summer, man?"

Thad pushed himself up. "Of course I am. You guys are ready for camping, right?"

Danny's face fell. "Oh, er, sure ... yeah." He sounded as sure as snow in June.

Thad grimaced and gave his two friends a wicked look. "I got my parents' permission. I said we're camping back behind Derek's house. What about you?"

Derek perked up. "You did?" he asked. He sounded impressed. "Really?"

Thad nodded. "Yeah. I figure it's close to the woods near the park, right?"

Derek's face fell. "Oh, yeah, sure." He bit his lip and then brightened. "My dad will be gone that week. He'll be flying to Germany, so it might work!"

Danny groaned. "You mean you guys are seriously trying to find old houses in the woods at night?"

Derek and Thad looked at him. "Of course!" they said together.

Danny looked at both of them. "What ... what if one of the houses is haunted?" he asked, his voice quavering slightly.

Thad gave a sardonic smile. "Believe me, after this weekend I'll be ready for anything."

"Huh?" Danny asked. Derek also gave Thad a hard look.

Thad grinned tightly. "Don't worry about it. I'll tell you on Monday. Uh, speaking of that, I'll be busy on Saturday and Sunday."

Chapter 9

Saturday afternoon came, and just past four o'clock Thad found himself stuck in the van on the way to his sacrifice. His mother kept taking her eyes off the road to make sure Thad's hair was perfectly combed. She eyed his ever-rising cowlick with concern. Twice she'd licked her fingers and made to push it down, but Thad wisely leaned the other way.

"Remember, Thad. These are important people. You have to look your best and be on your best manners. Mr. Tranner is used to high company. He's a respected member of the school board."

"Mom, okay." Thad sighed, not really knowing what the school board even was or did. "I just want to get this over with." He tugged at his tuft of hair in the back. The more nervous he got, the more he tugged at his cowlick. By the end of the weekend he figured his mother wouldn't have to worry about it any longer. He would pull it straight out of his head.

"Well, this is it!" Mrs. Utley gave Thad a bright smile as she turned into a driveway in a well-kept neighborhood a few streets over from Derek's house. "You'll have a great time—I know it."

"I bet." Sitting in front of the minivan, Thad put his hand on the door but made no move to open it.

From the front windshield he saw a surprisingly normal-looking two-story house, with light blue siding and red shutters on the windows. A brick chimney stuck up on the left, next to a two-car garage. From the driveway, a cement sidewalk led to a small uncovered porch with a deep red door. Trees dotted a large front yard lined with thick, dark green grass. A wood fence was visible on either side of the house enclosing what seemed to be a sizable backyard. From behind the fence Thad could hear the screams of kids. They were either killing each other with terrible deaths or having a great time.

"Thaddeus Utley, you put a smile on your face and go out there and have a wonderful time. Don't forget the present and your bag."

Thad didn't move. "I won't."

"Here, let me fix your collar." Maybe Mrs. Utley, due to the screaming, started having second thoughts, because she kept the engine running as she leaned over and straightened Thad's shirt.

A blinding white polo shirt, it tucked tightly into his khaki shorts and was cinched firmly at the waist by a brown leather belt. His old sports sneakers had been traded for a pair of freshly polished Reeboks. Thad didn't go to many sleepovers and when he did, his mother made sure he didn't embarrass her. Instead, she embarrassed Thad.

Thad squirmed, but still did not leave the safety of the van.

Just then the screaming increased. Suddenly, a gate swung open in the fence to the left of the house and a young girl raced out. Seeing the van, she jerked to a stop and waved a hesitant hand.

Thad's heart jumped in his chest. The girl appeared to be near his age and had long, silky, black hair hanging past her shoulders. Her thin face appeared intelligent and lively. Tan shorts and a thin white shirt covered a one-piece bathing suit. Wet splotches dotted her clothes and she had no shoes. In her hands she held a large water gun. Thad stared at her. Gulping, he looked over at his mother.

She also stared at the girl. "This boy ..." she said slowly. "He isn't a girl, is he?"

Then the girl flicked hair from her eyes and opened her mouth. "JAK!" she cried. "YOUR FRIEND IS HERE! YOU'D BETTER COME OUT!"

Thad lifted his eyebrows toward his mother and then stared back at the girl. "I think it will be fine, Mom."

"Well, maybe … Look, Thaddeus, I have a confession. Well, the only reason I initially agreed to this is, well, Mr. Tranner." She took a deep breath and started speaking faster. Her hands went to the steering wheel and clinched tightly. "He works at the school board, and, um, he's pretty high up, okay? Well, he may be able to help my job … oh, what am I doing? Thad. If you want to go home, there's still time. We can still find a babysitter."

Thad could only imagine what it would look like if the van backed out right now and left. He might never see the girl again. "That's okay, Mom." He started to open the door.

"Honey, really, I don't know …"

The red door swung open and a petite woman rushed out balancing a baby on her hip. Seeing the van, she lifted her free arm and waved vigorously. "Susan? Is that you? I'm Mary Tranner. You're just in time!"

She looked like an older version of the young girl. Caught, Thad's mother put on a big smile and quickly opened her door. "Don't unpack yet," she said tightly from the side of her mouth. "Oh, hi! I'm Susan Utley, Thaddeus's mom."

"I'm so glad you made it! Michelle, go get your brother and tell him his company is here."

The girl made a face. "I already did!"

"Then take Peter and go find him."

"Oh, fine." The girl wrinkled her nose but took the baby from her mother's shoulder.

Thad quickly exited the van and moved shyly to his mother's side.

"Oh, I'm so sorry, this is my daughter, Michelle, and my youngest, Peter. This must be Thad!"

Michelle smiled brightly at Thad and lifted the baby's flabby arm to give a wave. "We'll be back!" she sang. "Nice to meet you, Thad!"

Thad swallowed and half waved as she disappeared behind the fence.

"Not a problem," Thad's mother said, forcing a smile. "I didn't realize you had so, um, well, that your son had siblings."

Mrs. Tranner laughed. "Oh, that's most of them. Jakavos and Michelle are in the middle. The poor boy has three more older sisters. Peter is his first brother."

"Really? What are their ages, if I may ask?"

Thad stifled a groan. His mom was always way too protective. He knew she would not want him stuck in a house full of girls picking on him.

"Well, let's see. Catherine is a senior next fall and turns eighteen in July. Barbara is fifteen and Elizabeth just turned thirteen."

"Oh, um, are they, you know, are they okay with a sleepover?"

Mrs. Tranner laughed. "You don't have to worry about a thing. The girls are all going out with me for a shopping trip."

"What?" Michelle came through the fence with the baby and still carrying a dripping water gun. "Mom! I hate shopping!"

"Michelle, I told you yesterday! Oh, my, what are you wearing? Quick, give me the baby and go get ready."

"But Jak won't come out!"

Mrs. Tranner rolled her eyes at Thad's mother. "I live in a circus. Fine. Go show Thad where he is and then go get ready. Thad, I'm really, really glad you came." She took a deep breath. "To be honest, he wasn't so sure you would make it."

Thad squirmed. "Oh, um, er, no, I can't wait."

"Yes, neither can Jak." Then she got a better look at Thad. Eyeing his clothes a bit critically, she frowned momentarily, but quickly hid it with a kind smile. "I think you'll have a great time. Why don't you run off and I'll talk to your mom for a minute. Michelle, don't point that thing this way! You'll squirt somebody's eye out!"

"Sorry, Mom," Michelle said, sounding anything but.

Mrs. Tranner took the baby and pushed Michelle toward the backyard. "Tell Jak to come back quick to get his friend's bags!"

Michelle grinned and said, "Sure, Mom!"

Thad swallowed and followed one of the prettiest girls he'd ever seen. He never knew Jak had sisters! But of course, to be honest, he didn't know jack about Jak. The weekend promised to be very educational.

Leading Thad through the gate, Michelle raised a hand and gestured to a wide space with large patches of dirt and dotted with trees. The little grass remaining looked to be the victim of a long war it had no hope of winning. A hose lay across the middle of the yard and streamed with water, creating a good-sized mud pit.

Michelle didn't have Jak's mischievous slanted eyes, but they still possessed plenty of spark. Grinning at his reaction when seeing the yard, she pointed to the back corner at a stack of logs.

"He's behind those logs," she whispered. "We're in the middle of a water fight, so watch out. I think Barbara is up in one of the windows with balloons."

Thad swallowed nervously. "Oh, uh, okay ..."

"Just follow me. Oh, and take this." She pushed the water gun in Thad's middle and gave him no choice.

Hunching her shoulders, she crept toward the log pile with long graceful steps. Along the way, she stopped by the mud pit and picked up another water gun. Waving a hand forward, she pointed to the logs. "On the count of three," she hissed, "we rush him."

Gulping, Thad nodded. Water leaked from his gun and busily wet the front of his shorts. Sweat dripped down the back of his neck. Suddenly he wished he'd taken his mom's advice and left. Instead, he pushed the gun in front and waited for the signal.

Mouthing the first numbers, Michelle yelled "THREE!" Dashing to the logs, she jumped on top and yelled. Thad hurried to catch up and found her staring at a bare patch of earth.

"Huh?" Michelle asked in befuddlement. "Where'd the little monster go?"

"Right here, loser!"

A stream of cold water drenched Thad's back and then Michelle's.

"Hey!" shouted Thad. Whirling, he saw Jak standing in the middle of the mud wearing a bathing suit and holding the hose. Holding a finger over the nozzle, he did a dance while shooting a steady stream without letup. Suddenly he recognized Thad and yelped. Dropping the hose like it burned him, he stared in wonderment.

"I thought she was joking!" he said in amazement. "You really came!"

Just then a large water balloon fell from the sky and smacked him in the side of the head.

"Direct hit!" yelled a teenage girl from the top middle window. Then she also noticed the company. "Oh my gosh! Oops!" She ducked back inside and the window slammed closed.

Thad, dripping with water, blinked stupidly.

Jak, now on his knees in the mud, wiped hair from his eyes and grinned. "Aren't you glad you're here?"

"You bet," Thad said weakly.

Michelle thought quickly and suddenly turned her gun on Thad. "Um, that's it! Boys against girls! Take this, invader!"

A stream of water struck him in the face and went up his nose.

"This way!" called Jak, gathering up the hose again. "I'll cover you!"

Michelle squealed as the hose sprayed her and she ducked behind the logs.

Not knowing what else to do, Thad moved behind Jak, nearly slipping in the mud. He really wished his friends were with him. He wouldn't feel like such an idiot, and, he had to admit, they would be having fun.

"What do we do now?" he asked Jak.

Jak turned his slanted eyes at him and grinned. "We soak my sister!"

"Wait!" Michelle cried from her fortress. "Tell your friend to take off his shoes before they get ruined!"

Thad looked down and stifled a groan. Too late. Standing two inches in mud, his bright white Reeboks looked to have been dipped in fudge ... or something else. Brown spatters covered the laces and tops.

"Don't worry, we can rinse them off later," Jak said. Suddenly looking shy, he squeezed the hose tight so no water escaped. "Do you, um, want to go inside and do something else?"

"Oh, well, no, that's okay. I can put my shoes by the house, if that's okay. I can go barefoot."

"Sure," Jak said doubtfully. "Sorry, um, for getting you wet … I didn't think … um …"

Thad shrugged like it was no big deal. "That's okay … I really hate these shoes anyway. My mom made me bring them. Here, wait a sec." Thad kicked off his shoes and peeled off his socks. After a brief moment of hesitation, he pulled off his shirt too. This he at least folded neatly and put on top of the shoes. "All right, I'm ready now."

Smiling, Jak kicked the water gun toward him. "You go first and I'll follow."

"You sure?" Thad asked timidly.

Jak grinned wickedly. "Trust me."

Gulping, Thad slowly approached the woodpile. Michelle had kept awfully quiet and out of sight. Jak, he noticed, made no move to follow.

Suddenly a water bomb exploded in the dirt by his right leg, spattering him with mud.

"Hey!" cried a voice from above. "You're not Jak!"

"Right here, loser!" Jak sprung from the edge of the house and unfurled the hose. A wild stream of water shot up and sprayed right into the surprised face of an older sister that had reappeared at the top window.

"Jak!" she screeched. "You're soaking my room!" Hastily she moved back and slammed the window again.

"You're going to get it now, boy." Michelle stood behind the pile and shook her head.

Not knowing what else to do, Thad squirted her in the face. That was when his mother walked into the backyard and just about fell on her face.

"Thaddeus Utley!" she cried in dismay. "What—what are you doing?"

Chapter 10

Thad, Michelle, and Jak froze in place.

Mrs. Tranner quickly followed after and surveyed the damage with a well-practiced eye. She'd dropped the baby off somewhere and placed her hands on her hips. "Michelle! You're supposed to be getting ready! Jak, get over here and …" she paused. At first Thad thought she was angry, but instead she put a hand to her mouth to stifle giggles. "I'm sorry … I just … my kids." She looked up toward the sky. "Why me?"

Mrs. Utley looked at her and then at her soaked son standing with a water gun still aimed at a soaking girl. She also started to giggle and it turned into outright laughter. "I guess sleepovers for boys are a little different than for girls. Thad," she choked. "You're a mess!"

Looking sheepish, Jak went over to his mom, wiping mud from his hands on his sides. "We were just playing," he mumbled.

"I can see that. Here, you got mud on your face, on your back, and your hair! Jak! That had better be mud! Go take a shower and get your room ready for Thad. If it looks anything close to you, we're in big trouble." She gave him a sharp but playful spank and sent him to the back door. "Stay off my carpets and go straight to the tub! Don't pass Go and don't collect any more mud!"

She looked over at Thad apologetically. "I promise, this wasn't planned. If it's okay, you can take the second bath."

"Uh, Mom?" Michelle asked. "What about me? Can I just stay home?"

"No, ma'am. You get your stuff and use my bathroom. Now hurry! Your father is coming home with the pizza and I promised to be out of here by then."

Mrs. Utley shook her head. "Thaddeus, I mean, uh, Thad, I'll leave you here now. I think you'll have a good time."

Wiping mud from his face, Thad grinned. "You bet."

Thad waved a last goodbye to his mother's departing minivan and struggled to put his heavy travel bag on his shoulder. His other hand held a large gift bag containing Jak's present. Taking a deep breath, he turned to the front door.

Without a free hand, he struggled to reach the doorbell and finally managed to knock it with his elbow.

Almost instantly it swung open and a pretty brunette teenager of about fifteen stared at him. "Oh," she said as if surprised. "You're still here! We thought you'd gone."

Thad blinked stupidly.

"Barbara!" scolded Jak's mom. "Don't say that! Here, Thad, sorry, but I had to fight to get these for you. Come in. You're probably freezing!" Mrs. Tranner ran down the stairs behind the teenager with a load of towels. "Don't worry about making a mess. My son already did that. Just wipe your feet and I'll show you to Jak's room. Here, put down your bags."

Barbara grinned and stepped back. "Sorry about the balloons earlier. I'm glad I missed you." Her hair was slightly damp in front and her black shirt was rumpled as if still drying. Otherwise, she was very pretty and a few inches taller than Thad. "I can take the gift bag—I hope you didn't get anything too good for my brother. He certainly doesn't deserve it."

"That's, um, fine," Thad mumbled awkwardly, shuffling into a tiled foyer.

"Oh, leave the poor boy alone." Mrs. Tranner took Thad's travel bag and stuffed his arms full of towels.

Still shirtless and shoeless, Thad uncomfortably started wiping off the mud and water.

"I already put your shirt in the wash and cleaned your shoes. They're drying out back."

"Oh, um, thanks," he mumbled.

"Barbara, go get Peter ready. I need to see if Michelle is ready. Thad, I'll be right back. I'll drop your bag in the room."

"I can get that—"

"No trouble." She'd already started up the stairs. "Catherine, you and Elizabeth need to get off Minecraft and get ready to go! We leave in five minutes!"

Feeling nearly overwhelmed, Thad used the brief moment of peace to look around as he finished drying. The interior of the house seemed bigger than it looked from outside. Stairs directly in front of him led to the second floor. To his left was a small closet next to the entrance of a comfortable den. He could see couches and a large rocking chair set close together and facing a flat-screen TV with a large oriental carpet in front. The walls were lined with bookshelves. To his right was a spacious living room with more couches and another rocker. More bookshelves lined the walls where there were no windows. There had to be more books in the two rooms combined than his school library. This, he decided, was not how he expected Jak, the little spaz, to live.

"Thad?" called Mrs. Tranner. "Are you coming?"

Putting down the towels, Thad went quickly up the stairs and followed Jak's mom. The upstairs hallway was carpeted and Thad saw a trail of mud leading to a room on the right.

"That's the bathroom," Mrs. Tranner said with a roll of her eyes. "It was cleaned earlier today, but I'm not holding my breath now."

He followed her down the hall to a closed door holding a large poster of a soccer player on it. A short hall to the left led to another room, this one open.

"If you didn't know, Jak is a soccer nut," called a voice from the other room. "I'm Elizabeth!"

"And you're a soccer nut, too," an older voice chided.

Turning, Thad saw a girl a few years older coming toward him being followed by a young woman. Both were dressed nicely in shorts and blouses and wore identical ponytails.

"I'm Catherine," said the older girl. "I'm glad you made it up in one piece."

"Yeah," Elizabeth said wickedly. "We were sure you wouldn't come, and if you did, you'd leave screaming in five minutes."

"That's enough, you two," their mother said. "Downstairs on the double and let's get ready to go."

"Sure, Mom," Elizabeth said. To Thad, she smiled and said, "Nice to meet you!"

Catherine patted Thad's shoulder. "Really, we're glad you're here."

"I can drive, right, Mom?" Elizabeth asked, winking at Thad.

"Sorry, Elizabeth," Mrs. Tranner said as if used to the question. "Catherine has the license."

Thad blushed as the two girls brushed past on their way to the stairs.

Mrs. Tranner smiled. "Don't mind them, Thad. Jak hasn't gotten a lot of guests lately. Now come in!"

Thad's eyes widened. It was true. Jak was a soccer nut. Entering his room was like entering a shrine dedicated to soccer. Posters and framed pictures of teams and players covered the wall and even some parts of the ceiling. Pushed back in the right corner was a small bed decked out in soccer covers. A small goal a foot high lay next to the foot of the bed and held three soccer balls. A desk faced a window on the wall across from the door and held a pile of soccer books. To Thad's left stood a dresser supporting a bookshelf. Among the books were soccer trophies and soccer trading cards. A toy chest was stuck in the left corner near an open closet. Thad spotted at least one more soccer ball peaking from the closet. In the center of the room lay a large rug in the shape of … a soccer ball. Thad's bag lay on top of the rug with a sleeping bag next to it.

"I hope you'll be comfortable here," said Mrs. Tranner. She sighed. "He decorated it himself with the help of his sisters."

"Oh, it's, uh, great," Thad said. "Really." He wished his room looked half as good.

"Well, go ahead and get what you need for a shower and I'll get everything ready downstairs. John should be here any minute with the pizza." Mrs. Tranner's face suddenly turned serious and she placed a hand on Thad's shoulder. "Thank you for coming."

Embarrassed, Thad nodded. "Yeah, erm, thanks for having me …"

"It'll be our pleasure." Giving his shoulder a squeeze, she left the room.

Sighing, Thad knelt by his bag and tried to process everything. As the only boy with an older sister, entering Jak's house was like entering a public zoo … only he was the animal everybody wanted to see. Before he could collect his thoughts, the door burst open and Jak raced in.

Seeing Thad, he stumbled to a halt and rubbed his thighs. Damp hair hung from his head and beads of water still clung to his neck. His black and red soccer pajamas also had damp spots. Thad hoped he'd at least used soap. "Uh, hey."

"Hey. You, um, have a nice room."

"Uh, yeah, it's okay … Are you going to use the shower?" Jak wiped water from his cheek. "You better hurry before one of my sisters gets in there. Once that happens, you're stuck. Trust me. They take hours in the bathroom."

Thad's mouth twitched. "Uh, okay."

"And make sure you lock the door. The lock is broken, so you have to open the drawer next to the door. I'll show you how. Trust me. You don't want anybody walking in, especially one of my sisters."

Now Thad squirmed. "Uh, no … not at all." Swallowing, he quickly gathered his pajamas and other necessities. He followed Jak with great trepidation to the bathroom. For a moment he feared that maybe Jak had led him into a trap—perhaps this was all part of an elaborate revenge plan …

Thankfully nothing happened, and using Jak's makeshift lock, Thad finished a very hasty shower with his eye on the door the entire time. When finished and wearing his own pajamas, he found Jak waiting by the stairs. He'd spent almost an hour at home debating whether or not to even bring pajamas. It was a good thing his mom made him bring them. He'd been planning on wearing shorts and a T-shirt.

"Hurry, the pizza is here!" Jak told him.

For Thad, staying at Jak's house was proving to be a very different experience.

Chapter 11

Mr. Tranner turned out to be a bulky man with dark brown curls and a wide friendly face. With solid muscle filling out his dress shirt and khaki pants, he stood just over six feet and resembled a small bulldozer. Seeing Jak coming down the stairs followed by Thad, his face lit up in a friendly grin. Quickly he shoved two gigantic pizza boxes into his wife's hands and snatched Jak up in a bear hug, lifting him up high in the air.

"I told you your friend would show up, buddy boy!" Putting Jak down, he tousled his wet hair. "You did use a towel, right?"

"Dad, come on!" Jak still couldn't stop smiling.

Mr. Tranner then thrust a meaty hand, the size of a dinner plate, at Thad. "I'm John Tranner, Jak's dad. It's great to meet you!"

Thad felt as if his hand would be squeezed to pulp. "I'm Thad."

"Well, I hope you're hungry!" Releasing Thad's hand, Mr. Tranner slapped his back.

Nearly flying to the floor, Thad nodded. "Yes, sir."

"Oh, no. No friend of Jak's is going to call me sir. Just call me ... ouch!"

Michelle had snuck up behind him and jumped up to latch both hands around his neck. Her feet dangled from the ground.

"Okay. Ouch," Elizabeth said dryly. "We'll see you later." She smiled at Thad. "Good luck." She and the other girls were gathered behind their mother, all except Michelle, clutching purses. Michelle still clutched her dad's neck.

Mrs. Tranner shook her head and passed the pizza boxes to Catherine before pulling at Michelle's shirt. "Okay, Michelle, not in front of guests! He's going to think we're barbarians!"

Mr. Tranner winced as his daughter released her grip. "Please take your horde, madam, and leave."

"Oh, honey," Mrs. Tranner said, "have a great time."

"Come back soon and I will." He wiggled his eyebrows.

Jak groaned and covered his eyes as they kissed.

Standing at the bottom of the stairs, Thad scratched his head. What would his mother think if she saw this, he wondered.

Before leaving, Mrs. Tranner pressed a cell phone in Thad's hand. "Just in case you want to call home or if there's an emergency, okay? We'll be back in a few hours."

Thad doubted he would need the cell phone. Mr. Tranner proved to be friendly and not quite what Thad's mother made him think he would be like. He wasn't boring at all.

Taking the pizzas to the kitchen, located behind the stairs, he set them on the counter and turned to the boys. "Okay, guys, what are the plans?"

"What type of pizza did you get?" Jak demanded.

"I wasn't sure what you wanted, so I got a little of everything. This one has the little fishies and the other is just olives and broccoli. I figured you boys could get your veggies while eating pizza." Seeing Thad's face, he laughed.

Jak gave him a sorrowful look and crossed his arms over his skinny chest. "Not funny, Dad," he said, shaking his head.

Mr. Tranner chuckled. "Don't worry, kids. I got Paul's New York classic. One cheese and one pepperoni. I hope you like New York style, Thad."

Thad grunted. "I never had it," he admitted. His mom wasn't big on ordering out pizza.

"Then get ready for a miracle," Mr. Tranner assured him. "Why don't we sit in front of the television and put on a movie while we eat."

"Really?" asked Jak, his eyes searching for a joke.

"Of course!" Mr. Tranner said. "There are no women around! This is what men do! Thad, you want a beer? All I have is root beer," he said before Thad could think of a response. "Now what movie do you guys want?"

"Not a western!" Jak turned to Thad. "All my dad watches are old westerns."

Mr. Tranner shrugged. "That's what I thought you would say. So I brought a soccer movie. Do you like soccer, Thad?"

Thad nodded. "Uh, sure."

"Great," Mr. Tranner said. "Here, catch."

Mr. Tranner produced a DVD case from his back and tossed it to Thad, who caught it in surprise.

Jak moved to his elbow to see. "Sh-shoow … a … lin soccer?" he tried.

"*Shaolin Soccer*, buddy boy," Mr. Tranner said coming up from behind them. He slapped a hand on Jak's back. "Let's see how good it is."

It turned out great—for the next two hours Mr. Tranner sat with Jak at his side on the couch while Thad took the big rocker. At first they feasted on pizza and talked about school. Mr. Tranner asked about Thad's mom and mentioned that he knew her by reputation—all good, he assured him. He worked mostly in the middle schools and looked forward to seeing them next year in the sixth grade. After that, he promised no more school talk … though he did know a lot of jokes about school.

After a while they put on the movie and became lost in the world of martial arts and soccer. They laughed hard at most of the movie and at one point Mr. Tranner almost threw up his pizza from laughter. Once dinner was over, Jak got out his Xbox controls and introduced Thad to video game soccer.

At home, Thad had no cable, no video games, and very few movies. He spent most of his time playing computer games without Internet or reading. Just recently he'd started to write. This made him go wide-eyed with wonder at everything Jak had to offer. The two boys ended up being on the same team because Thad proved hopeless with the controls. They played for about an hour while

Mr. Tranner cleaned up. Play was interrupted when he returned from the kitchen carrying pints of ice cream and bowls.

"We're supposed to wait for your sisters, Jak, and have cake, but I think we can sample the ice cream."

Nobody argued. After multiple helpings of mint chip and candy-bar-flavored ice cream, Jak and Thad started doing their own version of Shaolin soccer, using a pillow for the ball. Mr. Tranner went around the room to do his best as goalie and prevent any pictures or vases from shattering.

Finally, sweaty and exhausted, the three collapsed on the couch. Mr. Tranner put his arm around Jak and looked at the ceiling. ESPN played on the television and everything seemed perfect.

Thad actually felt bad for all the boys who refused Jak's invitation. They were really missing out. Feeling lazy and content, his eyes traveled around the room and took in the family pictures.

"So," Mr. Tranner said after a long moment of silence, "you boys know each other well?"

"Uh, yeah, Dad," Jak said, looking up. "I invited him, right?"

Mr. Tranner tickled Jak's stomach. "Oh, so you did. What do you know about Thad, then? And what does he know about you?"

Both boys wriggled uncomfortably. Thad sat on Jak's left on the end of the couch. He couldn't meet the smaller boy's eyes. Even though they'd sat near each other in class for an entire school year, neither ever took the time to learn much about the other.

Mr. Tranner chuckled. "Well, now's a good time to change that. Jak, why don't you tell Thad about yourself? And then he can share with you, if he wants."

"Like what?" Jak asked. "He already knows I like soccer."

"Oh, yeah?" Mr. Tranner pulled Jak close and squeezed him around the shoulders. "Do you like soccer? Really? I never knew that."

"Dad!" Jak squirmed, but couldn't hide a smile.

"All right, then," said Mr. Tranner. "Tell him about your family."

Jak lifted his eyebrows. "I can tell him about my big annoying dad."

Mr. Tranner immediately slid his arm behind Jak and grabbed him by the waist and tickled his side. "You think I'm big and annoying? Do you?"

"Yes!" screeched Jak. "Okay, okay!"

Letting go, Mr. Tranner tousled his son's hair. He looked over at Thad. "I see you looking at all the pictures. Any questions?"

Thad reddened. He'd been looking mostly at the pictures of Michelle. "Um, not really … well, uh, what grade is Michelle in?" he blurted. Instantly he regretted asking and he felt his face burn.

Mr. Tranner nodded wisely and nudged Jak's arm. "Ah, so you noticed. Jak, you want to tell him, or should I?"

Jak shrugged. "You," he said simply.

Mr. Tranner nudged Jak again. "Come on," he said. "Tell Thad how you and your sister are the same age but not twins and not in the same school."

Jak sighed and rolled his eyes. "Daadd …"

"Oh, fine." Mr. Tranner leaned back in the cushion and patted Jak's shoulder. "We found Jak in Romania when he was two. We were visiting a monastery over there when one of the monks introduced him to us."

Jak moved to rest his head against his dad's shoulder. "I was playing soccer then, wasn't I?" he asked.

"Yes, you were." Mr. Tranner grinned, relaxed. "The monks wanted to get you away from their quiet home, and my noisy brood of girls seemed perfect. And once seeing you, buddy boy, I knew it had to happen." He looked up at Thad and smiled. "Our old priest had arranged the trip as sort of a pilgrimage. He's the one who helped us get Jak in the end. I tell you, adoption is not an easy process. But you, buddy boy, were worth every hardship." He squeezed Jak's knee absently.

Jak slid his head down so it rested on his dad's knee. He curled up his body and relaxed. Mr. Tranner smoothed down his hair as he continued.

Thad didn't dare move a muscle. As he learned Jak's story, he couldn't help but feel guilty for being so reluctant to come to the birthday party.

"Michelle is actually a few months older. But," he now made a fist and knocked lightly on Jak's head, "unlike some guys in the family, she actually pays attention in school. She used to do Elizabeth's homework before starting kindergarten. She got so far ahead that she ended up skipping fourth grade. Next year she'll be in the seventh grade."

Thad swallowed. That meant next year he'd at least be going to the same school as her.

Mr. Tranner gave a huge yawn and sat forward. "Oh, boy. It's way past bedtime." He clapped Jak's thigh. "You guys ready for sleep?"

Jak barely lifted his head. "But Dad," he murmured, "you said I didn't have a bedtime tonight!"

"I know I did." He grunted. "I meant it's past my bedtime. We have church tomorrow, remember? You guys are riding with me early, right? Either that or you're stuck in the van with the girls and the baby."

"Um, sure, um, Mr. Tranner," Thad said. Secretly, though, he wouldn't mind riding in the same car as Michelle. "What time should we be ready?"

"I try to leave at nine thirty, but we can be a few minutes late. Oh, Thad, I'm sorry to say, but we don't eat breakfast before church because of Communion. Don't worry, though. We have cereal, frozen waffles, or toast. Just say what you like and I can have it ready before leaving."

"Oh, um, that's fine," Thad said quickly. "I don't need anything either. I can wait."

Mr. Tranner looked at him doubtfully. "Well, uh, I don't know how much you know about our church, but it's Romanian Orthodox. You can't receive Communion unless you're Orthodox—it's a rule to make sure you know what you're doing."

Thad could just imagine stuffing his face while Jak and Michelle watched. No way would he let that happen. "That's okay," he said. "I'm not really hungry in the morning."

"Well, all right. Let me know if you change your mind. Why don't you boys start another game and ..." he trailed off. "Uh, Jak? Jak?"

Mumbling, Jak only curled up tighter against his dad. His eyes were shut.

"It's been a long day, huh? I guess the cake will have to wait." He glanced over at Thad. "Are you doing all right?"

"Sure. It's been great, really. Thank you, Mr. Tranner."

Mr. Tranner waved a hand dismissively. "Believe me. It's worth all the trouble." He grimaced and ran a hand through his hair. "We moved here last summer from Florida for my job … Starting over somewhere new has been hard, especially for the kids. You ever move, Thad?"

"Um, no, sir—I mean Mr. Tranner."

"Ah, just call me Ouch. Poor Jak had to leave all his friends, his soccer team, and his home. At the same time, we had Peter and, well, Jak didn't transition too well. Sorry to tell you all of this, but I thought you should know. We're all trying, but moving can sure make life difficult."

Thad nodded uncomfortably. "My best friend is moving next week … He's going to California."

"I'm sorry to hear that. It's not easy losing friends … nor is it easy making friends. Make sure you guys have fun together before he leaves, okay?"

"Uh, yes, sir."

"Ouch," Mr. Tranner said. He grinned at Thad's confused look. "With Jak around," he explained, "I say 'ouch' a lot, so that's what I'm called a lot."

They spent the next few minutes watching ESPN. Mr. Tranner frowned when the sportscaster began a story about another doping scandal in sports.

"I remember when sports were about playing and not this junk," he muttered. "Do you play any sports, Thad?"

"Uh, a little soccer."

"Oh, yeah?"

Thad's face reddened. "Not for a real team or anything. I just play recreation in the fall."

"Hey, that's a good place to start." He nodded tiredly at the television. "Just make sure if you ever go into high school sports you steer clear of those jokers." He gestured at the screen. "This junk is happening all over … I spent all afternoon in a meeting because of a rumor that some of our high school players are using steroids and may be passing them down to middle school. Middle school, for crying out loud."

Thad brought his knees to his chin and kept quiet. He'd thought having cable meant watching great sports all the time. Instead, much like in the rest of life, evil was always trying to creep in and ruin everything.

Mr. Tranner sighed and clicked off the television. "Sorry, I guess I am getting tired. You want to stay up and watch something else?"

"No, that's okay … I'd rather get some sleep."

"All right …" Getting up quietly, Mr. Tranner gathered Jak in his arms and carried him up the stairs.

Feeling wiser, tired, but also happy, Thad followed.

Chapter 12

Jak woke up to brush his teeth with Thad and then crawled under his covers. First, though, half-asleep, he dragged all his blankets off the bed so he could be on the floor next to Thad. The lights went out as Mr. Tranner left after a final good night.

"Thad," Jak whispered, "are you sleeping?"

Getting into his sleeping bag, Thad shook his head tiredly. "No, but aren't you?"

"No way … It's a sleepover … We have to stay up late, right?"

"Sure." Thad put his head on his pillow. "Uh, what do you want to do?"

"I don't know … play soccer?"

Thad didn't know if Jak meant it so he only grunted. For a moment, he thought Jak had fallen asleep, but the rustle of the sheets next to him said otherwise.

"You never told me about you, Thad."

Thad swallowed. "Well, uh, like what?"

"I don't know … just tell something."

"Uh, okay …" Thad's legs twitched. He hated talking about himself. "Well, I like your family. I mean it. All I have is one sister and she mostly ignores me. I hardly even see her anymore. I didn't know you had all those sisters."

Jak coughed hard. "Trust me. You don't want too many sisters. I mean, they can be torture."

Thad grunted and didn't dare answer. For Jak to call anybody but himself a torture had to take some guts.

Suddenly Jak giggled. "We soaked Michelle and Barbara pretty good, right?"

"Uh, yeah ..." Thad felt his own face grow hot and his stomach gave a jump. He clearly saw Michelle's face dripping with water where he'd squirted her.

Misreading his reaction, Jak went quiet. "Thad ... you're glad you came, right?"

"What? Oh, of course! I was just thinking ... er, Jak, have you ever gone camping?"

"Camping? No way." He sounded disgusted. "Trust me, with four sisters, I'm lucky to do anything without makeup or shopping involved."

"Oh ..."

Thad stared up into the darkness with a lot on his mind. While it had been a great time, he had no idea what to tell the others. How would he act on Monday morning when back in school? Jak turned out to be okay, just young and maybe a little too lonely. Thad smiled in the dark. Who'd ever believe Jak to be lonely? All he needed was a friend who understood. Yawning, he started forming answers when sleep overtook him.

"Wake up, sleepyheads!" announced a voice somewhere over Thad's head. "You didn't stay up for cake and ice cream!"

Thad struggled to open his eyes. Blinking, he found himself staring up at a large poster of an Argentinean soccer player pumping a fist while screaming. He hoped it hadn't been the poster talking to him. Groaning, he sat up and wiped his eyes.

"Finally," said the voice in disgust. "What are you two doing? Nobody is supposed to sleep at sleepovers!"

Thad went still.

Michelle Tranner stood in the doorway wearing gray sweatpants and a lime green T-shirt. Her long dark hair was rumpled but seemed to shine in the early morning light.

Suddenly self-conscious, Thad pulled up his sleeping bag. Looking over, he saw Jak's still form curled under his sheets.

"You can't come in here," Jak's sleepy voice mumbled. "Mom said no girls allowed."

"I'm not in the room, snot face." She said it kindly, but Thad could tell she was annoyed. "How come you ate all the ice cream without us? We couldn't even have cake!"

Jak sat up suddenly. "Cake?"

"Yeah, remember? You two were supposed to wait for us!" Michelle shrugged her shoulders. "Oh, well. Catherine and Elizabeth took forever picking out shoes. It was awful. Hey, Jak, want to do a quick game of soccer?"

Stretching, Jak's lips curved into a smile. "Sure."

Groaning again, Thad searched wildly for a clock. The sun had barely risen. "What time is it?"

"Just past six," Michelle said, stepping into the room and going to the small goal with the soccer balls. "We have to be quiet so we don't wake up anybody."

Gulping, Thad nodded. "Yeah … that would be bad."

"Come on, Thad," Jak said excitedly, throwing off his covers. "We have to clear the space! Trust me, it'll be fun!"

Soccer in Jak's room consisted of going one-on-one in a dribbling battle. The ball had to start from the edge of the rug away from the goal and then make it in the small net for a point. If it was lost, the other player had to take it back to the edge before trying to score. At first, Thad sat and watched through bleary eyes. Then he started rotating in—it was the first to two goals and the winner stayed on.

Thad started too hesitantly and was easily beaten by Jak twice and then he lost once to Michelle. Jak used his quickness and skinny body to do a dizzying array of moves. Michelle, on the other hand, used more surprise and power. Against Thad, she faked a long shot and then moved right. Going slow, she waited for Thad to follow and then all at once cut left and sent a left-footed shot in for the goal. For the next point, she went straight for the goal and right through Thad's tentative tackle.

"Come on, Thad!" Jak cried, bouncing on his bed. "Don't let her score so easily!"

"Ha!" said Michelle to her next challenger. "You try to stop me!"

Jumping from the bed with a thump, Jak grinned. "Trust me. I won't try."

The two siblings actually took it easy against Thad. Against each other, it was more like WWF. Shoving, grabbing, and kicking each other more than the ball were all part of the rules. Being quiet was forgotten.

Thad sat back on the bed and shook his head. Once again he wished his friends were there … then, thinking about it, maybe they were. All at once he forgot about being shy in front of strangers. Taking a breath, he cleared his throat. Whenever he played sports with Derek, Danny, and Donald, one of them usually took the job as the sports announcer.

"Lady and gentleman," he began slowly and then with more confidence continued, "welcome to the brother-sister grudge match! The winner—"

"Gets a wedgie!" laughed Michelle as Jak slid-tackled the ball into the net for a point.

"Uh, okay," Thad said. "Let's join the action. The sister has the ball at the top."

"Call me Michelle!" gasped the sister.

"Call her loser!" suggested the brother.

"Um, Michelle dribbles to the center. Now Jak goes to meet her and is tossed down by Michelle! Hey, isn't that a yellow card?"

"Only if he wets himself!" Michelle tried to move away, but Jak reached out and grabbed her foot.

"Down goes Michelle! Now Jak is up! Now he's down!"

Just after Michelle took Jak down in a full tackle to prevent a winning goal, the door burst open and Elizabeth and Barbara stuck their heads in.

"What's going on here?" Barbara demanded. "Jak, you can't be serious!"

"Michelle, you woke us up!" Elizabeth accused.

"You do realize it isn't even seven yet," Barbara added, shaking her head.

Catherine arrived next, rubbing her eyes. She carried a flashlight and a crumpled white sheet tucked under her arm. All three girls wore sweatpants and long T-shirts. None looked very happy to be awake. Their hair stuck in all directions.

Thad nervously wriggled on the bed. Suddenly he realized how stupid it was to be in pajamas playing soccer in a bedroom with four older girls watching. He expected Catherine to be livid. He knew his sister would be—she hated to be woken up before ten unless absolutely necessary and she doubly hated stupid games.

Instead of being angry, Catherine moved into the room and tossed Michelle the white sheet. "I think for the good of the cause, we'd better set up a puppet show."

Jak groaned and picked himself off the floor. "Aw, man!"

Michelle grinned. "Yes!"

Thad watched dumbly as the girls quickly spread the white sheet over the dresser. Looking thoroughly embarrassed, Jak moved to sit next to Thad. He rested his chin on a knee.

"Sorry," he mumbled embarrassedly. "My sisters …"

"That's okay. What do they mean by a puppet show?" Thad asked him.

"You'll see!" Michelle said brightly. "You'll like it!"

A puppet show consisted of blocking the window with a shade and making the room as dark as possible. Then Catherine turned on the flashlight and aimed it at the white sheet. She sat behind Jak. Jak resisted as she tried to put an arm around him.

"Okay, who's first?" Catherine called cheerfully. "Remember to keep it down so we don't wake Mom and Dad."

"Or the neighbors," snorted Elizabeth.

"I'll go!" Michelle said. "You too, Barbara."

"Fine," Barbara said sourly, "but make it quick. I still need the shower."

"We're going to do the story of the fox and the hunter," Michelle announced.

"Great," groaned Barbara. "I'm too old for this!"

Elizabeth moved next to Jak's side and rubbed his back. "That's your favorite, Jak!"

The boy made a sour face, but Thad noticed him sitting up straighter. Turning to the show, he watched as Michelle and Barbara started making shadow puppets with their hands.

"That's not a fox!" Catherine reprimanded. "That looks like a deranged rabbit!"

"Fine, it's the rabid rabbit and the hunter," Michelle said.

"More like a space alien than a hunter," snorted Elizabeth.

Jak couldn't stifle a laugh and even Thad had to crack up.

"Okay, okay!" Michelle amended. "The space alien and the rabid rabbit! One day an alien came to Earth …"

Thad cracked an eye. He'd just had a nice dream about a crazy rabbit biting a space alien and giving it rabies to save the world … he sat up with a jerk and found himself at the head of the bed still in his pajamas. Jak lay at the foot of the bed and appeared to be fast asleep. Everything came back to Thad. The white sheet remained, but all the girls had vanished. In the distance he could hear voices and the sound of a shower running.

"I'm getting the boys now," he heard Mr. Tranner say behind the closed door. "I hope they got enough sleep."

Reaching across the bed, Thad tugged at Jak's ankle. "Jak!" he whispered. "Wake up!"

Kicking, Jak rolled to his back but didn't open his eyes.

"Jak!" Thad said desperately. "Your dad's coming and I need the bathroom!"

"Okay, sleepyheads, rise and shine!" Mr. Tranner banged on the door. "You guys awake? Departure time is in thirty minutes!"

Mumbling, Jak finally sat up and grinned crookedly at Thad through rumpled hair. "I think we're too late. I think the girls got the bathroom."

Thad swallowed down panic. He'd been holding it for a long time. "What do I do?"

The boy scrunched his nose. "We can try downstairs, but that's probably taken too."

"Great! Then what?"

He yawned. "Then we water the back bushes."

Thad found out that with four sisters in the house, Mrs. Tranner's bushes were well watered. They still didn't seem to grow very well.

After washing their hands in the sink, the boys had just enough time to run up and change for church before it was time to leave. Michelle let the bathroom open just long enough for them to brush their teeth.

"In the Orthodox Church," she told Thad seriously, "it's important to brush your teeth. Otherwise you stink up the priest's nose at Communion."

Clueless, Thad only nodded wisely.

They left a house full of screaming girls rushing around trying to press dresses and apply makeup at the same time.

Mr. Tranner breathed a deep sigh of relief as he backed out his blue sedan from the driveway. He and Jak both wore dark pants and blue short-sleeved dress shirts. While Jak's shirt was open at the collar, Mr. Tranner sported a long red tie.

Sitting in the back next to Jak, Thad wore long khakis and a blue polo shirt. His family belonged to a nondenominational church but only went a few times a month. Sundays were usually reserved for rest and getting up was difficult. He was surprised to hear that the Tranners went every Sunday. He wondered what their church would be like. He'd never even heard of the Orthodox Church.

"I think you'll find it interesting," Mr. Tranner said, as if reading his thoughts. "I'm sure Jak will help you understand what's going on, right?"

Jak yawned. Then he perked up. "Dad, can Thad go on the altar with me? Father Alex said I could serve in the summer if I came."

"Uh, well ..." Mr. Tranner looked in the rear mirror. He sounded doubtful. "I guess, uh, if Father Alexander says it is okay."

Thad looked at Jak. "What do you mean, 'serve'?"

Jak got his mischievous look and grinned at him. "Trust me. It'll be fun."

Thad swallowed nervously.

"He means you help the priest on the altar," said Mr. Tranner worriedly. "Uh, Jak, I think altar boys need to be Orthodox." Mr. Tranner shrugged. "Oh, well. Attendance has been sparse in the recent weeks. Maybe you boys can spice things up." He winked at Thad and said no more.

Chapter 13

Saint George's Romanian Orthodox Church was a twenty-minute drive from Jak's house, located in a downtown area littered by strip malls, restaurants, and several other churches. Thad had been by it many times but had never really noticed it before. From the outside, it didn't look like much. A large block building made of red brick loomed over a mostly empty parking lot. Tall stained-glass windows rounded at the top lined the sides and a small dome in the shape of an onion occupied the roof over the front entrance. Thad could make out another larger dome in the middle of the otherwise flat roof. Inside, though, he would find himself in a different world.

Jak raced ahead as soon as Mr. Tranner parked the car.

"Come on, Thad!" he called back impatiently.

Mr. Tranner turned to grin back at Thad. "Good luck," he said. "We're a little early, so take your time. Think of this as a new experience if nothing else."

After nodding, Thad hurried out of the car so he wouldn't lose Jak. He ran up the brick steps to meet Jak at the front. Two large wooden doors loomed in front of them. They reminded him of gates to a castle found in fantasy movies. He wasn't too sure what to expect, but he started to feel nervous about Jak's mischievous eyes lighting up. It took both of them to pull one of the doors open, and then took Jak pulling Thad's sleeve to get them inside. A sweet, smoky smell and dimmed lighting greeted their entrance.

Thad found himself in a small square room facing two more massive doors. At either side of the doors, wooden stands held large elaborate paintings of what Thad guessed to be holy people.

Gulping, he followed Jak deeper into the room with uncertainty. His heart started to beat wildly.

Candles burned in two boxes packed with sand next to the pictures. The boxes were level with his shoulders. What kind of church let people play with fire? Thad wondered. Didn't they know about Jak yet?

From the main church building, Thad heard a deep voice chanting in a strange language. It sounded smooth, slow, and sort of peaceful.

"Hurry up!" urged Jak, tugging at his sleeve. He'd retrieved two candles from a table to the left while Thad gawked at the unfamiliar surroundings. The church his parents usually went to was more like a warehouse with a giant stage for concerts.

Jak moved like ants had crawled up his pants. Quickly he thrust a candle into Thad's hand. A man in a dark suit standing behind the table with the candles stared balefully at them but made no comment. His gray bushy moustache twitched when Jak ran to the nearest lit candle.

Thad followed at a much slower pace. "What are you doing?" he asked.

"You light candles when you come in."

"Why?"

Jak shrugged his shoulders. "I don't know," he admitted. "But it's fun. Once Michelle lit her hair on fire ... Well, maybe I helped. Hurry, I don't see any servers yet."

Feeling very lost, Thad lit his candle and stuck it in the sand. He avoided looking at the man behind the table. He felt his gaze burning a hole in his back. Nodding awkwardly at the nearest holy picture, Thad then followed Jak through a small side door on the left leading to the main church.

Through this door, Thad lost his breath. Rows of pews faced an elevated platform on the other end of the church. On the platform, standing before the pews, he saw a long wall of gold panels. Set in the gold, several bright paintings of what Thad guessed were other holy people stared at him. Thad recognized Jesus on one side and a woman holding a baby. Two angels, both taller than the boys, stood at either end of the gold wall. They carried swords and wore armor—one had a red robe and the other a blue robe. Thad couldn't help but feel slightly intimidated.

Looking closer, he saw that the angels were actually small doors. In the center were two much larger gates—thrown open wide, these were elaborately designed and looked to be made of gold. More bright paintings of holy men and women looked out over the pews from the side walls. In fact, the paintings went up to the ceiling and then even on the ceiling.

Thad stared up in wonder as he saw inside the large dome in the middle. Angels and what had to be Jesus stared down at him. The paintings were everywhere, even on the walls between the windows. It felt as if hundreds of eyes were staring at him.

He swallowed hard as he took in everything. Lit lanterns hung over the paintings on the gold wall and stands of larger candles were placed under them.

To the right of the altar, a man in a black robe stood behind a stand and provided the chanting. A sweet fragrance filled the air, threatening to overwhelm Thad.

Thad suddenly felt very out of place and dizzy. Suddenly he wished he'd eaten breakfast. Fear locked his knees.

At his church everyone wore mostly shorts, T-shirts, and sneakers. A few wore polo shirts and slacks. Then they all sat in chairs facing a stage where a group of people played loud music with guitars. The walls and stage were always bare. In this place, that could never happen. Everyone here dressed in nothing less than ties, dress pants, and dress shoes.

Just then the double main doors at the gold wall opened and a tall bearded man stepped out. He wore sparkling white robes and had a matching cape hanging from his shoulders. Facing the pews, he lifted his hand to the pews before going back inside. If he'd noticed the boys, he gave no sign.

"That's Father Alex," whispered Jak urgently at Thad's side. "You'll meet him. Come on."

"Uh, I don't think I ..." But Jak wasn't listening. Helplessly, Thad followed Jak down toward the golden altar. The pews, thankfully, were mostly empty. Only a few older women and men stood in the back. The men looked formal in suits, while the women all had long dresses. Scarves covered their hair. One woman met Thad's eye and grimaced. He quickly ducked.

As they reached the raised altar, Jak confidently turned left and led the way to a plain wooden door Jak hadn't seen before.

"This is where the altar boys go," he whispered over his shoulder, pushing through.

Thad rushed to follow. The room was surprisingly bare. A closet stuffed with gold robes was on the left. To the right, next to an open entrance leading to behind the altar, a rough wooden stand held two lanterns on poles. A single long pole holding a decorative cross leaned between the lanterns. Opposite the door, a small counter held various items, including a basket of bread and a hot-water heater.

Jak already stood at the closet pulling down robes. "One of these will fit you," he muttered. "Mine is easy to find, because it's small."

"Who's this?" muttered a deep voice, sounding more grouchy than kind.

Thad jumped. Father Alexander, or Father Alex, stood in the doorway and looked down at him severely.

Jak dropped the robe he was holding and it took down two others.

"Jakavos, who's your friend?" asked the priest in a grumbling voice. His dark eyes flashed under thick bushy eyebrows. They never wavered from Thad.

Father Alexander had long stick-like arms and no slouch about him. Tall, thin, his long narrow face appeared stretched further by a sharply pointed beard hiding his neck. A mustache, even thicker than Thad's father's, hid his mouth entirely and quivered under a long, hooked nose. Bristling dark with tinges of gray, the priest's hair went from his chin to the top of his head. It was thinning in the front and Thad couldn't help but think of a wizard. An evil wizard.

Jak looked back from the closet and opened his mouth without speaking.

The priest frowned. "Are you two alone?" he practically barked.

Slightly cowed, Jak nodded. Then he licked his lips nervously. "This is, um, Thad. He's visiting."

Father Alexander closed his eyes briefly and then lifted his eyes upwards. Thad was positive he heard him mutter a prayer asking for mercy. Then, opening his eyes, the priest nodded gruffly at Thad. "It's good to meet you." He offered his hand, palm down.

"Uh, thanks," Thad gulped. He took the hand and shook awkwardly.

The priest nodded and did nothing but lift his eyebrows. Turning, he stretched his hand out to Jak.

Jak immediately placed his open right hand on his left palm and cupped the priest's hand in his own. Bending, he quickly kissed the top of the priest's hand. Father Alexander grunted and then went back to the altar without looking at Thad.

"Get ready and be out here in two minutes," he said gruffly over his shoulder as he left.

Face burning, Thad tried to steady his beating heart. He didn't know what had just happened, but he felt as if he'd just failed a test. Somehow he doubted Father Alexander was very impressed, or even happy, with his two servers.

"Um, Thad," Jak said sheepishly, "do you know how to put on these?" The shorter boy held up a gold robe in one hand and a long red sash with gold trim in the other.

Thad looked at him with frightened eyes. "Are you serious? Don't you know how?"

"Um, most of the time there's a big guy who helps."

Thad pulled uncomfortably at the gold robe covering him from his shoulders to his feet. He felt like he was wearing a dress.

They'd been able to find a picture of a server wearing the sash on the wall. Somehow it circled the waist and managed to have both ends hanging down the front like twin banners pointing to the feet. After struggling for several minutes, the boys had been rescued when Father Alexander stuck in his head and saw the mess.

The boys had been standing in a pile of robes that they'd tried on before finding ones that fit. With twitching eyebrows, he'd taken a moment to frown severely. Then he'd silently marched over and grabbed the sash from Jak's hands. Deftly, he'd had Jak raise both arms before wrapping the sash around his waist. Crisscrossing in the back, he'd neatly tucked the ends down the front. Doing the same to Thad, he'd then pushed the boys ahead of him to the door.

"My son graduated last year," he'd growled. "Now I'm stuck with you, Jakavos. It's a cross I must bear. Now pay attention. I need the censer in a few moments."

Thad had no idea what to do. The Orthodox Church was like a different world complete with a different language. Standing beside Jak, he felt like a house cat dumped in a lion's cage, as they faced a giant table where Father Alexander stood with his back to the pews. The great priest, with his mane of hair, looked ready to pounce at any moment.

Trying his best to still his beating heart, Thad focused on the table in front of him. Placed in the center of the altar, the table held a large gold-encrusted book and what looked to be a miniature gold castle. Thad had no clue what was happening. Sometimes Father Alexander spoke in a strange language he guessed was Romanian and sometimes in English. A man in a black robe stood outside the altar behind a stand and answered whatever prayer the priest said. Mostly it seemed to be a lot of asking for mercy. Thad fully agreed.

Just when he thought the worst was over, the priest turned and snapped his fingers. Glaring at Thad and then Jak, he snapped them again. "Candles, hurry!" he said shortly.

Jak jumped and quickly went back to the room.

Thad found him holding a lighter and flicking it at one of the lanterns on a pole.

"What are you doing?" he hissed in alarm. "You're going to burn the place down!"

Jak frowned at him. "We always do this. Here, you need a candle too."

"What for?" Thad asked, horrified.

"We have to carry one out. You know, a, uh, procession."

"No, I don't know!"

"Just follow me," Jak said, grinning. "It's easy."

Thad groaned, but dutifully took the candle Jak had finally managed to light without burning his fingers.

The procession never started well and never got better. After standing near the side door with the angel in red on front, the boys heard a sharp cough. "Go," commanded the priest.

In his haste to pull open the door, Jak bumped Thad's candle and nearly knocked it over.

"Hey!" hissed Thad, turning away sharply. He had to bend over to keep the candle from falling. A stream of melted wax, resembling a tear, fell to the tiled floor.

"Sorry," Jak muttered as he slipped through the door. Thad rushed to keep up. In the process, his sleeve caught on the edge of the door and abruptly closed it as he exited. Father Alexander, following closely behind them carrying the gold-covered book over his head, nearly smacked his face into the door.

"Jak!" hissed Thad. "Help!" He was caught fast on the door.

From the pews, a few murmurs were heard clearly. The chanter's voice went up an octave and increased in volume.

Jak quickly went back and helped Thad pull free his robe. He then pushed the door open, this time nailing the priest in the face. Father Alexander had not moved.

The two boys stared up fearfully as the priest muffled a grunt and the door abruptly closed again. The door slowly swung open. Staring down, Father Alexander kept the book held high, but his eyes were smarting.

"Just go," he muttered. "Go before something else happens."

Something else happened. Jak gripped his candle tightly and turned to lead the way. Not wanting to be left behind, Thad followed closely. His right foot stepped squarely on the back hem of Jak's robe. Not being able to find the smallest robe in the packed closet, Jak had ended up wearing one much too large.

With a startled grunt, Jak fell to his knees and barely prevented a face-plant by jabbing his candle in front of him like a cane.

Father Alexander, his eyes closed, walked into the back of Thad, nearly tripping. Stumbling, Thad poured melted wax on the back of Jak's robe, some splattering on his bare neck, and barely kept his balance.

As if stabbed with a pin, Jak leapt to his feet and arched his back. Gritting his teeth, he practically ran from Thad to the front of the altar, stopping next to the painting of the woman with the baby. Thad quickly followed while Father Alexander paused and seemed to be muttering either a prayer or an oath. The chanter was practically yelling his chant now.

"Move over there," Jak hissed. "You're on the wrong side!"

"Huh?"

Jak demonstrated by crossing to the other painting. Thad quickly followed.

This caused Jak to shake his head in exasperation. "No, we're supposed to be facing each other!"

Thoroughly confused, embarrassed, and scared, Thad looked at him. Finally, he planted his feet firmly and Jak crossed back to the other side.

Clearing his throat, Father Alexander finally moved between the boys and faced the altar. He didn't look at either boy as he raised the book and started chanting a heartfelt prayer in Romanian. The chanter joined in, and after a moment the priest walked through the center doors.

Thad let out a deep breath when Jak moved to the center. Thinking he meant to follow the priest, he started to step through the center gold doors.

The entire congregation audibly gasped.

"No, Thad!" Jak nearly shouted as he grabbed the back of Thad's robe. "You can't go that way! We go back the way we came! Only priests go there!"

Thoroughly confused and embarrassed, Thad stopped. "Wh-what?" he stammered.

"Just follow me." Jak let go of Thad's sash, which, pulled loose, fell limply to the floor.

Thad's knees locked up and he refused to move. His entire body started to shake. "I-I don't understand ..." He felt his face burning as every eye in the church stared at the back of his head. Sweat dripped from his face. His vision started to fill with spots.

A loud hiss escaped the pews. "He's going to faint!"

The chanter lifted his voice high to the heavens, drowning everything else out.

Then, just as Thad felt ready to surrender to blackness, a slight kick delivered to the back of his knees caused him to buckle. Immediately a firm hand grabbed his elbow.

"Trust me, it'll be okay." Jak spoke gently in his ear. "Just breathe and follow me."

"O-okay." Face still burning, Thad managed to stumble after Jak back to the altar. His sash trailed behind him like a tail between his legs.

The procession finally ended and so did Thad's life.

He wiped sweat from his face when they'd made it to the safety of the back room.

"Only priests are allowed through the big doors," Jak explained. "If you go through there you have to become one."

"Oh," Thad said weakly. "I feel sick."

"Don't worry," Jak said cheerfully, replacing his candle. "I used to mess up a lot too. You'll do better next time."

"Next time?" blurted Thad. "How many more processions are there?"

Jak scrunched up his eyes. "Two or three, I think." He shrugged. "The last one we need to carry the censer."

Thad slumped to the ground, letting Jak take his candle from nerveless hands. His heart pounded wildly. Then he jerked up his head. "Jak, what's a censer?"

Jak grinned. "I'll show you. But first you need to fix your robe."

Thad got a bad feeling as he stood back up. He doubted he would enjoy it.

Chapter 14

The censer turned out to be a golden bowl with a movable lid attached in the middle to a thin chain. A series of other chains ran from the perimeter of the bowl and held bells. About two feet in length, the chains met at the top, disappearing into a small rounded handle. Only the center chain could be moved and was used to slide the lid up and down. Currently the lid was propped open and revealed a glowing piece of charcoal in the bowl.

Something flammable, just what we need, Thad thought morosely.

Placed near the altar table, the censor hung on a metal stand with a plate of small white rocks on top.

"That's incense," whispered Jak, when showing Thad the pebble-sized stones. "You put it on the charcoal and it makes all the smoke."

"Right," Thad said doubtfully. Letting the biggest troublemaker in school play with fire and lit charcoal didn't seem like a really good idea. "Are you sure about this?"

Father Alexander, who had totally ignored the boys since the procession, now turned from the table and glared. "Hurry," he snapped. "Censer!"

Jak grabbed a handful of stones and threw them into the censer's bowl.

"Just watch."

Nothing happened.

"Hurry!" demanded the priest.

Frowning, Jak tossed in more incense. "There should be smoke."

"Let me try." Thad found a spoon on the incense tray and, taking a big spoonful, dumped it on the glowing charcoal.

The priest snapped a finger impatiently. "Censer, now!"

Jak snatched the handle and pulled it free. Immediately the lid clanged closed and the bells jangled loudly. The chanter continued to nearly shout the prayers and was by now going hoarse.

Father Alexander took the censer from Jak and impatiently waited for Jak to kiss his hand. Then facing the altar, he lifted the lid and raised the censer above the gold book. Instantly a gigantic cloud of gray smoke poured out and completely enveloped his head.

The prayers became coughs. Choking, the priest closed the censer and thrust it back at Jak. Stumbling away from the table, he turned toward the pews and choked out something in Romanian.

"See?" Jak said, putting the censer back. "I told you it smoked."

"Oh, yeah," muttered Thad, feeling light-headed again. "It smokes."

They had no time to get in trouble.

Father Alexander turned and coughed. "Candles," he wheezed. "Quick!"

The next procession went much better. Father Alexander remained on the altar this time, reading from the gold book that turned out to be the Bible. The boys stood on either side with their candles. Thad had carefully followed Jak this time and made sure to copy everything he did. By focusing on his partner, Thad managed to keep it together. No major mistakes happened.

Afterwards, though, there was no time to relax.

"Censer!" the priest said as soon as the boys entered the door. Then the priest froze. His beard quivered. "Jakavos, I fear you have to carry it on the next entrance."

Jak's face lit up. "Really?"

The priest closed his eyes and nodded. "Go light another charcoal," Father Alexander said, then cleared his throat. "Thad, you make sure he doesn't burn the place down! Oh, and, Thad, carry a candle. We'll go out one more time, thank Heavens, and you'll lead us."

Thad's mouth went dry. He barely nodded. He very nearly whimpered.

Jak was already in the back room rummaging for the charcoal.

While Jak managed to avoid burning the church down, he did come close.

Having found the charcoal, Jak grabbed a piece with a pair of tongs and held it up. With his free hand, he took the lighter and placed a flame on the charcoal. After a few seconds, sparks started to shoot out.

Thad watched dubiously, realizing the priest's orders were no joke. "Jak, I think it's lit."

By the time the lighter lowered, sparks flew out of the charcoal in every direction. The boy's dark eyes practically danced when he tossed the lighter to Thad.

Father Alexander coughed loudly from the altar. "Jakavos. Censer."

Thad hurriedly lit his candle and took his place at the altar door. He couldn't believe it. Yesterday the sleepover had been a lot of fun, but now it had turned into a nightmare. The scariest part, Jak served as the leader ... and seemed to be good at it. He was very different here than in school.

"When do I go?" Thad hissed to Jak nervously.

Jak busily dumped more incense on the sputtering charcoal. Thad knew how it felt.

"Wait. I'll tell you!" he hissed back. Jumping up, he carried the smoking censer to the glaring priest.

It took a while, but after censing the altar and then outside the altar, Father Alexander returned the smoking censer to Jak. By this time, a thick cloud hung over the entire church and smelled like a mixture of flowers and spices. If they'd been smoking out hornets, they would have done a good job. The censer looked to be holding a small forest fire.

Thad covered his nose and wondered if he'd missed the entrance. Apparently he wasn't so lucky.

The priest went to the back of the altar to a small table holding a tray of bread and a large chalice. Covering them with a cloth, he turned and nodded. "Let's go."

Jak faced the priest and awkwardly swung the censer in front of him. While shuffling backwards, he turned his head to Thad. "Now!"

"Where?" Thad whispered hoarsely back.

"The Great Entrance!" Jak hissed.

Taking a deep breath, Thad opened the door. He stopped still. Standing in the front row, all looking at him, was Jak's entire family. Mr. Tranner had been there before, but alone and near the end. Now the rest of the family had arrived. Mrs. Tranner, standing next to her husband with the baby perched on her shoulder, looked at Thad with a white face. Mr. Tranner seemed to be trying hard not to smile. The girls were all in the middle, directly in front of Thad and staring. Michelle met his gaze and grinned wickedly.

"Hurry," hissed Jak, nearly at his back.

Jerking, Thad quickly held his candle high and carefully continued the procession. It was his third time and this time he knew what to do. Moving to the spot in front of the painting, he stopped. From the corner of his eye he was horrified to see Jak still moving, but going to the right instead of the center. Already down the steps, he headed for the pews. Thad had messed up again.

Then Father Alex's deep voice grunted. "Jakavos, follow your friend. We'll take the shortcut today."

Jak nodded and did an abrupt turn, heading toward Thad.

Clearly relieved, Father Alexander lifted up the covered chalice and tray high.

That was when Jak, still walking backwards to face the priest, tripped on the final step and ended up sitting down solidly. The censer banged on the marble and sent out sparks. Miraculously, the charcoal stayed put.

"Watch out!" Mr. Tranner said as his wife gasped in horror.

Father Alexander stopped with his foot poised over Jak's middle. Balancing, he appeared to be sweating profusely.

Scrambling back, the boy got to his feet and continued censing.

Mr. Tranner let out a deep sigh of relief as the priest made it up the steps without catastrophe.

Still sweating, Father Alexander moved to the center and turned toward the pews.

Thad had no idea what he said, but whatever it was, he agreed with it wholeheartedly, especially when the priest abruptly turned and went back into the altar. Anything to get away from the pews and Jak's family. Bowing in the center, he hurriedly followed Jak back through the side door and away from, at least he hoped, his last procession ever.

The service continued and seemed endless. Without any processions to worry about, Thad began to get bored. Jak had tried going to the back room, but Father Alexander stopped him with a stern snap of the fingers. Sometimes they sat, sometimes they stood. Once Jak went to heat the water, for communion he said, but mostly the boys remained by the smoking, and occasionally sparking, censer.

Thad felt his eyes starting to glaze. Still tired from the night before, he found it difficult to pay attention, even if the language wasn't half Romanian. Then suddenly he smelled something burning. It wasn't the sweet, spicy smell of incense. This smelled like burnt vegetables. Looking around, he noticed a trail of black smoke rising from behind Jak.

The small boy stood by the censer and was staring obliviously into space.

"Jak," hissed Thad. "I think you're on fire!"

"Huh?"

Father Alexander had just asked people to lift up their hearts. Hearing Thad, he turned with a frown.

Thad's heart lifted clear up to his throat. A clear orange flame leapt from the back of Jak's robe. He remembered spilling the wax on that area. A spark from the censer had probably ignited it and now Jak was about to turn into a human torch.

"Let us give thanks to the Lord!" Father Alexander called loudly, turning to bow to one of the paintings.

As the chanter responded with it "being proper and right," he gestured toward the smoking altar boy with fear in his eyes.

The priest heaved a sigh and walked over to Jak.

Looking behind him, Jak saw the flames and went still with shock.

Thad looked hurriedly around for a fire extinguisher, but Father Alexander moved faster.

Grabbing Jak by the arm, the priest abruptly sat in a folding chair set up for the altar boys. Throwing Jak over his knees, he proceeded to beat out the flames with three hard whacks. He added two more, the last probably harder than necessary. Then without ceremony, he pushed the surprised boy back to his feet and mussed up his hair.

"Jakavos, one day you will burn with the Holy Spirit, but not today." Rising, the priest calmly went back to the table and resumed the prayers.

From then on, Thad and Jak watched him with awe. For the rest of the service, they jumped at his every command.

After the service, Thad had the honor of holding a large basket of bread in front of the father to be handed out to the people. There were few in attendance and soon the priest was left with Thad.

Jak was in the back room fingering the three holes in the back of his scorched robe.

"Thad, I thank you for your help today," rumbled Father Alex. "You're not Orthodox, are you?"

"Uh, yes, sir. I mean, no, sir."

The priest smiled and his eyes softened. "Well, that's okay. You did fine for your first time. Jakavos is lucky to have you for a friend."

Swallowing, Thad nodded. All weekend he held it in, but now it burst forth. "Well, actually we don't really know each other." He winced. Something about all the incense and smoke made him feel light-headed and not think straight. Why would he admit this to a strange man who looked like he belonged in a fantasy movie? At the same time, it felt good to tell somebody. "I, uh, well, he invited me for a sleepover."

Patting Thad's shoulder, the priest nodded. "Sometimes we do good things without knowing why."

Thad grunted and stared down at his shoes. "Actually, I only did it because my parents promised I could go camping with my friends if I did." Then he looked up and said earnestly, "But I really did have fun."

The priest smiled. "You mean during the service?" He chuckled at Thad's sickening expression. Suddenly he no longer looked quite so severe. Under his bushy eyebrows, his eyes even seemed to twinkle. "Orthodox services are not for the faint of heart, especially if Jakavos is helping."

Thad couldn't help but grin. "He does have a nice family, though."

"Yes, he does. I think he also has a nice friend. Now come, Thaddeus. We'd better get Jakavos. It's been almost five minutes and I'm getting worried. Before you leave, I'll give you a blessing for a safe camping trip. With friends like Jakavos, you're going to need it."

Thad frowned as he followed the priest. How had he known his name? he wondered.

"Uh, I do have a question."

The priest stopped and turned with surprise. "What is it?"

"Why, why did we go out on so many processions? I mean, you just carried stuff around from the side to the front." Thad's face grew red when the priest stared at him with narrowed eyes.

"A good question, young Thaddeus." He thought for a moment. "It has a lot to do with gifts ... They're hidden back in the altar and I bring them out to share with the people. Together we offer the gifts for the world and for ourselves, and in return the gifts are given back to us in communion ... if that makes sense." The priests stared across the pews with a sigh. "Unfortunately there weren't many people to share them with." He grinned sadly at Thad. "We all have gifts, Thad. Gifts we can either hide, or share. Many people choose to hide their gifts, especially on Sundays. It's important we share them with as many people as we can." He cleared his throat and smiled. "Sorry, I'm starting to preach. Bad habit. Does that help?"

"Um, I think so. Thanks."

"No, thank you. Thank you for keeping Jak from burning the place down. We'd better hurry—I smell smoke."

A lot of things puzzled Thad about that Sunday morning and his head spun from thinking about it. In the end, he settled on one main thing. Sometimes appearances could be deceiving and it took real understanding before a good judgment could be made.

They found Jak holding a piece of bread over the lighter. "Um, just making toast," he said guiltily when Father Alexander cleared his throat. "Want some?"

Chapter 15

Jak's parents waited for them outside the main church and said the girls were already eating donuts. It turned out that after every service, coffee, donuts, and juice were served in a small reception hall behind the church. A patch of grass separated the two buildings and Jak told Thad they could play soccer there later.

Before Thad could run off inside, Mrs. Tranner pulled him to the side.

"Thad, I'm really sorry. I had no idea Jak would drag you up to the altar."

Thad's face burned. He just felt relieved to have the whole experience behind him. "Oh, it was fine, Mrs. Tranner. I, um, had, uh, fun."

"Really?" she asked doubtfully. "Jak didn't cause any trouble, did he?"

Like almost burning himself up? Thad thought. The burn marks had been in the back and had never reached Jak's clothes. Only the chanter had witnessed the near disaster.

Thad swallowed and stared at his shoes. He tugged at his cowlick. "Oh, um, no," he managed to say. "Not really."

"Next time show up early and you'll see," Mr. Tranner said ruefully to his wife. "The first entrance was a masterpiece." Before Mrs. Tranner could ask what happened, he clapped Thad on the back and told him to run after Jak before all the good donuts were eaten.

Later that day, Thad's thoroughly exhausting and enlightening sleepover finally drew to a close. Back at Jak's house, he shared a late lunch of birthday cake and ice cream and watched Jak open his presents. While he clearly enjoyed the books and soccer jersey, Jak claimed his favorite was the Lego soccer set brought by Thad. Soon afterwards it was time for Thad to return home.

"I thought you would never call," his mother greeted him as she parked the minivan. "So I decided just to drive over to make sure you were okay." Thad had been in the front yard with Jak and Michelle kicking a soccer ball around, working off all the sugar.

Thad wiped sweat from his face and grinned. "Sorry, Mom," he said ruefully. "I'll go get my stuff and say goodbye."

"Make sure you thank Mr. Tranner!" she called.

As Thad and his mom drove off, he looked back and saw Jak waving from the front door in the midst of his sisters. They gathered around him like a host of mother hens. Jak's face wore something akin to desperation.

"Well, I think you must have had some fun," his mother said after a minute. "Mrs. Tranner said you were welcome back any time. Apparently you were a big hit."

Thad grunted. He wasn't thinking of going back just yet. Instead he was thinking about a camping trip coming up …

"Well, what did you end up doing? Thad?"

Thad had his eyes closed and head slumped against the window. A small smile crossed his face as he entered the world of dreams.

That night, Thad called his friends and told them to meet at his house after school the next day. He never said what for but only it was important.

"Does this have anything to do with where you were this weekend?" Donald had asked. "I tried calling you for two days!"

"Maybe. You'll see. Donald, just make sure you come."

"I'll be there. I want to know why you're so secretive."

School went by in a blur. It was Field Day for the entire school and Mr. Freeman's class was separated into different teams as soon as they walked in. Thad and Jak were split and only had time to nod and wave. Donald had been placed with Thad's team and watched the friendly exchange between Jak and Thad.

"So what's going on?" he asked, standing next to Thad.

Thad only smiled. "You'll see. Now, are you my partner for the balloon toss or what?"

"I'll be your partner, Thad. Just watch out for one in the kisser. I'm going to nail you there first chance I get."

"Only if you aim at Mr. Freeman," Thad retorted. "Your aim is so bad you couldn't hit the ground if you dropped the balloon."

"Huh. I'll drop you and hope you miss the ground. All you're good for is pollution."

Thad laughed. It was back to old times. In two short weeks, Donald would be moving, but that would only be a problem in two weeks.

The good humor seemed to be catching. Over the weekend Mr. Freeman had regained his own humor and promised an ice cream party the next day if nobody got hurt during Field Day.

After school, Thad waited impatiently for the others to show up. Everything had seemed perfectly clear before, but now he was having second thoughts. Would the guys be ready to accept Jak? He'd kept tight-lipped on the bus, despite Danny nearly throttling him to get him to spill the beans.

Donald arrived first. Derek and Danny showed up soon after.

"Hurry up and talk, man," Derek said, barging into Thad's room.

Danny followed and echoed these thoughts. "It looks like a storm out there and I'm not walking home in the rain," he said, wiping his nose with the back of his hand.

"It might do you good," Derek said cruelly. He elbowed Danny in the ribs. "The rain might melt some of your fat."

"Shut it, Derek," Danny said. "I'm just husky. I'll be skinnier than you one day."

Derek snorted. "Yeah, when you're dead and rotting!"

"Cut it out, guys," said Donald. He and Thad sat on the floor and were in the middle of a card game. "Just sit down and listen to Thad."

Thad sighed. "What are we going to do when you leave, Donald?"

"Celebrate," Derek said, taking a running leap from across the room onto Thad's bed.

Danny crawled after him. "Okay, Thad. We're listening, now tell us."

Putting down his cards, Thad bit his bottom lip and looked at his friends. Each one, even Derek, looked back with interest.

"Well, guys, I guess you wonder where I went yesterday and Saturday."

"Not really," Derek said, shrugging. "I don't care."

"Yes you do! You called me yesterday asking!"

"You shut it, Danny!"

"Just tell us," Donald pleaded.

"Well, remember Jak's invitation?" Everyone went quiet. Only Donald grinned. "Well, my mom made me go, and—"

"You went to the little spaz's sleepover?" Derek's jaw dropped. "Are you serious?"

Danny fell back on the bed and was somewhere between laughing and crying.

"Come on, guys! Cut it out! It really wasn't that bad! He's just like a little kid. Besides, his sisters are nice."

Again there was complete silence. Even Donald stared bug-eyed at Thad.

"The little spaz has sisters?" Derek finally asked after several seconds.

"Four of them, actually," Thad said. "Er, one is actually our age, but she skipped a grade. We'll see her next year in school." Thad's cheeks flushed.

Donald chuckled. "I bet you can't wait!"

Face still burning, Thad put his arms around his knees and squeezed. "That doesn't really matter, okay? What matters is that I think we should invite Jak on this camping trip."

"No way!" roared Derek. "Are you crazy?"

"He'll mess everything up!" Danny said.

"Wait, guys," begged Thad. "He just moved this year. He just needs a chance!"

"A fat chance," muttered Derek.

Danny nodded. "Thad, you know what he's like."

"Well, he's different at home," Thad promised. "Really. Besides, if he comes, we can guarantee an adventure."

Derek shook his head. "Maybe, but my dad's tent is only big enough for four people."

"He is small," Danny said slowly.

"Not that small," Derek said, glaring at Danny. "Not with you around."

Thad tried again. "Maybe we can sleep outside the tent ..." Thad could tell he was losing. After all, the same arguments he was hearing were basically the same ones he had used just a few days ago with his parents about the sleepover.

"He can take my place," Donald said suddenly. Everyone looked at him. "I won't be able to sleep over. My parents will never let me. Besides, I don't think I could stand the bugs ... or the smell of all you guys."

"But you have to go," Danny burst out. "This whole thing is for you!"

Thad ducked his head. "Yeah," he said weakly.

Donald chuckled. "Guys, I'll still come. I just won't sleep over. I'll go partway on the first day and then you can meet me back the next day. You all are looking for a secret clubhouse, right? If you find one, you can bring me before I leave ... after you clean out all the bugs."

Thad nodded in excitement. He slapped Donald's back with real feeling. "That's an awesome idea."

Danny spoke up. "Does that mean Jak can go?"

"Since I'm going to be the leader," Derek began, "I should—"

"Hold on," interrupted Donald. "There are no leaders yet. Let's have a vote. All in favor of letting Jak go raise your hand."

Not surprisingly, the vote was split down the middle.

"Come on, guys! You need to give him a chance!" pleaded Thad.

"Well," Derek said after a moment. "Will he introduce us to any of his sisters?"

Donald shook his head. "That's it. He's going. He has my spot."

The next morning, Thad greeted Jak by asking him if he wanted to go on a campout once school ended. Jak had just arrived in the classroom. His book bag slipped from his back and he nearly hit the roof with excitement. Immediately he tried using the class phone to call his mom to ask permission. When Mr. Freeman told him to sit down, he lasted less than five minutes. Raising his hand, he finally asked to use the bathroom.

"The way you're squirming in that chair I think it's too late," Mr. Freeman said dryly. "Go ahead."

Ten minutes later he got a call from the office saying Jak had been found on the phone in the library. Brought back by a red-faced principal, Jak wriggled in her grip but gave Thad a quick grin and a nod. Apparently, he'd gotten the okay.

Thad tried his best to look innocent when Mr. Freeman stared between the two. Finally, he threw up his hands. "That's it! No ice cream party today! Everyone get out a book and read."

Thad, Donald, Derek, and Danny moved to sit with Jak at lunch and they started their planning. Jak kept mostly quiet and sat between Thad and Donald. He seemed happy just to be included. Totally ignored, the Beast sat a seat over from Derek on the opposite side. She ducked her head toward her tray and ignored them back.

The rest of the week passed slowly, but with growing excitement. The boys agreed to meet at Derek's garage on Sunday afternoon with all their supplies. Then they would decide on what to take and what to leave behind. Final plans would be made and a leader would be chosen. On Monday morning, just past sunrise, they would reconvene at Derek's house and start the trip. A lot had to be done before then. Parents had to be convinced and the supplies had to be gathered. Nobody let on to their parents about the real plan. All they said was that they would be playing in the woods behind Derek's house. Except for Donald, they'd leave

Monday morning and come back Tuesday afternoon. Donald would go with them partway on Monday and meet them on Tuesday. He was the safety valve. If anything happened and they didn't come back on Tuesday, he would at least know where they'd be.

The last day of school finally came and the entire fifth-grade class of Knox Elementary school was promoted. Nobody could wait to get out and celebrate. After the final bell, Mr. Freeman was the first out the door.

Chapter 16

"**O**kay, who goes first?" Derek asked. It was Sunday afternoon and the boys were gathered in the shed back behind Derek's house. Thad had ridden his bike to Jak's house and then together they'd biked to Derek's place. Donald and Danny were already waiting. Each boy carried a heavy backpack on his back. All their schoolbooks and notebooks had been long abandoned. Having waved to them from the side of his house, Derek had led them to the back and to the shed.

"This is a pretty nice place," Danny said, looking around. Roomy, the size of a normal bedroom, it had old wooden chairs along the walls and a square table in the middle. The only downside was a musty, sour smell. Two round windows on either side were both opened and provided a breeze.

Derek grunted. "We have to be out here. We have to be quiet and can't use the garage. My mom's inside resting with a headache."

"Sorry," said Donald sympathetically.

Derek snorted. "Don't be. She gets them a lot when my dad is gone."

"Hey, Derek, why don't we use this place as a clubhouse?" asked Danny. "It's perfect!"

"Because we can't!" yelled Derek. He seemed to be on edge. "For one thing, my stupid older brothers come in here a lot and so does my dad."

"Okay, okay. sorry."

"Just go first, okay?" He nodded at the table. "Dump out your bag and let's see what junk you brought."

"It's not junk."

"Sure," scoffed Derek. "We'll see."

They sat on the wooden chairs and had their bags at their feet. Hefting his, Danny moved a little shyly to the table. "Well, first I have a whole bag of peanut butter and jelly sandwiches." Dropping his backpack to the wood surface, he unzipped it and pulled out a large, clear shopping bag stuffed with sandwiches wrapped in napkins. Purple and red jelly leaked and smeared the edges.

Donald raised an eyebrow. "You mean you brought sandwiches today for tomorrow?"

"Yeah, why?" Danny said. He frowned as everyone stared at him.

Derek wasn't as kind. "You stupid moron! We can't eat those! By tomorrow they'll be a sour, soggy mess!"

Danny looked crestfallen. "Oh."

"Why don't we eat them now?" Jak said. He fidgeted in his chair as all eyes went to him. He shrugged. "I mean, we might as well."

"Yeah," Donald said hurriedly. "I'm starving."

"Great thinking, Danny," added Thad.

"Yeah, you're a real genius," Derek said sarcastically.

"Uh, yeah ..." replied Danny thickly. Giving the bag of sandwiches to Thad, who was closest, Danny went back to his backpack. Hurriedly he produced his other items. "I have a flashlight, sun screen, extra clothes, and a box of granola bars, a pack of chocolate, and a water bottle."

"Of course you'd bring candy," snorted Derek. "All right, who's next?"

Danny quickly stuffed everything back into his backpack and slumped back to his chair. He didn't look at Derek.

"I'll go!" Jak jumped eagerly off his chair and lugged a bag behind him. Unzipping it, he pulled out a coil of rope, two high-powered flashlights, three pairs of socks, a water bottle, a large bag of trail mix, one set of extra clothes, and, with his face reddening slightly, a small homemade first aid kit. "I told my sisters I was going and they made this," he confessed.

A pocket-sized pouch with *Good luck, Jak!* sewn in small neat letters on front, it contained bandages, Band-Aids, and ointment for cleaning cuts.

Derek smirked. "Very cute, but otherwise not bad. Thad, you're next."

Stiffening, Thad slowly rose to his feet.

"I don't have much," he muttered.

Derek grunted impatiently. "We'll see, won't we? Now hurry up." Derek, never the nicest person in the world, certainly seemed to have gotten up on the wrong side of the bed.

Thad produced similar items—flashlight, clothes, and granola bars. He looked at Danny and offered a kind smile. "I think you're the only one who brought food for all of us."

Derek laughed. "That's what you think!"

Donald, since he wasn't camping out, didn't have to bring anything. He sat munching on a sandwich and kept quiet.

"I figured you all would forget," crowed Derek.

"Forget what?" Danny asked, tearing open one of his soggy sandwiches. Everyone else had a sandwich, except Derek.

"For one, I, of course have a tent." Derek went to the back of the shed and held up a large tent bag with a smaller case holding collapsible poles. He threw both on the table.

"We knew about that," Thad said. "You already told us!"

"Yeah, but did I tell you about this?" Derek proceeded to produce a cooking pot made for camping and five bowls with metal spoons. Dumping them on the table next to the tent, he went back and returned with boxes of macaroni and cheese, toaster pastries, and instant oatmeal. For the kicker, he tossed in a box of matches.

The other boys stared in stunned silence. Nobody had ever thought of making a fire.

"Aw, man," Jak finally said. "This will be so cool!" His eyes gleamed with excitement.

Thad got to his feet, licking his lip hesitantly. "Um, Derek, are you sure about bringing all of that?"

"Of course!" he said. "We need to eat breakfast, lunch, and dinner, right?"

Thad cleared his throat. "Yeah, but lighting a fire—"

Donald spoke up. "You guys will be on Park land. It's illegal to light fires there."

Derek grew red. "What are you talking about? It's probably illegal to trespass in the first place! I know how to make fires easy and safe! My dad takes me camping all the time! Don't be babies."

"I, I think it'll be okay," Danny said.

"See?" crowed Derek. "Even the biggest wimp thinks it'll be fine."

"Thanks," muttered Danny.

Sighing, Thad looked at Donald, who shrugged in response.

"Fine," Thad said, "but we'd have to be careful."

"No kidding," Derek returned. "Now, who's going to be the leader?"

It was no contest. With all his contributions, Derek became the undisputed leader.

"All right, then," he said, standing up proudly. "Meet back here no later than six fifteen in the morning. If you're late, you'll be left behind."

"Do I still make more sandwiches?" Danny asked. "They took a long time to make and a lot of bread—" He surveyed the half-eaten sandwiches around him sadly. Only Donald had finished his.

"Don't waste your time," began Derek, but Donald cut him off.

"You had a good idea, Danny," he said gently. "Why doesn't everybody make two sandwiches and we can trade with each other at lunch. Remember, you guys will be gone for two days and will need lunch twice."

"Uh, yeah, but, uh, make it *three* sandwiches each," Derek said.

"Okay … Say, Derek," said Danny, "can we get a drink from your house? These sandwiches made me thirsty."

Jak nodded in agreement.

For a moment Derek look frightened, but then he sneered. "You guys brought water bottles, use them!" He glanced toward his house. "Let's split now and get ready for tomorrow. Remember, don't be late!"

At the crack of dawn, Thad's alarm buzzed in his ear. Already awake, he groaned and turned to switch it off. It was mostly dark as he stumbled from his bed to the bathroom. After flushing, he washed his hands and splashed his face with cold water. Quickly the tiredness left his body, only to be replaced with excitement. Just one week before, he would be dreading another school day. Now, with summer stretched in front of him, like a blank canvas waiting to be painted with adventure, he couldn't wait to get started. Hastily changing from his pajamas into old jeans and a thick T-shirt, he gathered his backpack and hurried down to the kitchen. Both his parents were fast asleep and wouldn't stir for at least an hour. Having their blessing, he didn't even worry about a note.

Putting his backpack on the counter, he went to the fridge and hurriedly pulled out bread, ham, and cheese. Minutes later, he stuffed three sloppy sandwiches in a plastic bag and crammed them into his backpack. Then, searching the closet, he grabbed an opened package of chocolate chip cookies. Getting a glass of milk, he ate a hurried breakfast. He figured eating milk and cookies was all part of a balanced meal—flour, eggs, and milk, right?

Finished, he put everything back, dropped his glass in the sink and grabbed his backpack. Just as the sky began to lighten over the houses behind him, Thad rolled down the driveway, pedaling toward the adventure of a lifetime.

Few clouds marred the deep blue sky and the air felt cool and still. Early mornings seemed much more peaceful than any other part of the day. Accompanied only by singing birds, Thad traveled the empty roads feeling free and unburdened. Minutes later, he coasted into Jak's driveway and found the boy waiting impatiently at the door.

"I thought you forgot!"

Thad braked his bike and stared at him with raised eyebrows. "It's not even six, Jak."

Jak stood and stretched. "Still, I've been waiting for a long time." Like Thad, he wore old jeans, but unlike him, his shirt was blue with white sleeves down to his wrists.

"You might get hot, you know. I think it should be in the nineties."

Jak made a face. "My dad said to cover my arms and legs because of ticks." He grinned. "Don't worry, I got a plan."

The door opened behind him and Mr. Tranner peeked through. "Good morning, guys! You all set?"

"Uh, yes, sir," Thad said, caught by surprise.

Mr. Tranner yawned and waved a hand at Thad. "Remember, call me … oh, never mind. I hope you guys stay safe and have fun."

Thad sat back against the seat of his bike and looked down. "We will."

"Just in case, Thad, I want you to take a cell phone." He tousled Jak's hair as he stepped by and headed to Thad. He wore a white robe and sandals. "I would leave it with my son, but he tends to lose things. It's actually Michelle's, so be careful. She's not as forgiving as I am." Grinning, he offered a slim, black phone that Thad took with care.

"Uh, thanks, Mr. Tranner," he said.

The adult nodded. "Use it if you need it. Otherwise, just bring it back."

"I will." Handling it like a delicate rose, Thad carefully put the phone in his side pocket. Later he would move it to his backpack.

Jak put on his backpack and raced to the garage for his bike.

Mr. Tranner watched him go and grinned. "I remember when I was your guys' age … sure seems like a long time ago." He smiled tightly. "Hopefully you have better sense than I did. And whatever you do, keep an eye on Jak, huh?"

Thad swallowed. "Yes, sir. I promise."

"Okay, then. Have a great time." He took Thad's hand and shook firmly.

Jak pulled his bike from the garage and walked it to his dad.

"Jak, be careful, okay?" Mr. Tranner said. "Whatever you do, don't get eaten by a bear."

Jak rolled his eyes. "Sure, Dad. That'll be easy."

Mr. Tranner snorted. "I know." He gave Jak a hug. "No bear would dare touch a smelly thing like you."

Jak smirked. "That's not true, because you're the only bear I know."

Mr. Tranner slapped Jak in the back of the pants. "In that case, go before I get angry."

Thad looked away and waited for Jak to start pedaling. Then he waved to Mr. Tranner and started his bike.

"Remember," Mr. Tranner called, "we'll see you tomorrow before five! If not, you're grounded, Jak!"

He could have been talking to the wind.

Chapter 17

Donald and Derek were waiting in Derek's driveway when Thad and Jak arrived.

"Any word from Danny?" Derek asked, glancing at his watch. "I hope he didn't chicken out."

"More like overslept," yawned Donald. "I'm tired." He shook his head to clear it. "Are you sure we have to leave *this* early."

"Of course!" Derek said importantly. "We need time to find the mysterious houses, right?" He eyed Thad. "If they're even there."

"They're there," Thad said evenly. "Jak saw them."

Jak nodded. "We just need to find the pond."

Derek sniffed. "No, we need to find Danny!" He stomped his foot. "Where is that fatso?"

"While we're waiting, where should we put our bikes?" Thad asked.

Derek grunted. "Just put them behind the shed. They'll be safe." And no parent would spot them easily.

"Relax," Donald said. "We have plenty of time."

Derek made a face. "Not true," he grumped. "Didn't you say the trail to the park goes through people's backyards? I'd rather them be asleep than awake when we go across their lawns."

Thad and Jak placed their bikes with Donald's and returned to the driveway. Danny still hadn't shown up.

"We could call him, maybe," Thad said doubtfully, reaching for Michelle's phone. *Michelle's phone!* Just the thought sent shivers down his spine.

"Wait! Is that him?" Jak pointed to a figure that had just turned the corner and was pedaling like mad in their direction.

Danny had an older bike that had been in its fair share of accidents. As a result, the pedals clicked against the bent frame. The familiar clicking sound could clearly be heard.

"About time," muttered Derek.

"I'm so sorry, guys," Danny puffed when he reached the driveway.

"Keep it down," growled Derek. "My mom has another headache. What took you so long?"

"Well," wheezed the boy as he climbed from the bike, "I ran … out of bread … for sandwiches … So had to find … something else."

Donald looked at him blankly. "Um, what did you find?"

Danny grunted. "Onion bagels."

"I'm not trading anything for your peanut butter and jelly onion bagel, Danny!"

"Ah, come on!" Danny said. "It can't be that bad!"

The boys had gathered all their supplies and had started their journey. Leaving Derek's backyard, they'd entered the tree line and found a narrow deer path leading toward Donald's old street. Since Donald didn't have a backpack of his own, he carried the tent and a bag of food slung over his shoulder. He also carried a can of bug spray. Having offered to spray anybody who wanted it, he now held it in his hand and kept a sharp lookout for any bugs or insects.

Still creeping slowly over the horizon, the sun lit the way without bringing scorching heat. That would come later. Until then, they enjoyed the pleasantly cool air and chirping birds.

The trees were mostly new growth, from less than fifty years, which meant they were clumped close together and fought desperately for sunlight. The deeper they went, the more the trees leaned in crazy directions, their leaves desperately searching for a hole in the wooded canopy to drink in the sun. Green leafy plants and thick ivy clustered together under the trees, also fighting for survival. This meant it was important to stay on the path. Straying too far meant wading into a thicket of thorns, or worse, a patch of poison ivy.

Derek and Donald led the way. Danny followed close behind, still trying to get Donald to trade sandwiches at lunch. Three sandwiches—each one barbecue—were all Donald brought with him from his house. The rich aroma of pulled pork and sauce wafted from the top of the food bag provided by Derek.

"It's not even lunchtime," Donald said, exasperated. "We have hours yet."

"So?" Danny growled. "This is important!"

Behind Danny, Jak chirped up. "I'll trade, Danny."

"What type of sandwiches do you have?" Danny asked doubtfully.

Jak shrugged. "I don't really know. My sisters made them last night."

"Well, okay," Danny said. "If Donald won't …"

Donald shook his head firmly. "I'm not trading, Danny. Sorry."

"In that case, thanks, Jak." Danny sounded like he meant it.

Bringing up the rear, Thad rolled his eyes. Some adventure this was turning out to be.

After several minutes of walking, they came to a steep ravine. The trees were much farther apart in this area. Looking over the ravine, the boys saw why. A stream ran at the bottom. Extending over the stream, sticking into either side of the ravine, was a long, black pipe as thick as a tree log.

"What do we do?" Danny asked, dumping his backpack down and taking a seat. "Man, this thing is heavy!"

Derek looked at Donald. "Is this part of the trail?"

Donald shrugged. "I guess. My mom lived on the other side, so we have to cross."

"Wait," Danny suddenly said. "Thad, you said you guys found a stream, right? Could this be part of it?"

Thad shook his head doubtfully. "Look over there, Danny. There's a neighborhood behind us and another one in front of us.

There are lots of streams around here. We're trying to find one away from neighborhoods."

"Trust me," added Donald, putting down his bags. "We haven't even reached the trail yet."

Danny groaned. "Oh, man, I thought we were almost there."

"So we have to cross this thing?" Derek went down the side of the ravine slowly and nearly slipped. He raced back up to join the others. "This pipe must be a water pipe to the neighborhoods."

"Or a sewer pipe," Danny said.

"Don't contradict me. I'm in charge, remember?"

"I think what's important," Thad said slowly, "is how to get across." Squatting, he set his pack down, too. His shoulders already ached.

"Crawl or walk," Donald said with a sigh, not looking too happy. "I don't see any other way across the stream."

Where the pipe ran, the stream opened up and formed almost a small creek. Tall river grass grew on the edges from thick mud. Walking across did not look friendly, or very possible. The only good news, the pipe was only about six feet high at its highest point. If anybody fell, it wouldn't do too much harm.

"I'll go first," Jak said excitedly. Without waiting, he started down the ravine.

"Whoa! Wait, Jak!" Thad made a grab, but it was too late. Biting his lip, he grabbed his pack and followed after, careful not to slip. As he neared the pipe, the ground leveled and he reached the edge of the pipe just as Jak climbed on top.

"It's pretty stable."

"Right." Thad looked back. The others looked ready to give up already. Thinking quickly, he stared to the other side. "Okay, Jak. But I'll follow after you, okay? We'll go together."

"Let's go, then!" Jak said impatiently.

"Hold on!" Thad told him. "We have to be careful." Tentatively he put a foot on the pipe and then another. Spreading out both hands, he started walking.

Jak—much more careless—walked rapidly ahead of him. "See, it's easy—"

His sneakers suddenly slipped from beneath him and he fell hard on his left thigh. Just in front of him was a wood support that held the pipe up in the water. The supports ran every ten feet or so. Reaching with both hands, he grabbed the support and kept himself from falling totally off the pipe. "Oops."

"Jak, be careful!" yelled Thad, his heart starting to beat again.

"Okay," the boy said tightly, clearly shaken. "Sure ..." He sat on the support and waited for Thad to walk gingerly to him.

"Are you okay?" Thad immediately asked when reaching him.

Shrugging, Jak grinned. "I didn't fall into the ravine at least."

The others had gathered at the pipe but didn't look too excited to continue.

"Maybe we should go back," Danny said hopefully. "We can just camp out around here, or something."

Thad shook his head. "We can make it. The pipe is okay. Crawl if you need to, but let's go."

He took hold of the back of Jak's backpack and had the smaller boy go first. Following slowly, he was ready to sit and pull Jak back at any moment. Section by section, they made it across the pipe. Reaching the other end, Jak jumped to the edge of the ravine in triumph. "That was cool!"

Wiping sweat from his face, Thad only gulped. On two separate occasions he'd almost slipped and pulled both of them into a wet, muddy bath. Looking back, he was relieved to see Donald leading the way. Crawling with his bags hanging beside him, he carefully made it all the way to the middle. Behind him, Danny was also crawling and looking close to crying. Derek, surprisingly, brought up the rear. Straddling the pipe with his legs, he was slowly inching forward. His backpack was held in front of him and slowed his progress even more.

Putting down his backpack, Jak crouched and rested his elbows on his knees to support his chin. "They're taking forever," he moaned. "Can't they hurry?"

"Quiet," Thad snapped impatiently. "You nearly fell, remember?"

Jak fell quiet. Growing bored, he started searching for rocks and throwing them into the stream.

"Tell the little spaz to stop!" cried Derek, hugging his pack close. He'd barely reached the midway point and his face was chalky white. "He might hit one of us!"

Jak gave a scornful look, but tossed down the stone in his hand.

Thad told Jak to find a path to the neighborhood and went to the pipe's edge. "You guys are doing fine," he said. "Almost there."

"Easy for you to say," Danny huffed. "You're already there!"

It took several more minutes, but first Donald, then Danny, and finally Derek made it safely across.

"Man, let's not do that again," Danny said, wiping sweat from his face. "I nearly puked!"

"Wasn't so bad," Derek said, running a hand through his hair.

"Good," Donald reminded him, "because you'll have to cross back tomorrow." Donald would be meeting an aunt in one of the houses ahead and not have to worry about the return journey.

Derek blanched.

Jak raced to the edge of the ravine above them. "Hey, guys, I found a way out! Come quick!"

The way out of the woods led to the backyard of a large triple-story house, with a full-sized swimming pool and a playground resembling a mini resort.

"Too cool," breathed Jak.

"I would love to live in that house," Danny mumbled. "I bet they get room service every day."

"It's not a hotel, it's a house," growled Derek.

"So? I bet they hire maids to serve them! I know I would if I had all that money."

"Let's just hope they don't have dogs," Donald said. "We have to cross that to reach the road."

Thad wiped his nose. "Or a security system," he added.

Jak grinned. "One way to find out." His eyes gleamed with mischief.

Thad groaned as Jak boldly walked from the trees and onto the thick, bright green, grass carpeting the backyard.

"Like you said, Thad," Donald said wryly, "bringing Jak would bring more adventure. Let's go."

Thankfully, nothing happened and they reached the street without incident.

Nobody dared mention how they would get back the next day.

"Now, uh, guys," Donald told them as they reached the safety of pavement. "You may not have noticed, but this is a pretty rich neighborhood. Follow me and don't do anything stupid."

"Then we'd better hurry," Derek said. "Between the little spaz and Danny, stupid is just around the corner."

"Just follow me." Donald led the way around the bend.

Following, the group stared with open-mouth wonder at all the imposing houses looming into view. Each one was built as if trying to outshine the next. Many were three majestic stories tall and seemed to gloat about it. Perfectly kept lawns seemed to sprout in front of each house. Running fountains, pearly white birdbaths, stonewalled gardens, and elaborate birdhouses were just some of the yard decorations they passed. Even Jak seemed cowed by the majesty and kept quiet.

Finally, after turning down two streets, Donald stopped in front of a modestly sized stone house with a series of paths lining the expansive front yard. Trees dotted the yard before ending in an open field of grass that stretched behind the house. Beyond the grass rose a steep hill about six feet in height. A wooden fence stretched along the top of the hill. Thad guessed the fence to be at least six feet tall.

Donald crossed his arms. "That, guys, is where we find the trail. Should we go on?"

"How do we get over the fence?" Danny wanted to know.

Derek frowned. "Forget that, how do we get up the hill?"

"Run really fast and jump?" Jak's voice piped up.

They all looked at the smaller boy.

"Wait!" Thad snapped his fingers. "Jak, you have a rope, right? Why don't we tie it on top of the fence? We can use it to climb over that way."

"We can try," Donald said doubtfully.

Jak was already excitedly pulling the coil from his pack.

"Okay, genius," Donald said, "but how do we tie it on top of the fence?"

"We'll figure that out when we get there," Thad told him. "Come on!"

Taking one look at the silent house, Thad moved quickly up the front yard. Mulch and stones lined the paths and he had to be careful not to trample anything. Reaching the grass, he grabbed his backpack and ran the rest of the way to the bottom of the hill.

Jak joined him first and tossed him the rope. Thick and rough, it was at least thirty feet.

"This is perfect. Here, Jak, you come with me. I'll boost you to the top of the fence and you can tie the rope. Okay?"

The boy stared up at the fence and nodded. "Got it." Built of sharp pointed planks, the fence had plenty of places to tie the rope.

"Let's go before the others get here." Thad waved for Donald to hurry and then grabbed Jak's arm. "We'll leave our packs here. I'll go first, okay?"

Jak slapped him on the back. "Go."

Sprinting, Thad raced up the sharp incline and reached the fence. Going to a knee, he locked his hands together and extended his other leg to keep from sliding. Then he turned so his back was against the fence. "Hurry up!"

Jak charged up after, carrying the rope. Reaching Thad, he planted his right foot in Thad's hands and leaned on his head. Jerking his arms up, Thad gave Jak a boost to the top of the fence.

"Hurry before I drop you," Thad grunted. It was a good thing Jak was so light, because Thad's arms already ached from carrying his pack.

"Almost done!" said the boy over his head.

"HEY!" shouted an angry voice from the house. "What are you kids doing!"

Chapter 18

Yelping in surprise, Thad dropped his hands and leaned back. Instantly he started to slide down.

"Help!" wailed Jak. He fell back, but managed to grab the rope. This didn't stop his slide. Feeling his skin burn, he abruptly let go and landed on top of Thad. Then he started rolling. He cried out as he next started sliding down headfirst.

Thad dug in his heels and grabbed Jak's feet to stop their fall.

"You okay?" he asked.

Jak sounded more shaken than hurt when he answered. "I hope so."

"You kids better get out of here!" yelled the voice that started it all. A white-haired man stepped from the back of the house and shook a fist in their direction. "Go back home!" Then he went back into the house and slammed the door shut.

Donald, Derek, and Danny quickly ran the rest of the way to the hill.

"What do we do?" Thad asked.

Donald nodded at the rope. "Get out of here! I don't think the guy saw you two. He only yelled at us."

Thad got up gingerly. "He must be blind and deaf then."

"I don't care, as long as he doesn't call the police!" Derek took off his backpack and, using both hands, flung it over the fence. Grabbing the rope, he soon followed. The others quickly copied.

"How do we get down on the other side?" Danny asked when nearing the top.

"Jump!" Derek answered.

Danny swallowed hard. "That's what I was afraid you'd say!"

Thad went last and at the top of the fence he paused to untie the rope and throw it over. He was pleased to see that the surface was flat on the other side. Hopping down, he landed lightly on his feet.

"Everyone okay?" he asked.

"I think so," Danny said, sounding surprised.

"Man," Derek wheezed. "I thought you wet your pants," he said to Thad. "When that guy yelled, you two practically took the fence down."

"Then we'd be in real trouble," Thad said ruefully. He brushed all the leaves and dirt from the back of his jeans.

Danny helped knock the stuff from his back.

"Man, you almost look camouflaged," he teased, pulling a fistful of pine needles from his shoulder.

"Well, guys," said Donald. "Should we take a break? The trail to the park should be just over there."

"Definitely." Danny went to his pack and grabbed his water bottle. Drinking greedily, he wiped his mouth. "Man, it's amazing how great water tastes when you're thirsty."

"Yeah," grunted Derek. "You learn to appreciate how good we have it."

Danny suddenly looked very uncomfortable. "Um, speaking of which, guys, where do we go to the bathroom?"

Donald lifted an eyebrow. "Like they did in the old days, Danny. Look around you and find a tree."

Danny's face reddened. "Okay, right. But, er, guys, what if you have to, you know, go—"

Jak snickered and Derek broke into a chuckle.

"What's wrong, Danny?" Derek asked. "You look sick."

"Come on, guys!" the stricken boy wailed. "This isn't funny!"

Derek squatted at his backpack and reached in the front zipper. Feeling around, he pulled out a squashed roll of paper. "Is this what you're looking for?"

The relief on Danny's face was more than apparent.

"See now why I'm the leader?" Derek said, gloating. "I knew none of you guys would think of something so vital!"

"Great," Danny said, "now give it to me!"

"Oh, no," teased Derek. "This is important paper. You'll have to work for it."

"Good grief!" Danny fell to his knees. "Anything, I'll do anything! But hurry up!"

Thad squirmed and scratched his side. "Come on, Derek. I, uh, I may need it too," he muttered. The cookies for breakfast were quickly becoming a bad idea.

Derek threw back his head and laughed. "I know. You guys can compete for it! The first one to say I'm the greatest leader in history twenty times wins."

"That's stupid!" moaned Danny.

"Guys, really?" Donald said with a frown. "Don't be gross. Besides, the people on the other side of the fence can hear you, you know."

Derek ignored him as he started cracking up. "Somebody better hurry!" he sputtered. He hid the paper behind his back.

Grimacing, Thad looked at Danny.

In return, Danny gripped his thighs in frustration. "Okay, Derek …"

At that moment, Jak darted behind Derek and grabbed the paper before the bigger boy could react.

"Hey, give it back!" Derek cried. He lunged to his feet.

Instead, Jak quickly tossed it to Thad.

Thad caught it with both hands and sighed. "That's enough, Derek," he said. Then he underhanded the paper to Danny, who, once he caught it, immediately took off running into the trees.

"What?" demanded Derek. With a final glare at Jak, he turned to Thad. "I was only having a little fun. Man, you guys are all party poopers."

"You got the last part right," Donald said dryly.

Sulking, Derek took a seat and drank from his water bottle. He again glared over at Jak. The smaller boy grinned back.

After a long break where Thad also was forced to find relief in the wild, the boys gathered their packs and resumed their journey. True to his word, Donald led the way to a worn trail, smooth and gray against the forest floor. Stepping onto it, the boys knew they were heading to adventure. Here, the trees were older, thicker, and more spread out. In some areas there were patches of grass, but mostly leaves covered the ground. After five minutes of walking, they were surrounded by nothing but trees. Civilization seemed far behind them. Lulled into silence, they stared up at the bright green leaves hiding an assortment of birds. Squirrels raced across their path and Derek spotted a snakeskin.

Moving on, they twice startled deer and once came across a turtle sunning itself on a rock.

"I think we're getting close," Thad said.

"How do you know?" scoffed Derek. "Do you recognize that tree?"

"No, I just feel it."

Derek snorted. "Yeah, right …"

Thad was proven right when shortly after, the path abruptly ended on top of another ravine. Below the drop-off was a cobblestone tour road.

"See," he exclaimed excitedly, "this is the road we came out at! Remember, Jak, when you took us on that shortcut and we got lost? We found this road and followed it to Mr. Freeman."

Jak nodded. "The pond has to be close by."

"Good," wheezed Danny. "I'm starving."

"Me too," Donald agreed. "I vote we find the pond and have lunch."

Derek grumped. "I'm in charge, remember. Besides, it's not even noon yet."

"But it feels like we've been walking forever," groaned Danny.

The sun now peered down from up high. Even in the shade the air was hot and stuffy.

Even Jak looked wilted. Face flushed, he wiped sweaty hair from his eyes. "I'm ready for swimming."

"You should roll your sleeves up," Derek said, "before you're swimming in your own sweat."

"Let's just keep going before a car comes by and sees us," Thad said. "They might report us or something. We'll see what time it is when we reach the pond."

The threat of being caught spurred the boys onward without further complaint. Finding a rough trail down to the road, they crossed to the other side and continued their journey. There was no path to follow now. Thad took the lead and tried to remember by instinct where to go. He didn't worry about getting lost. Going forward would eventually lead them to the battlefield, while going backwards would lead to the tour road. Also, he knew the tour road led to the main road near Knox Elementary. In any direction they would find civilization, eventually.

For the time being, though, all they found were flies and bugs. Donald had dropped to the rear and was employing his can of bug spray to full effect.

"Argh!" he screamed. "Spider!" He squirted a stream and then another when a large horsefly flew across his vision.

Derek looked back. "Donald, you're going to waste it all!"

"I don't care," Donald wheezed. "Just as long as the bugs don't eat me!"

"That one won't," Danny said with a grunt. "You got it."

They crossed three more hills; each one Thad was sure would be the last. The pond would be below. Then, as he stumbled up the fourth hill, he was finally right.

Below him, nearly hidden behind a wall of green vegetation and water grass, he could make out blue water.

"Look!" he shouted. "The pond! See, I told you!"

"You also told me this would be fun," gasped Danny from far below. "I think … I hate you … forever."

Derek staggered to stand by Thad. He smacked his shoulder. "Never doubted you … Guys," he called back, "let's have lunch!"

Danny suddenly doubled his speed.

With renewed energy, the boys made it down to the pond and found a small opening next to the pond's edge. The stream Jak had followed weeks before was farther along, but an easy distance to walk. The hard part, the group knew, was behind them. They fell tiredly to the ground and took time to recover their breaths.

"Time for sandwiches!" Derek announced after a few moments. Nobody argued with the leader.

All the sandwiches were a little squashed, but everybody was too hungry to care.

True to his word, Jak traded one of his sisters' to Danny.

"Oh, my goodness, Jak, you're the best!" Danny exclaimed. Hungrily, he tore through wax paper to reveal a large sub sandwich stuffed with grilled chicken, vegetables, cheese, and ranch dressing. His eyes lit up. "Jak, I love your sisters! All of them!"

Thad jerked his head up and immediately flushed. He'd fingered the phone in his pocket several times already and had yet to move it to his backpack. Michelle's face swam in his mind and he quickly splashed it away.

Jak shrugged with disdain. "You can have them," he mumbled. He munched on the onion bagel sandwich and seemed perfectly content.

Swallowing a bite of his dry sandwich, Thad looked at Jak. "Uh, do you have another sandwich you want to trade?"

"Sure," Jak said a little bitterly. "My sisters make them all the time for me. I'm sick of them."

Danny stared at him like he was crazy. "Jak, the next time you have a sleepover, I'm going!"

Derek snorted and shook his head. "Whatever," he mumbled.

After lunch, which saw Jak trade all his sandwiches away, the boys started to wander and explore the area.

"Look!" cried Danny. "There's a blue heron! And I think that's an egret!"

The pond looked murky and gross. Mostly covered with green scum, pools of dark water spotted the scummy surface. Bugs zipped across the water, flying through a faint stench of rotting plants. The birds were on the opposite shore and seemed content to stare into the murky water, hunting for lunch of their own. A family of ducks also patrolled the middle of the pond, taking no interest in the boyish invaders.

Derek barely glanced at the birds.

"Ah, what do you know," he said with scorn, plopping down on a low-lying rock by the pond's edge. Larger rocks were piled to his left and jutted out over the water. He spat in the shallow water.

"More than you think!" Danny followed Jak up a large fallen oak tree that tilted over into the pond. Its thick heavy branches kept it from falling completely into the water and it offered a grand view from on top.

Donald, meanwhile, wandered down a trail toward the edge of the pond in the direction where they had come from.

"Where are you going?" Thad called.

"Just to use the bathroom … and maybe for a short walk."

"Well, I'll follow after." Thad started to go then, but looked back at Danny and Jak. The two were laughing about something in the pond.

"Just watch your step," snorted Derek. He slapped at a mosquito. "Man, it's so hot!"

Feeling torn, Thad looked once more where Donald had left and then started for the fallen trunk.

At least four feet in diameter, the massive tree still clung to its extensive root system. A gaping hole sat under where the twisted roots once strived. Staring at the hole, he wondered if that was what it felt like to have a friend move away. Like the earth just gives out under you, and down you fall.

He heard Danny laugh from above and then start to choke. All at once, Thad remembered what Mr. Tranner had said about moving … about how hard it was to start over, especially for kids.

Groaning, he smacked his head. All this time, he'd been worrying about himself. Not once did he think about what it must feel like for Donald. After all, when Donald left in just a few more days Thad would still have Danny, Derek, and now, thanks partly to Donald, Jak to hang out with.

Just as he turned to run after Donald, he heard Danny shout in alarm. Turning, he saw Jak hop down from the trunk and struggle to peel off his shirt.

"Guys," Danny called. "You'd better do something!"

"What's the matter?" Thad asked, puzzled.

"Jak—he's trying to go swimming!"

"So what?" Jak asked. Wriggling, he managed to get the sweat-soaked shirt off over his head. He tossed it by the rock where Derek sat.

"Are you crazy?" Derek asked.

"No, just hot." He kicked off his sneakers and started undoing his jeans. "I'm melting."

Derek shot to his feet and glared. "Thad, you'd better get over here! Your little spaz is going off the deep end."

"It's not that deep," Jak assured him cheerfully. "Trust me, it'll be okay." Slipping down his jeans, he calmly peeled off his socks and walked up the outcrop of rocks.

"I don't even trust you as far as I can throw you, because I can throw you pretty far," growled Derek. "And I just might prove it!"

Jak ignored him. Only his dark blue boxer shorts remained.

Thad hurried from the tree. "Jak, stop right there! Don't go in there!" All he could think of was Jak not being able to swim in the scum and drowning ... or getting some horrible pond disease. And then he would have to face Jak's family ...

Pausing, Jak looked over his shoulder and grinned. "Why? Wanna stop me?" Then he took off in a run and leapt out over the water.

Tucking his knees to form a cannonball, he smacked hard into the water, breaking the pond's stillness.

Ducks squawked from where they swam in the center and a large heron flapped in the distance.

Jak's head broke the surface and he grinned. "You guys should come in! Trust me, it's great!"

"Isn't it shallow over there?" Danny asked, awed at the boy's boldness.

The boy in the water shook his head. "I looked from the tree—there's a deep hole over here. Look, you can't see the bottom, but trust me. I touched it. It's just a little past my head."

"Sand?" asked Danny hopefully.

Jak grinned. "Nope. Mud."

Derek stood on the rock and put his hands on his hips. "Look, Jak. I'm in charge here! I didn't give you permission. Now get out of there!"

Jak splashed where he treaded water. "Sure, but I'm going right back in."

"I don't think so!" Derek snarled. "You're too stupid to know better."

Jak merely paddled a few feet in and stood up in the shallow water. Wiping water from his hair, he grinned. "It feels good. Really, you guys need to try it!"

"Nobody is going in there," Derek said firmly.

"Well, I kind of want to," Danny said hesitantly. "It's burning out here."

Derek turned to stare at him incredulously. "Are you serious? There are leeches in there!"

Danny jumped back as if bitten. "What! Really?"

Jak laughed. "No way!"

"Who asked you?" snarled Derek. "You're just a little spaz!"

Jak stepped from the water and onto the soft mud to face Derek. His thin frame dripped with dirty water, but he looked anything but cowed. An impish gleam entered his dark, slanted eyes.

"What's wrong?" he asked innocently. "Are you scared?"

Derek, who'd turned to Danny, whirled back on the smaller boy. "What did you say?" he said dangerously.

His face unreadable, Jak shrugged. Then the corners of his mouth tugged upwards. "You just sound a little scared."

"No, I just don't want leeches on me, idiot!" shouted Derek. Leaning forward, he suddenly shoved Jak in the shoulders.

Caught by surprise, Jak fell back with a sick splat in the mud.

"There!" spat Derek. "Now it looks like you messed in your pants. I guess you want my toilet paper now!"

Struggling to stand, Jak got up awkwardly. A thick layer of mud covered the entire back of his boxers and muddy goop dripped downwards. His skinny chest heaved, but his mouth curled into a dangerous smile.

"Too bad you have it," Jak said tightly. "So you use it!" Reaching back behind him, he grabbed a large gob from his boxers. Narrowing his eyes, he flung it at Derek.

It landed with a hard splatter against Derek's shirt.

A great silence descended at the sound of the splat. For a second nobody moved.

Chapter 19

Danny sidled back to stand beside Thad. "We'd better do something," he said out the side of his mouth.

Thad shrugged helplessly. "Like what? I think they both asked for it."

Derek stared down in shock at the muddy splotch. Like the others, he wore jeans and a T-shirt—only Jak had brought a long-sleeved shirt. However, Derek's clothes were much newer.

"Do you know how much this cost?" he finally cried out furiously.

"A lot less now," Jak observed. Mischief still burned in his eyes.

Derek stared at him and shouted, "It cost a whole lot more than your worthless life, you creep!"

Jak merely shrugged. "I would trade you, but your shirt is stained and now smells. Sorry!" Turning, he dashed back into the pond and dove into the deeper water.

Fighting to control his breathing, Derek looked back down at his shirt and then at where Jak had disappeared beneath the surface. "I hope you drown, little spaz!" he spat. Turning, he stormed back to his pack without looking at either Danny or Thad.

Thad sighed. "Well, that ended well."

Danny blinked and slowly grinned. "Yeah, but Jak is right. It is really hot."

"Uh, you're not going in, are you?" Thad asked in alarm. He was more surprised that Danny would cross Derek than him wanting to swim. He watched, too stunned to speak, as Danny pulled off his shirt.

Danny briefly hesitated, but then shrugged. "Why not?" he said as if talking to himself. "It looks like fun." He started pulling off his sneakers. "I'm sick of sweating."

Out in the pond, Jak swam toward the ducks while trying to make honking noises at the same time.

"But what about Derek?" Thad finally managed to ask. "He isn't going to like it."

Danny looked up at Thad. "He can clean his shirt if he wants. I'm sick of being bossed around." As long as Thad remembered, Danny had always followed. Now he'd either found a new leader or, much more likely, he'd found himself. "Wait up, Jak!" Danny called. "I'm coming in!"

Thad watched almost wistfully as Danny raced to the pond in his shorts. It did look very refreshing and a lot more fun than standing around dripping sweat.

He glanced over at where Derek knelt with a wad of tissue, wiping furiously at his shirt.

No matter what Thad chose to do next, he could be right, or very wrong. Going in the pond meant getting Derek even madder. Staying with Derek meant being hot and bored. He decided to go neutral and find Donald. Despite his size, Danny was a strong swimmer, and so, it seemed, was Jak. The two boys were splashing near the middle of the pond. Derek would have to make his own choices.

After following the path for a few minutes, Thad found Donald staring at a small pine sapling as thin as a pencil. Growing next to a patch of wild fern between two giant oaks, it looked like a lost little kid in a crowded tree mall.

"Think it will make it?" Thad asked.

Turning, Donald saw him and grinned sadly. "Maybe. Are you guys ready to move out now?"

Grinning, Thad went over to Donald and shook his head. "Something like that. Jak and Danny are swimming in the pond and Derek is throwing a tantrum because of it."

"I thought I heard somebody in the water." Donald shook his head. "Those guys are crazy."

"Yeah, how am I going to control them with you gone?"

Donald turned to one of the great oak trees and started picking at the bark. He'd left his bug spray with his pack and no longer seemed to care about the bug life. "You'll do fine. They all listen to you."

"Only because you're always with me." Thad wiped down his cowlick and scratched the back of his neck. "Really, Donald. Thanks for coming."

"Ah, it was nothing. It's better to be here than at home. My parents are running around trying to pack everything. If I didn't come, I would either be babysitting my little sister or packed in a box on a truck." He turned to Thad and grinned. "Besides, it's been fun."

"Even the bugs?"

Donald slapped a mosquito on his arm and winced. "Except for the bugs. I hope there aren't any bugs in California."

The two boys fell silent and Thad kicked a pinecone off the path. Putting his hands in his pocket, he looked up at Donald.

"You know, we don't have to say goodbye forever. I can get e-mail."

"Definitely," Donald said. "And Facebook."

"Yeah."

Donald turned and grabbed Thad's arm. "I really will miss you."

"Me too."

Grinning, Donald nodded. "I'd better get back now. My aunt is probably looking for me."

"Already?"

"Thad, it's probably close to one! My parents dropped my sister off at noon."

"Oh … but how are you going to get back? I mean, what about climbing over the fence?"

Donald flashed a brilliant, white smile, causing his brown face to light up in humor. "Go around it. I would have told you before, but you wanted to use that rope so bad. The fence isn't that long."

Thad groaned. "But we almost got busted! I thought that guy would call the cops!"

"Well, now you know on the way back tomorrow! I'll see you then, right?"

Thad grinned and nodded. "Right."

Donald started back toward the tour road, but suddenly stopped. "Oh, Thad?" His voice sounded tight. "You guys better be careful. Look."

Thad hurried to him and saw where Donald pointed. Just off the trail was a pile of fresh dog droppings. He remembered. Wild dogs were loose in these woods …

Thad decided to walk with Donald to the tour road before heading back. He'd hoped the dog sign was not an omen of things to come.

Back at the pond, Derek furiously threw down his wad of dirty tissue and sat back against his pack in disgust. His shirt was smeared with water, pond grime, and shredded tissue. From the water, he could hear Danny and Jak whooping and hollering. Three times they'd jumped off the rock, and now they were playing water wrestling.

He kicked Danny's mostly empty water bottle away and got abruptly to his feet. He'd used Danny's water to try to clean his shirt.

Sure, he was angry at Jak, but that was to be expected. The little spaz always did stupid things. Derek was only trying to control him. Besides, the pond was probably full of leeches and water snakes. But when Danny also jumped in, well, that really hurt. Danny had always supported Derek … until now. All because of the little spaz.

And then Thad had also abandoned him.

A new surge of anger went through Derek. Kicking a pile of leaves, he decided to take a walk. He started toward the stream. Maybe he'd find the houses alone. Then he would hide in one and wait for the others. Allowing a grin, he thought about taking his tent and food with him. The others would think he'd left and really be scared. But that would take too much work, and besides, if the others thought he'd left, they'd probably leave too. Derek was still the leader.

As Danny's and Jak's voices grew fainter, Derek's anger softened. He knew he'd been in a bad mood, but everyone had bad moods. Danny should know this by now! Really, Derek decided, it was Jak's fault, but Danny was still to blame.

Suddenly, Derek froze. Whirling, he saw nothing but trees. At the same time, he had a prickly feeling run down his back.

A breeze rustled the green leaves over his head and he heard a woodpecker somewhere to his right. Otherwise it was awfully quiet. Straining his ears, he couldn't even hear shouting from the pond. His heart pounded in his chest. Despite the quiet, he couldn't dismiss the very uncomfortable feeling that he was not alone.

Looking in front of him, he saw the stream feeding into the pond. Beyond it was the hill where Thad claimed you could see the houses from. All at once, Derek did not want to see any houses— at least not alone.

Gulping, he slowly turned back to the pond and started running, ducking branches and dodging logs. He didn't stop until seeing the backpacks still lying just where he'd left them.

Letting out a deep breath, he slowed to a walk and tried to control his breathing. Of course it had been his imagination. Then he went still. It was still quiet—especially in the pond.

Thinking the worst, Derek dashed to the edge of the water. The surface lay flat and still. A few ducks swam near the center, but no bodies were visible. He was about to call out to Danny and Jak when he heard a faint giggle.

Shutting his mouth, he listened intently.

"Oh, the sun feels good," groaned Danny's voice from the left.

Derek carefully stepped to the edge of the water and hid behind a tree. Looking left, he saw Danny and Jak several feet from him. The boys were sunning themselves on a small open grassy area and were oblivious to his presence. Danny lay flat on his back with his arms spread out and his feet dangling in the water. Next to him, Jak lay on his stomach, resting his cheek on his hands, facing the water. Derek saw his eyes were closed.

Grunting, Derek controlled the urge to yell at them. Danny looked like a beached whale—his arms and legs were tanned, but his big belly was as white as snow. Next to him, brown all over, Jak resembled a river otter. Both looked very content and peaceful. Looking to his right, Derek saw the rocks they'd been jumping off earlier. That was where it had started, where Jak had left his clothes.

Quickly moving back, Derek left the two boys to sleep in peace. He grinned and hurried to the rocks. He had a terribly awesome plan.

Danny woke up with a burning sensation on his stomach. Staring up, he saw bright sun shining down with a single turkey vulture circling overhead. He sat up with a jerk. "Ow!"

Looking down, he saw his stomach was completely red. He must have dozed off. "Great," he groaned. "Just what I need."

Next to him, Jak lay dozing.

Scratching his itchy back, Danny looked around him. He guessed they'd been sleeping for over an hour, at least. The sun had gone higher and hotter. Heavy, dark clouds were in the distance. The pond appeared empty except for the ducks, now swimming way on the other side. There was no sign of the other boys.

"Jak?" he said. "Jak, I think we'd better go find the others."

Murmuring he would later, Jak didn't move, so Danny kicked his foot. "Jak, wake up!"

The smaller boy woke with a start. Propping himself up on an elbow, he grinned lazily back at Danny.

"Should we go swimming again?" he asked.

"No, I think we need to find the others." Danny sounded worried. Getting to his feet, he brushed off the dirt behind him. "I hope they didn't leave us."

Yawning, Jak stretched out his shoulders and then arched his back. "Nah, they wouldn't do that." Then he froze. "Would they?"

"Let's just go, okay?"

Jak rolled over and Danny helped him to his feet, wincing as he did so. "This sunburn is going to kill me," he moaned.

The boys carefully picked their way through the bushes behind them and walked gingerly through the spikey-gumball-infested leaves.

Chapter 20

"**M**aybe we should've stayed in the water," Danny said, sucking in a breath as his foot found a sharp pinecone. He only half meant it. While the sun had dried their skin and most of their undershorts and hair, in the shade and with a breeze, they both felt slightly chilled.

Lighter on his feet, Jak reached the rocks first. He stopped and stared before putting his hands on his hips.

"Danny?" he asked, his voice sounding puzzled. "Where're my clothes?"

"Right where you left them—ow! And mine should be behind you—hey! Our backpacks!"

Near the rocks where they had stopped for lunch, only Derek's and Thad's packs remained.

Ignoring the pain, Danny hopped and skipped to Jak's side. The two boys stared despondently before them. Their clothes and shoes had vanished.

"Great," moaned Danny. Stepping back, he lifted his head. "Derek! Thad! This isn't funny anymore!"

Nobody answered.

Jak crouched down grimly. Slowly a small smile played across his face. "It's a little funny," he said.

"No, it's not!" Danny stalked angrily away from the pond and shook his fist. "Come out here and give us our clothes!" After still no answer, Danny rubbed his face. "This is a nightmare! I've only dreamed of this happening!"

Jak laughed but then shrugged. "I guess we can look around," he said doubtfully. "Maybe they just hid them."

"Derek, Thad! If you hid our clothes you better come out now!" A troubled look crossed Danny's face. He turned to Jak and gulped. "Okay, we'll look, but first, I need the bathroom." He scurried painfully into the trees. Searching wildly for any sign of Derek or Thad, he found a smooth deer path and took it a little farther before ducking behind a large oak tree.

Finishing, he was still fuming about never trusting Derek and Thad again when he went back to the deer path. "I hate you, Thad!" he yelled out. "I hate you, Derek! You too, Donald, if you're part of this!" Heading back toward the pond, he searched the trail for sharp obstacles. He never saw the figure appear on top of the hill above him until too late.

"Hey!" cried a surprised voice. "What are you doing?"

Spinning, Danny looked up in horror to see Mandy the Beast staring down at him.

"Ack!" Covering his shorts with his hand, he dove off the path and rolled into a pile of green plants.

"Hey, I hope you know that's poison ivy you're in!" the Beast said.

"Aaaack!" Jumping to his feet, Danny ran down the path, screeching in a very high-pitched voice. Reaching the pond, he found Jak staring at him with bemusement. "The Beast!" he screeched. "The Beast is coming!" He stamped his feet and waved his arms. "She's here!"

Jak's eyes widened and he looked past Danny hopefully. "Really? Where?"

Danny gave him a wild-eyed look and dropped his jaw.

Thad found them a second later, running from where he'd said goodbye to Donald at the tour road. "What's going on?" he cried "I heard you screaming a mile away!"

Danny spun on him in terror. "The Beast is here! She stole our clothes!"

"What?" Jak and Thad asked together.

"I hear you guys, you know," Mandy's voice called from up the trail. "I'm coming down."

Jak stared at Danny in horror. "I thought you meant a wild dog!" he yelped. "Are you crazy?"

"That's the same thing!" Danny cried. "She's the Beast and she's coming!" Dashing away, Danny ran full speed into the pond, falling with a splash.

Jak made to follow but ducked behind a tree at the last minute. Disappointment and shivers wracked his body.

Thad was left standing alone with a bewildered look as Mandy descended the hill.

"What are you doing here?" he finally asked just before she reached him. He couldn't help but sound stupid.

"You guys need to be quiet," Mandy said, ignoring the question. "I saw some guys with guns around here earlier and they don't look friendly."

"She stole our clothes!" screeched Danny from the pond. He sat in the shallows with only his shoulders, head, and neck visible. "Make her give them back!"

Mandy stopped a few feet from Thad and flicked back her hair. She wore her usual old jeans and T-shirt and had nothing with her.

"Did you take some clothes from around here?" Thad asked her, pushing down his cowlick furiously. He looked back, desperately wishing Donald had decided to come back. He would know what to do in this situation.

Mandy glared at him. "No! Why would I do that? Why isn't Danny wearing his clothes? I mean, I just got here, dope. I told you, I saw some guys with guns. Maybe they took them."

Danny started to rise, but abruptly sat back down. "Don't lie! You have them!"

Derek's voice cut in. "Ah, she has nothing, you idiot!" Looking furious, Derek stood behind a clump of bushes a little way from the backpacks. "I took them." He held a pile of shoes and clothing and stomped toward Danny.

"Why did you do that?" Danny shouted. "We've been stuck in our—" his sunburned face turned a deeper shade of red.

Derek glared at him. "It was just a joke, okay! I was only going to keep them for a minute, but you guys fell asleep!"

"So what?" Danny cried. "We've been awake for a long time!"

Derek looked down at the ground. "Well, I fell asleep too. Then you woke me up screaming like a banshee." He sneered at Mandy. "And where did she come from?" His voice dripped with venom.

Mandy, used to such scorn, ignored him. She looked at Thad.

"See, I told you so," she said. "I'm not a thief."

Thad grimaced and stuck his hands in his pockets. "Fine, but you have to leave."

"Why?" Mandy asked.

Derek sneered. "Just do what he says. Go hunt somewhere else."

Mandy tightened her mouth and looked at Derek for the first time. "For your information, this is more my land than your land, so maybe you guys should leave."

"Uh, first can we please get our clothes back?" Danny asked. He softened his voice. "Sorry, Beast, for thinking you took them." He glared at Derek. "I didn't know some other jerk did."

Mandy waved away the apology.

"I'm serious, man," she said. "There are guys with guns around."

Scowling, Derek walked to the edge of the pond and dumped the clothes and shoes onto the leaves. "Help yourself."

"Thank you." Danny started for the shore, but stopped. "Now, uh, Beast, do you, uh, mind?"

"She's leaving," growled Derek, turning his wrath on her. He stomped to stand next to Thad. "Tell her, Thad."

Before Thad could decide what to do, a sharp bark from behind Mandy caused everyone to freeze.

Jak gasped and ran from behind the tree. Ignoring everybody, he raced up the hill before slowing midway up. Going to his knees, he offered out a hand.

"Here, girl!" he crooned. "You can come down."

"What's he doing?" Derek asked nervously. "He's going to get bitten."

Thad only shook his head and gulped. Mandy took a step back.

"I hope he got his rabies shot," she said to no one in particular.

Ten feet from Jak, a large, brown mutt with round dark eyes stared down. Almost everything about the dog was brown—the long, pointed snout ending in a soft black nose, floppy ears, and skinny tail. The deep, dark brown eyes fixed on Jak. A long moment passed. Then the dog bowed her head.

Woofing softly, the dog took a step down and sniffed in Jak's direction. Briefly, the tail lifted in a small wag. Then with a final bark, the dog spun sharply and ran out of sight.

"Whew!" breathed Derek, stepping back with rubbery legs. "That was close."

Disappointed, Jak rose and slumped down the hill. "She almost came," he lamented. He kicked a stick and immediately hopped with pain.

"Uh, that's a wild dog, you know," Mandy told him.

To confirm it, a long howl sounded in the distance. Faint barks followed of more than one dog.

"She's still friendly," Jak said after a moment of hesitation. "Right?"

Everyone else just stared uneasily around them. The barking died down, but apprehension remained.

Muttering, Danny exited the pond and quickly started gathering his clothes. "Don't look, Beast!" he ordered. "Man, now I'm all wet again!"

Jak joined him and the two started sorting their clothes.

Derek grunted. "The dogs followed the beast," he said halfheartedly.

"That's not true!" Mandy turned on Derek and made a fist at him. "I already said I saw some guys with guns around here! I bet they're hunting those dogs!"

"Yeah, right!" Derek said derisively. "You didn't see anything. What are you doing out here to begin with?"

"Yeah," said Thad with more with curiosity than anger, "you said you had more right to this place than we did."

"I live around here," Mandy said with an air of challenge.

Derek snorted. "There aren't any trailer parks around here. Good try."

"For your information, my mom got a house last month just on the other side of those trees!" Mandy sounded mad and the others went silent at her outburst.

For a brief moment Thad thought she'd meant the old houses in the woods, but she pointed in the opposite direction. Then he thought quickly. "There are houses there, but then you would have ridden our bus to school," he said tentatively.

"Yeah." Mandy's voice dropped. "My mom drove me to and from school." Her anger spent, she gazed down in shame, hiding her eyes behind tufts of hair.

Nobody spoke for a moment. The bus was a cruel world. Being labeled a beast and ridiculed constantly was not an easy life. None of them had ever thought of the consequences of their actions. It had all been a game, with one loser.

"Well," Thad finally said after clearing his throat, "how did you know we were even out here?"

Now it was Mandy's turn to be embarrassed. "I heard you guys talking at lunch during the last week of school. You dopes didn't even notice me."

"So you were spying on us!" Derek said nastily.

"No! I was just walking in the woods when I saw the guys with the guns! I've been looking for you to warn you!" She didn't sound very convincing as she kept her eyes hidden behind her bangs and directed toward the leaves.

"There were no guys with guns!" Derek practically shouted. "We're the only ones out here!"

"There were too!" Mandy shot back. "I heard them talking! They even said they would be seeing Billy Boston here tonight!"

Derek burst out laughing. "Billy Boston? You're joking!" Billy Boston was Kevin's older brother and considered the best athlete in the county, possibly in the state. "Why would Billy be out here at night?"

Mandy shrugged. "I don't know, but I heard it!"

Derek refused to believe her. "No way! My brothers know Billy! He'd never be out here—he's afraid of the dark!"

Danny stepped behind the tree with his pants on and shirt in his hands. "What? Billy Boston is afraid of the dark? But he's like a superman!"

"Trust me, I know," Derek said. "My brother went to a football camp with him and said Billy sleeps with a light on." He shrugged. "Lots of people are afraid of the dark. It's no big deal."

Mandy shrugged again. "I just know what I heard."

Derek waved a hand like fending off an unwanted mosquito. "You're just spying on us! Get lost!"

"No! I know you're going to those old houses up there and I'm going too," Mandy said stubbornly. She jutted her jaw forward and dared anybody to argue.

Thad gulped. "You mean you've been there before?" he asked.

"No," she admitted, "but I heard you talking about them."

"Hmmph," Derek said. "I bet they don't even exist. Let's just set up our tent and stay here. The Beast can go back to her hole. I mean home."

"Hold on," Danny said, now fully dressed and looking up from where he was tying his shoe. "Where's Donald? Did the dogs—"

"He had to go back," Thad said, sighing. He really wished Donald had stayed. "Derek, we can't stop now. Remember, Donald wants us to find the clubhouse."

"He's moving," Derek said, going to his pack and grabbing his water bottle. "To California. Remember?"

"Yes, I do!" Thad said. "That's why we're out here! We need the clubhouse before he's gone!"

Derek scoffed. "Right, Thad. Donald hates the outdoors. We only came because you made us with your stupid story about houses in the woods. Well, I'm hot and tired. I want to stay here, and I have the tent. I doubt there are houses anyway."

Danny cleared his throat. "It's only a little farther, Derek. Why don't we make camp here and go look for the houses? We can come back here."

"Suit yourself," growled Derek, taking a seat. "I'm staying."

170

"I'll go," Mandy said.

Thad crossed his arms. "No." He ignored Mandy and stared only at Derek.

Jak, tugging on his shirt, stepped behind the tree and sat by Danny's feet. All eyes went to Thad.

"What do you mean, 'no'?" Derek asked dangerously.

"You're the leader, remember? More than that, you're our friend, Derek. We have to go together, or not go at all. You decide."

Derek stared at him suspiciously and then licked his lips. "What about the Beast?"

Thad licked his lips and tugged at his cowlick. "It's a free country," he said. "She can decide what she wants to do."

Derek waved his hand in defeat. "Fine. We'll go, but the Beast stays."

Mandy blew hair from her face and crossed her arms.

"Call me what you want," she said, "but I'm going too. If I go home, I'll just tell my mom and she'll call your parents! She'll tell them how y'all are trespassing on Park land!"

Thad licked his lips as Mandy and Derek stared each other down.

Danny broke the tension with a disgusting noise from his mouth. Jak giggled.

Derek muttered darkly and finally said to Mandy, "Okay, but you're still not sleeping out here tonight."

"Of course not!" the girl said in disgust. "I wouldn't want to smell you guys all night if you paid me!"

Derek made to say something nasty, but stopped.

"Hey, do I smell bad?" Danny asked, sniffing. He made a face. "Oh, yeah, I do."

Jak grinned. "We both smell like pond scum."

Chapter 21

The sun stretched high overhead as the day entered the late afternoon when Derek led the group across the stream. Finding several long-fallen logs, they constructed a crude bridge over the moving water and crossed without incident. Derek went first, followed by Danny, Jak, Thad, and finally Mandy.

The girl had refused to back down from her threat and Derek finally snarled for her to stay in the back. He'd tried to not let her use the log bridge, but Thad had pointed out how she could easily just jump over the narrow stream anyway (they had made the bridge more for fun than from necessity).

All of the hostilities ceased when they made it up the hill on the other side of the stream. Just as Thad had described, down on the other side, a paved road meandered through the middle of the forest, overgrown with weeds. Houses were also visible in the distance.

"Too cool," Jak said, even though it had been him who'd really discovered them first.

"Come on, let's go down!" said Derek. In the excitement, he forgot his bad mood. "I bet we're the first ones here in years!"

"Just watch your step!" warned Danny, sucking in his breath. His wet clothes chafed and his sunburn stung like the dickens. Still, he hurried down with the rest of them. Either the sense of adventure or the fear of being left behind spurred him on.

"It's like it's a magic road that just ends," Thad marveled when they'd reached the pavement.

Just under the hill where'd they come from, the road suddenly vanished. Pavement immediately turned into a layer of leaves, sticks, and tree-gumballs. The road itself was built in a long clearing with tall grass on either side. It was only visible from up high unless you were practically standing on it.

"Hmmph," Mandy said. "I bet the rest of it is just buried under the leaves."

"Or," said Thad, "maybe there's a magic portal here leading to a new world."

"Yeah, in your head," snorted Derek. "Come on. Let's follow it to the houses."

Feeling the air of adventure return, the group hurried up the road, rising in a gentle hill toward the cluster of buildings. They'd left all their backpacks and the tent back near the pond. Derek carried a flashlight and Thad still had the cell phone. Moving quickly, they passed by a cluster of trees before taking a gentle right and walking into a large clearing full of weeds, bushes, and buildings.

Derek arrived first at the clearing and quickly stopped, holding up a hand. "Stop here!"

Everyone crowded at his back and the carefree joking that had continued on the road ceased.

"What's wrong?" panted Danny, wiping his face.

Derek didn't answer. The feeling he had before of being watched had come back in full force. Even with the others, he felt a very uncomfortable presence.

Thad felt it too. Moving to Derek's right shoulder, he nodded at the houses. "Do you think we should go on?"

From where they stood they could see the front of a two-story house with a cracked, peeling, white frame. An old shed the size of a garage stood next to it. Strangely, though, this seemed much newer with a fresher coat of paint. A smaller single-story house with a collapsed roof faced them from across the road. This house had no paint and the wood looked to be rotting.

"Feels spooky," Mandy said.

Nobody disagreed. All the windows of both houses were completely gone or sported gaping holes in the glass. They looked like deranged eyes staring at them. An array of garbage lay scattered in the tall grass around them. Old glass bottles, rusted cans, broken ceramics, and even a cracked tub were just some of the highlights.

"I bet a lot of kids grew up around here," Thad said in a hushed tone. "Maybe their ghosts still live here."

"Don't say that, man," Mandy said. "You're giving me the creeps."

Jak shivered violently and wiped back his damp hair.

"Ah, that's a load of trash," Derek said suddenly, stepping confidently into the clearing. He stopped short, though, and waited for the others. "There are no such things as ghosts."

A loud mocking laugh answered him. It came from behind the white house.

Thad felt his stomach do a flip and Jak latched onto one of his arms. Danny took the other. They all froze as the laughter faded.

Thad felt his knees buckle.

"Pl-please t-tell me that wasn't real," Danny said shakily.

"You know," whispered Derek, backing up slowly. "Maybe we should go now."

"Not going so soon, are you?" asked a deep voice behind them.

Screaming as one, the group whirled in fright.

Their only relief came from not seeing an actual ghost. But after a moment, they almost wished they had.

A tall, brawny teenager with long, blond curls hanging to his shoulders stood on the road behind them. His thick arms cradled a small but wicked-looking pellet gun. Wearing combat boots, jean shorts, and a sleeveless T-shirt with a heavy metal band logo, he did not look friendly. Despite his grin, his pale yellowish eyes held only cruelty.

"Now what are you clown freaks doing out here?"

Derek found his voice first. "We're wondering the same thing about you."

"You don't ask the questions," the teenager snarled. Fuzz covered his chin and cheeks. Scratching it, he wiped his nose. It looked to have been broken more than once and tilted crookedly to the right. "You clowns are on my territory now."

"We have a girl with us," Danny said timidly. "Uh, we can go now."

Mandy glared at him as if insulted, but bit her tongue. Clearly she didn't think they should run.

The teenager shook his head. "Sorry, chumps. Not yet you don't." He cupped his hands and yelled. "Hey, Dave! Give the boss a call and tell him what we found!" He grinned wolfishly, revealing yellowing teeth. "He sent us out to find wild dogs and we got us a bunch of lame kids."

Derek suddenly blinked. "Hey, wait! You play football for Lincoln! I've seen your picture in the paper!" His older brothers played for Knox High. Derek followed their league religiously. Lincoln was the other large high school in the county and archrivals with Knox.

For the first time, the teenager looked mildly pleased. "That's right. I made all-state last year."

Frowning, Thad wondered what this meant when he heard a noise behind him. Turning, he saw two more teens coming from behind the white house. Both carried pellet guns and no signs of friendliness.

"Man, Charlie, what are we going to do now?" asked one nervously. Dressed in camouflaged hunting pants, boots, and a black shirt with short sleeves, he was several inches shorter than Charlie. He stood hunched at the shoulders and wore a hangdog look that made him look perpetually frightened.

His companion loomed over everybody and appeared much looser.

"See," he crowed loudly. "I told you I heard some kids earlier." Wearing a blue ball cap backwards, he wore a white, sleeveless T-shirt and tan-colored cargo shorts. These were slung low at his waist and freely displayed bright orange boxer shorts. An unlit cigarette dangled from thick lips turned up into a goofy grin.

"No kidding," Charlie snarled. "We heard you punks a mile away. Dave, did you call the boss?"

The scared teen flinched. "No, not yet."

"Then do it!" Charlie commanded.

"All right, man," Dave whined. "But I got to go up farther to find a signal."

"What are you waiting for?" barked Charlie. "We don't have all day!"

While the sun still remained visible, dark angry clouds threatened. Thunder rumbled in the distance.

Bobbing his head awkwardly, Dave turned with a jerk. Scuttling back behind the old white house, he fumbled at his pocket.

The big, goofy-looking teen laughed. "Dude, how did that idiot ever make the team?"

Charlie shrugged. "Who cares? Yo, you clowns stay right there. Nobody move."

"What are you doing?" Derek asked. His face went chalky white as the barrel of Charlie's gun swung in his direction.

"You'll see," the teen said slowly. To his companion, Charlie asked, "Where's your twerp brother? He might know some of these clowns."

The other teen shrugged unconcernedly. "He should be coming."

"Hey!" Mandy said suddenly. "What are you guys doing here?"

"Shut up," growled Charlie. "See this gun here? It may not look like much, but it's powered to kill a dog. If any of you clowns make any sudden movement, I'll gladly use it on you." He nodded at the other teen. "Yo, Ed, go fetch your brother."

Ed spat out his cigarette and cupped a hand to his mouth. "Hey, Eric! Come over here and meet your friends! Eric!"

A familiar voice answered. "What are you talking about? I don't have friends here."

Derek turned and looked at Thad. They all knew who would be coming. Sure enough, Eric Minters sauntered from behind the smaller house and went still. "What are you guys doing here?" he finally asked stupidly.

Ed laughed. "So you do know these idiots, Eric?"

"Yeah, they go to my school." His eyes narrowed. "One of them is the little spaz!"

"Little spaz, huh?" Ed looked at the group of kids and spat. "I bet I know which one that is." He grinned, displaying yellow teeth at Jak. "I heard a lot about you."

Jak ducked behind Thad.

"Shut up," growled Charlie, getting impatient. "My question is, what are they doing here?"

"We just wanted to see the houses," Thad spoke up. He swallowed hard. Now that he had spoken he couldn't back down. "We saw them on our field trip two weeks ago and only wanted to explore. That's all."

Charlie turned to Eric. "Is that true?"

"I don't know," Eric said disdainfully. "I wasn't in their class. I spent most of that trip smoking in the museum's bathroom." He tried to sound tough, but it came out nervous.

"I bet you did." Charlie spat in the dirt near Derek's sneakers. The teenagers seemed to like to spit. "Ed, go fetch some beers. Let's have a meeting with these kids while we wait for Dave."

"What do we do?" hissed Mandy in Thad's ear. "I don't like these guys. This is bad, man."

Thad swallowed and had no answer. While the teenagers talked, the kids shuffled together. Danny and Jak pressed close behind him and he could feel them shaking. Of course, it could have been just him. He knew his knees were trembling.

"Just play it cool," Derek whispered. "My brothers told me about these guys. They're all punks."

"Quiet!" barked Charlie. "Which one of you clowns is in charge?"

Eric snorted and crossed his arms contemptuously when seeing them all jump. At first he'd looked surprised and even scared. Now he relaxed and grinned.

"None of them have any guts. They're all a bunch of pansies," he said.

Face red, Derek stepped forward. "I-I'm the leader." He tried to deepen his voice, but it cracked and ended up more like a squeak.

"Sure you are." Charlie stared down at Derek for a long moment. "You're Joey's brother, aren't you?"

Derek nodded. "Uh, yeah, and Mike's brother, too."

Charlie relaxed and lowered his gun. "Cool, man. Then you're one of us."

"Him?" scoffed Eric. "He's a complete loser, man."

"Shut up," Charlie told Eric. "His brothers are all right. More than I can say for you and your brother."

Ed laughed as he exited the front door of the white house. He gripped his pellet gun by the barrel with one hand while cradling an armful of sweaty beer cans with the other. "He got you there, bro."

"Whatever." Eric stared balefully at Derek and then at the others.

Thad made sure to avoid his gaze. All at once, the adventure died. He desperately wished they'd never seen the houses. If only he'd listened to Donald and Derek, then they wouldn't be in this mess. He wasn't sure what exactly was going on, but he had a terrible feeling about it. These guys were serious bad news.

Danny fought tears on his right. To his left, Jak ... Jak was peering intently at the teens through slanted eyes. While no grin appeared, his lips were set in a very determined way. Thad started getting really worried.

Charlie took a beer from Ed and flipped it to Derek. "Here, drink up." Taking another beer, he cracked it open.

Derek managed to catch the can with both hands but looked too surprised to do anything else.

"Give me one, man," Eric asked.

Ed chuckled. "No can do, bro. Mom would kill me." He cracked open the last can and slurped nosily.

Derek held the can and went still. After a moment, he glanced quickly back at Thad and Danny. Both saw deep fear. Derek's hands trembled slightly.

"See," Eric scoffed. "I told you he was a pansy!"

Charlie frowned. "What's wrong, dude? Are you going to open it, or not?"

"Uh, uh, yeah ..." Hands still shaking, Derek managed to put a hand on the tab and press down. He flinched when hearing a sharp click. Suds fizzled from the opening.

"Come on, man," goaded Ed. "Real men do it. You're the leader, lead."

Derek's knees trembled. "I-I don't want to," he said softly.

Eric and Ed laughed, but Charlie only frowned.

"You better drink, kid," Charlie said. "I don't want to see a good beer wasted."

"Just good people," Ed cracked, taking another sip.

"You scared?" Charlie suddenly asked, stepping close to Derek. He bent low so their faces were about even.

Derek looked up at Charlie and took a deep breath. "N-no."

"Then take a sip," Charlie urged. "Then we can talk and I'll let you all go."

Jak all at once moved from Thad and walked over to Derek.

Thad tried to grab him, but was shaken off.

"Hey, maybe the little spaz wants a sip," Eric laughed.

Instead, Jak took the can and faced Charlie. "He said he doesn't want it." Deliberately, he tilted the can and poured out the beer. He glared at Charlie the entire time.

Eric stopped laughing.

Ed snorted. "That's a dumb move, kid."

Charlie tightened his grip on the pellet gun and then relaxed. "Eric is right," he said. "You all are pansies."

Derek's face flushed and he stepped forward. "Fine, but can we go now?"

Charlie stepped forward until inches from Derek and Jak. Looking down at Derek, he pretended to sniff. "Smell that? I smell fear."

"Maybe it's you," Jak said, his face set in a sneer. "You forgot to wipe."

Charlie looked over at him and smirked. "You're not afraid, are you? I bet you're the little spaz."

Jak sneered back. "And you're the big idiot."

Charlie made to shove Jak, but at that instant a low, dark growl erupted from the bushes to the right of Thad. The big brown mutt stepped out from a thicket and bared rows of sharp teeth.

"Hot potato, there she is!" cried Ed. He stumbled back so fast, he ended up falling.

"Shoot her!" Charlie stepped from Jak and started lifting his pellet gun.

"Leave her alone!" Jak leapt at him, knocking his elbow.

Snarling, the mutt started forward, but suddenly jumped a foot and yelped.

Ed, sitting on his seat, started pumping his pellet gun for another shot.

"What do we do?" Mandy cried in Thad's ear.

"Help Derek and Jak!" Danny yelled back, already running to the fracas.

Charlie had shrugged off Jak, knocking him into the ground, but stepped into Derek.

"Get out of my way," he snarled. "She's mine!"

Chapter 22

Barks and screams filled the air as chaos took over.

Charlie shoved Derek back, sending him crashing to the ground.

With a muffled roar, Danny went at him with a fury.

His attack never reached Charlie as Eric plowed in from the side, sending Danny flying.

Momentarily alone, Charlie swung his rifle toward the dog. Before he could get a shot, Jak got back to his feet and jumped on his back.

"Get off!" the teen screeched. "Get off!"

Jak held grimly on, locking his thin arms around Charlie's thick neck.

Eric and Danny started wrestling as Derek rolled away from them. He'd been kicked twice in the back by their flailing feet.

Barking once, the mutt jumped back as Ed hit her side with another pellet. Snapping her teeth, she all at once dashed back into the thicket and disappeared.

Thad started to go help Danny, but a pellet pinged off his shoe and skittered into the grass. He hopped back.

"Stay back," Ed hissed at him.

It ended quickly. Charlie ducked his head low and flipped Jak clear. Before the boy could get up, Charlie kicked him hard in the side and leveled his rifle at Derek's face.

"Anybody moves, this boy gets a free nose piercing!" he shouted.

Danny rolled away from Eric and sat up with a groan. Dirt covered his shirt and pain lined his face. He'd fallen on his sunburn.

"Now everyone, get back!" Charlie barked.

Derek raised both hands and stumbled backwards to Thad.

Eric walked up to him and all at once socked him in the gut. "That's for wasting the beer," he growled.

Crumpling to his knees, Derek fought for a breath.

"Jerk," Danny muttered, getting slowly to his feet.

Smirking, Eric only went to Jak and roughly pulled him up by the back of the shirt. "Now you know what I mean by little spaz."

Charlie snarled at Jak. "You touch me again and I'll break your arm!" To Eric, he said, "Throw him with the others."

"With pleasure," grinned Eric. He roughly dragged him toward Derek before tossing him rudely to the ground. Already limp with pain from Charlie's kick, Jak sprawled like a rag doll and rolled to where Derek still knelt. He breathed hard and stared balefully up at Eric.

"You guys all right?" Thad asked.

"Yeah," wheezed Derek. "No thanks to you."

His face turning crimson, Thad bent down and helped Jak to his feet. The smaller boy shook him off and sat hunched over in pain. Thad had never been in a fight before. He felt ashamed to have done nothing while his friends got the brunt of it.

"Hey, that guy had a gun on him!" Mandy said. "He would have shot him and me if we did anything."

"That's right," Ed said grinning. "And I still will shoot if any of you idiots try to run. Now what do we do, Charlie?"

"Now we go after those dogs!" A wicked glint appeared in his eyes. "First, though, we teach these clowns a lesson. Ed, you got everything out of the shed, right?"

Ed nodded. "Uh, yeah. The boss wants it all ready for tonight. It's in the house now."

"Good," purred Charlie. "Let's place these clowns in there for a few hours."

Ed's eyes widened. "You mean lock them in?"

"Why not?" asked Charlie, staring at Ed in a challenge.

"Uh, Charlie …" Ed lost his goofy grin and looked slightly scared. "The boss doesn't want any trouble for tonight."

"There won't be any trouble!" Charlie said sharply.

Dave ran back from behind the white house and frowned when he saw the empty beer cans. "I couldn't get a good signal and never reached him. Why don't we just let them go?" he said in a whiny voice.

Charlie shook his head. "Better yet," he said, "we lock them in the shed and go dog hunting."

"Good idea," Eric said.

"Shut up," snapped Ed. He reached in one of his pockets and pulled out a lighter. Flicking it, he lit his cigarette. "If we mess things up, man—"

"Nothing will happen," Charlie told him. "Once the dogs are ours, we'll come back and let them go." Charlie turned to the group of kids and sneered. "None of these pansies can do anything to us. If you guys tell your parents, guess what? You were trespassing too. Besides, it's for your own protection. Those wild dogs are dangerous."

"Yeah, I guess," Ed said, frowning. He didn't look too happy, but still wasn't ready to stand up to Charlie. He sucked in a deep lungful before blowing out a cloud of smoke.

"Then let's do it." Charlie walked to where Derek had finally managed to stand. "Lead your bunch of pansies and let's go."

"No," Derek told him, staring up at him with a glare.

The barrel prodded him in the back of the jeans. "You sure about that?"

"Just do it," Thad said tiredly. "We'll figure something out."

Charlie smirked. "Listen to the smart one and move!"

Feeling sick and angry, Derek had no choice. Thad miserably followed him, leading Jak by the arm. The smaller boy hadn't said a word. His eyes flashed with anger, but his body hunched in obvious pain. Danny and Mandy followed the solemn parade. If they had any ideas of escape now, Ed and Dave headed them off by keeping pace on either side.

Eric watched with a stupid grin and waved.

Charlie stopped at the white shed next to the larger house and pointed at an open doorway.

"Get in!" When Derek hesitated, he grabbed him by the arm.

"Okay," Derek cried. "I'm going!"

"Go faster!" Charlie practically flung him inside. The others quickly followed. The last sight Thad had before the door slammed shut was Ed flicking his smoking cigarette in disgust. Then there came darkness and a sharp click of a padlock closing.

"Get your rifles ready!" Charlie's muffled voice barked on the other side. "Make sure you have at least ten pumps. We're going to blow some holes in those mutts!"

"What do we do?" moaned Danny.

Minutes had gone by since their captors had left. In the shed, things were looking very bleak. Thad had already tried the door—solidly shut—and searched for a light switch, an equally hopeless task. The only light came from the cracks between some of the boards. Derek's flashlight had fallen from his pocket during the scuffle with Charlie.

"At least we have a roof over our heads," Mandy grumbled. Outside, the wind had picked up and thunder grumbled and rumbled. "There's going to be a storm."

"I want a storm in Charlie's face," Derek seethed. He paced angrily in front of the door, next to where Mandy sat with her back against it.

"And Eric's," Danny added. He and Thad sat in the middle of the shed. Jak, still very quiet, lay on his side behind them.

During his exploration of the shed, Thad found it to be nothing but a solid shell of wood. An elevated platform used for storage, four feet from the earthen floor, jutted from the back wall and extended five feet. It held nothing but animal droppings and a few pieces of scrap metal. Despite its age, the shed held together well and there seemed to be no weak spots to break through. They were truly stuck.

"Donald is lucky," Danny said after a while. "He's probably watching TV right now."

Thad sighed. "And just think," he said. "This would have been a great clubhouse."

"If those stupid punks weren't already here!" Derek stopped pacing and kicked the door.

"I wonder what they were doing," wondered Danny. "They seemed to have a boss, or something."

"They're the guys I saw earlier," Mandy said. "The ones I tried to tell you about, but y'all wouldn't listen."

"We're listening now," Thad said. "You said they were meeting Billy Boston here, right?"

"Yeah," the girl said. "I told you that."

Derek stopped pacing and looked at her. After seeing Charlie and the other teenagers, suddenly imagining Billy Boston being there didn't sound so far-fetched. But why? What exactly was going on here? To Mandy, he said, "Tell us again. Everything."

The girl sighed. "Well, I don't remember everything. I was just walking, when I heard some talking. At first I thought it was y'all, but the voices sounded too old. I hid behind a tree and saw Charlie and them carrying their stupid guns. Charlie was saying something about getting Billy Boston tonight, and that they would destroy everyone next year."

"So they're trying to take over the world?" Danny asked, half in jest.

Derek stomped his feet. "No!" he yelled.

"What's wrong?" Thad asked, alarmed. "Did a wasp get you?" He'd seen plenty of nests already.

"No, but I bet I know what's going on!" Derek cried. "Those guys, they're from Lincoln High."

"So?" Mandy rested her arms on her knees and shrugged.

Derek continued when nobody else said anything. "My brothers always talk about it. A lot of players try to transfer to schools they think will win. In fact, my brother Joey once told me he was offered five hundred bucks by a coach to go to a different school!"

Thad made a face. "Really?"

"Well, Joey does lie," Derek admitted. "But still, I know it happens. I bet Lincoln High is trying to get Billy to their school." Yelling in frustration, he banged a fist against the wall.

"Wait," Danny said. "What about Ed? Shouldn't he play with Billy? I mean, Eric goes to our school."

Derek grunted. "Eric's parents are divorced. His brother lives with his dad near Lincoln."

"Yeah," said Danny slowly, "but why meet out here in the woods? That doesn't make sense."

"We'll never find out while we're stuck in here!" roared Derek. He turned to Thad. "Check the phone again."

Sighing, Thad pulled Michelle's cell phone from his pocket. So far it'd only been useful as a faint light during his search of the shed. Like Dave had said, there was no signal for cell phones in this area.

"Sorry, guys," he said glumly. "Nothing."

"We'll get out somehow," Mandy said. "Together, we'll think of something."

Derek frowned. "You're not even with us."

"Derek," Danny said, slightly shocked, "leave her alone."

"No, I'm serious." Derek sat down and looked at Mandy's silhouette. "I know why the other guys stayed. They're friends … even the little spaz. But you could have run away when the fighting started. Why'd you stay?"

Mandy grunted. "For one thing, there were wild dogs out there, you dope."

"I still would've run," Derek said.

"Me too," echoed Danny.

Not used to this type of attention, Mandy visibly squirmed. "I don't know …" Suddenly she sniffed. "Hey, do you guys smell smoke?"

"Don't change the subject," Derek said. "Tell us—"

"Wait!" Danny tested the air and shot to his feet. "It smells like wood burning!"

Alarmed, Thad looked back at Jak, but the boy still hadn't moved. Only Jak would be dumb enough to try to burn their way out. Then he smelled it too. "Guys, I think there's a fire nearby."

186

"Maybe Charlie came back and they're making a fire," said Danny doubtfully.

Then Mandy yelped and shot from the door, beating at her jeans. "The door, I think it's on fire!"

Behind her, even in the gloom, thick smoke could be seen seeping in. Then a flicker of orange followed. The flame started to grow at the bottom of the door.

"That idiot!" Derek screamed. "Ed! He never put out his cigarette! That's what happened!"

Now Jak got up in alarm. Thad could see the whites of his eyes in the murky light. He looked scared.

"What's happening?" the smaller boy asked.

"We're being burned alive!" Derek shouted. "Stupid Ed threw a lit cigarette on dry grass and wood!"

Thunder cracked from overhead, but no rain fell. At the door, the flame licked the wood hungrily and continued to grow. Smoke poured in.

Coughing, Derek stumbled back. "We have to get out of here!"

"How?" choked Mandy.

"Can we beat out the fire with our shirts?" Danny asked. All of them were backing away from the smoke and flame.

"It wouldn't work," Thad said. "The fire is mostly on the other side where we can't get it."

Danny wiped his eyes. "Then we can at least duck so the smoke isn't so bad!" he said.

"Good idea, Danny," Derek coughed. "I'm glad you paid attention to fire safety." He didn't sound sarcastic.

On their hands and knees, they crawled under the platform where the smoke had yet to reach.

"Do you think we're safe?" Danny asked fearfully. The fire was still contained to the door but showed no signs of dying out.

"What do you think?" Mandy said bluntly. "We're in a building made only of wood."

"Not everything!" Jak said. He suddenly rolled to the side wall and started scraping at the dirt with his hands.

"Jak!" cried Thad. "You're a genius! The floor is dirt, so we can dig ourselves out!"

Derek snorted and instantly started coughing. "The floor is also as hard as concrete." He still went to join Jak.

After less than a minute, Thad was forced to agree with Derek. Even with all of them pawing at the dirt, they'd barely made a dent. They did more harm to their fingers than to the dirt floor.

"I broke a nail," moaned Danny. "This is the worse day of my life."

"That's okay," Derek said unkindly. "It's also probably your last day too."

"We need a shovel!" Mandy said disgustedly.

"Hold on, I got an idea!" Thad left the others and crawled into the thick smoke. Instantly he started coughing.

"Where's he going?" Mandy cried. "Are you crazy, man?"

"We all face the end differently," Derek said without humor. Sighing, he pushed himself from the wall. "It's hopeless."

"Hey, man!" Mandy shoved him in the shoulder. "You can't give up like that!"

"I'm not giving up like that!" Derek snarled at her. "I'm accepting facts!"

"That's giving up! Y'all been calling me names all year and I never quit!"

Derek stared at her and then abruptly got up and left. He went off into the smoke where Thad had gone.

"Where are you going?" Danny called after him.

"To find Thad and then die!" shouted Derek back.

Danny grabbed Mandy's arm as she made to go after him. "Let him go. He'll be back. You'll see."

Jak lay on his stomach and halfheartedly scraped at the dirt.

Chapter 23

Using all his effort, Thad threw a leg up over the platform and managed to pull himself up, rolling to his back. Every breath would bring thick smoke to his lungs, making breathing a nightmare. Shifting to his stomach, he squeezed his eyes shut from the stinging smoke and crawled forward. The whole time, he held his breath.

Once, at the pool, he'd been timed for forty seconds without taking a breath. He hoped to break his record. Waving his arms, he searched blindly for the metal pieces he'd seen earlier. Just when he thought it was hopeless, his right hand brushed against something sharp.

Grabbing it, he started pushing himself backwards, still on his belly. Keeping his face down in his shoulder as much as possible, he still didn't dare draw a breath. Moving became a strain and he could feel his strength leaving him. Gasping for a breath would only bring more torture. Dots appeared in his vision and he felt darkness closing in. Then, just as he thought it was hopeless, a hand gripped his foot and started yanking him backwards. He went toward momentary consciousness.

"Whatever you're doing, Thad," said Derek's muffled voice, "it's not worth it."

Just as his feet slipped in air, he managed to toss down the metal bar. Then he fell into darkness.

Derek grabbed Thad under the arms to keep him from striking the ground. "Thad, wake up!" Lowering him gently, he slapped at Thad's face.

Coughing, Thad opened his eyes and groaned. "Get the metal bar … we can use it to dig out."

"Do you need any help?" Danny called from the corner under the platform.

"I got Thad!" Derek hollered to him. "Come grab this thing! It might save us!"

Jak and Danny raced to help. Danny and Derek dragged a semiconscious Thad to fresher air while Jak took the scrap metal and crawled back to Mandy.

When Thad fully opened his eyes, he saw a glimmer of daylight and breathed in fresh gusts of air. He lay on the earthen floor of the shed facing a shallow trench being dug by Derek and Danny under the shed wall. As Derek stabbed and twisted a metal bar to loosen the dirt and stones, Danny scooped up the bits and tossed them aside. Jak and Mandy urged them on. Thankfully, most of the smoke from the fire went up to the ceiling and they were protected by the platform. However, flames started to illuminate the darkened shed. Waves of heat kept coming.

"You guys got it?" Thad croaked.

"Nice of you to wake up and join us," grunted Derek.

"Yeah, he probably saved our lives," Mandy said.

"Not yet!" Derek threw down the metal bar and breathed heavily. "It's like digging through stone." He'd tried to break the wood boards of the wall, but had only managed to knock off the bottom edge of the lowest board. The part touching the ground had been partially rotten, but otherwise the wood kept firm.

"Can," panted Danny, "somebody fit through yet? I know I can't."

Everyone looked at Jak.

"I can make it!" the small boy said, meeting their stares excitedly.

"It'll be tight," Thad said doubtfully.

"Just watch!" Going on his belly, Jak attacked the hole like a snake getting loose from a watering can. Sucking in his stomach, he went head first into the trench. Reaching out with his right arm, he found traction on the other side of the shed and squeezed out his head. Then he worked on his shoulders. Twisting and wriggling, with the others pushing from behind, he slowly started making it out. Then, with a wild kick, he snagged his pants on one of the broken boards. "I'm stuck!"

"Keep going!" Derek grabbed Jak's legs and pushed hard.

"OW!" screamed the trapped boy.

"Sorry, Jak, but it's either this or become human barbecue!" Derek pushed again.

Screeching, Jak turned his body and managed to pull free. Wood splintered and a large piece broke off, taking a fair amount of skin with it, but Jak rolled from the shed into the fresh air of a late afternoon.

Lightning flashed over him and another round of thunder boomed.

"What do I do now?" he asked, pushing himself to his feet, nearly running in place.

"Go find something to make this hole bigger!" Derek yelled. Seeing success had sent a fresh wave of energy. He gripped the metal bar and furiously attacked the trench.

"Shouldn't another person go out?" Danny asked. "I mean, who else can fit?"

"Jak barely made it and he's the smallest." Thad clamped Danny's shoulder. "Besides, I think you're next."

"We'll be here tomorrow if that's true," Danny moaned.

"We'd better not," puffed Derek. "Because then we'd be goners." He wiped sweat from his brow. "Here, one of you try digging."

Thad took the metal bar and knelt down. As he brushed the wall, he felt something wet. In the light, he saw it was a smear of red. Jak's escape was much tighter than he'd thought.

Meanwhile, Jak hastily searched the junk in the grass and found a solid metal pole about his length and two inches thick. Lifting it with two hands, he dragged it back to the shed.

"Will this work?" he gasped, dropping it outside the hole.

"Yes!" shouted Thad. "Bring it in."

As he moved to do so, the sky opened up outside and a torrent of ran started to fall.

"We're saved!" yelled Danny. "The rain will put the fire out."

"Sure," Derek said reasonably. "But we're still locked in the shed. Jak!" He had to shout over the sound of the rain drumming on the roof. "Give us the pole!"

Mandy helped pull in the pole and got her arm muddy in the process. "Perfect! The rain is helping the dirt soften!"

Once the pole was in the shed, Jak hopped from foot to foot excitedly as the rain continued to fall.

Inside the shed, things were not so good. Smoke continued to gather.

"Just use the pole to bash down the wall," Danny said.

"The wall's too thick," Derek shouted.

"Just dig out the trench," Mandy cried. "It's almost all mud!"

Derek also said no because the pole wasn't a shovel. Thad finally hit on the idea of using it like a crowbar. Tilting it at an angle, they could jab it between two boards and pry them loose. One end of the pole had a small four-inch hook that should be able to find a grip easily. He'd already found a knothole in one of the bottom boards that would be perfect. After more haggling, they tried it while Mandy continued digging in the mud.

At first it seemed like instant failure.

The three boys jammed the pole's hook between two boards, but it just slipped out.

"See, I told you," Mandy said.

Derek licked his lips. "Again!"

The next time, the pole caught and held fast. Leaning back, all three boys put their weight on the pole. For a moment nothing happened. The pole strained to lift and pull solid wood that had no place to go. Then came a loud squeak, followed by a sharp, sudden crack. The wood buckled before splitting up and open. A section of the shed fell away, leaving a gaping hole in the wall.

Thad peered out to see Jak sitting back in a mud puddle with a surprised look on his face. Soaked to the skin, the boy wiped wet hair from his eyes. "I thought you were crawling under."

"That's the little boy's entrance," Derek said, lifting a leg to step through the hole. "This one is for men."

"What about me?" Mandy asked.

"Oh, er, uh, and for women," Danny said hastily. "Here, you go first."

Quickly free of the shed, the kids didn't stay around much longer. The rain had petered out but had done its work. Only a smoldering mess remained of the fire. They were surprised when they took a peek at the front and saw such little damage. Only the door had been destroyed. Scorch marks surrounded the opening and marked the grass where the fire had begun, but mostly the shed had remained intact. The fire hadn't spread very far into the interior.

"Where do we go now?" Danny asked as they ran through the trees to the road. "Back to our camp or back home?"

"Those guys will be looking for us so I don't think the camp is a good idea," said Thad. "It's too close."

"Then we go home?" Danny sounded hopeful.

Derek slowed to a walk and shook his head. "No way," he said. "We have to be here tonight to stop them."

Everyone else slowed as well. Thad frowned. "Why not just tell our parents and call the police?"

"That wouldn't work," Derek said. "We have no proof. We don't even know who we're stopping. Besides, we're trespassing too, remember? If the police come now we'll be in just as much trouble and we couldn't help Billy. They might even blame us for burning the shed."

"Maybe he doesn't want to be helped," Mandy said. "If he's like Charlie, then I don't want to be near him."

"Billy's a good guy," Derek practically snarled. "My brothers are his friends. He wouldn't be with Charlie and those punks unless he's being tricked."

Thad sighed. "Fine, but we need to find a place to hide. Jak is hurt and those guys are still out there with their guns."

Jak scowled. "I'm not hurt!" Fresh blood soaked the side of his shirt where it'd been torn on the shed. The rain had washed away most of it, but it still bled. His shirt and jeans, soaked by rain, were plastered to his skin and his lips shivered slightly.

"I think we're all a little hurt," Danny groaned. "My sunburn … and," he twitched uncomfortably, "chafing."

"Yeah, Thad," Mandy said. "You're bleeding too."

"Just a few scrapes from climbing in the shed." He coughed. "Uh, Derek, I haven't thanked you yet, but you, uh, saved me."

Derek shrugged, embarrassed. "I'm still staying the night."

"Me too," Thad said with a sigh.

"Then where do we hide?" Danny said. He shivered. "We're soaked and stuck out here where those guys can find us."

Mandy grinned. "I know a place. Y'all just follow me!"

"Where are we going?" Derek asked her warily.

Mandy grinned. "My house, you dope. Y'all better find some manners, though. My mom hates rudeness."

Mandy took the lead and found a trail skirting the pond opposite where the boys had left their backpacks and tent.

Finding a path, she confidently led them to the tour road and took a right. "Just a few more miles," she called.

Danny groaned, but mostly everyone stayed quiet. Charlie and his groupies were still out there. The sun began to descend and none of them could believe that it hadn't even been one day yet. It felt like a week since they'd left that morning.

Nearing the end of the tour road, Mandy took a sharp left back into the woods. Following a well-traveled deer path, they meandered through young forests before reaching the back of a small cluster of old houses facing the road near Knox Elementary.

"I know where we are!" Danny cried. "Our neighborhood is just a few miles to the left. School is right over there! These are the poor—"

Derek punched Danny in the shoulder. "Quiet," he hissed.

Pretending not to hear, Mandy gestured to the nearest house. "That's my house there."

The size of a double-wide trailer, her house was a one-story flat with a molded roof. Weeds sprouted from an unkempt yard and the back steps sagged.

"Are your parents even home?" Thad asked, looking at the empty driveway.

"My mom should be. She parks in the front because our driveway has too many potholes. My dad works out of town."

Nobody asked any more questions. Suddenly they all felt shy and more than a little guilty.

As Mandy guided them to the back stoop, they heard a woman's voice from inside.

"Mandy? Is that you? Where've you been? You know better than to be outside during a storm!"

"I was inside, Mom!" Mandy called. "Oh, and I have friends with me."

"What?" cried the voice.

The door opened and a plump woman in a large, white bathrobe stared out. Her blondish hair, streaked with gray, hung on her wide shoulders. Wrinkles lined her worn face and her lips curled in a sneer when seeing the boys.

"These are your friends?" she asked without humor. "They're not the ones who tease you, are they?"

Chapter 24

Mandy shook her head vigorously. "No, Mom. I found them in the woods. They're camping out, but are in a little trouble."

"I'll say," Mrs. Purcell said flatly. She looked at Jak, who flinched. "You, boy, look like a wet rag with a ketchup stain." Her eyes hardened when seeing Derek, Danny, and Thad. "You sure these aren't the boys from school?"

"They are from school, Mom, but they're fine. Can we come in?"

Her mom's face looked pained. "But Mandy, I thought you didn't—I mean, I thought—"

"Mom!" Mandy said abruptly. "They were camping out and got lost. I helped them and they helped me. We're friends!"

Mandy's mom chewed her bottom lip. She put both hands to her hips and glared at the boys.

Nobody met her eye. Thad kicked miserably at the tuft of grass at his feet.

"So they're not the bullies that ruined your school year?" Mrs. Purcell said.

Mandy shook her head. "Mom, please!"

Mrs. Purcell suddenly looked deflated. "Oh, very well," she said sounding sad. "I'm sorry. I forgot my manners. Come on in." Moving back, she waved the boys into the house. "A few of you could use some cleaning up. Then you can tell me what's going on."

"Um, thank you, ma'am," Thad said, being the first to move.

Derek quickly echoed him, ducking his head.

"Don't thank me yet." Mrs. Purcell still eyed them a little frostily. Then she spoke to Thad. "Come to the kitchen and let's see some of your cuts." She put an arm on Jak's shoulder. "You too, boy. The rest of you can share a pizza. Mandy, you better go to the freezer and put at least three more pizzas on."

"Uh, you won't tell our parents?" Derek asked tentatively.

Mandy's mom laughed. "If I could! We don't have a phone here. I'll get a cell phone one of these days, but I'm afraid you're out of luck if you want to call anybody."

Derek shot Mandy a look but then shook his head. He remembered her threat to call their parents earlier.

Thad jumped. "Wait, I have a cell phone!" He instantly winced. The last thing he needed now was to call his parents. Thankfully Mandy's mom thought his look came more from physical pain.

"Not until you take your shirt off and get cleaned up. What did you do, crawl through a cheese grater?"

Thad gave a wan smile. "Well, something like that."

"Hmmph," sniffed Mrs. Purcell. "Guess you boys were camping, all right. You all smell of wood smoke. Hope you put the fire out."

"Well, the rain did most of that," Thad said. He and Derek shared a look.

Going through the back door, they found themselves in a surprisingly clean but cramped kitchen. A round table with two place settings sat in the center. A microwaved pizza box steamed from the counter and smelled like heaven.

"Before you go any farther, let's get introductions over with. I'm Mrs. Purcell. Who are you?"

After the boys introduced themselves, she had Danny and Derek sit at the table while Mandy scrounged for more pizzas from the freezer. Mrs. Purcell led Thad and Jak to the sink and disappeared into a room on the right to find her medicine box.

Jak shivered and glanced nervously up at Thad.

"I'm scared," he whispered.

Thad looked at him in surprise. "You'll be fine. She's nice."

Jak shook his head. "Not if she's like my sisters."

Mrs. Purcell returned with a small box and glared at the boys. "Don't be shy! Shirts off, let's go. I'm a registered nurse, so I know what I'm doing."

After a moment's hesitation, Thad shrugged off his shirt and sighed. While crawling in the shed he managed to scrape his chest and back. Nothing major, but both had bled.

To confirm it, Mrs. Purcell sniffed. "That's nothing." She sat on a stool and put her box on her knee.

"You, boy," she said turning to Jak. "You look like you're wearing a piece of Swiss cheese. I hope you don't like that shirt, because it's trash."

Flinching, Jak started to peel off his shirt and looked around to make sure nobody watched.

Sighing, Mrs. Purcell reached down, grabbed his shirt, and yanked it over his head. Dropping it away from her like it was repulsive, she stared at Jak's scrapes and sniffed.

"Okay, so what happened?" She spoke to Thad.

From the table, Derek coughed loudly. Mandy, opening two pizza boxes near the microwave, stopped.

"Oh, um, we were playing in the woods …" Thad began.

"Yes, go on." Going to her kit, she pulled out a cloth and brown bottle. Opening the bottle, she poured it on the cloth.

Thad swallowed. "Well, it started to rain …"

"You smell like smoke and this boy has splinters in his ribs. Oh, and this is going to hurt." She pressed the wet cloth onto Jak's side.

Eyes squeezed shut, Jak sucked in his breath, but he didn't cry out. Thad understood. Crying in front of Mandy's mom would be the ultimate embarrassment.

Thad tugged his cowlick. "Oh, uh, well, there was a fire …" he admitted.

"Uh-huh. We went over that," Mrs. Purcell said. Taking tweezers, she busily started picking wood from Jak's side. Jak winced at every prick, but bit his tongue. The others looked away in sympathy.

Thad took a deep breath. "I would tell you more, but, um, it'll have to wait until tomorrow. We're not done camping yet."

Mrs. Purcell stopped and looked up at Thad. "You mean you're coming back to visit tomorrow?" she asked.

Thad ducked under her gaze. "Well, if that's okay with you, uh, ma'am."

"That depends. Mandy, is that okay?" Mrs. Purcell asked loudly.

"Uh, yeah," Mandy said from where she was putting frozen pizza on the counter. She looked at Thad in surprise. "I mean, I guess so."

"Very well." Mrs. Purcell went back to defragmenting Jak. "That's all. It's bleeding again, but there's nothing too deep." She expertly applied bandages and taped up his side. She also put bandages on two of his fingers, both torn from digging under the shed. Finished, she sat back and admired her work. "Leave your shirt off and go get some pizza. We'll find you a new one." Jak quickly fled to the food. Then Mrs. Purcell turned to Thad and quickly cleaned his cuts and patted his arm. "You're good. Go eat too. You boys make sure you camp close by here, understand? You want to stay off the Park land. They don't allow fires. Do your parents know where you are?"

Thad quickly pulled his shirt over his head. "Kind of," he mumbled. "But I have a phone."

Mrs. Purcell grunted. "Make sure you use it. After that storm, I'm sure they're worried."

Thad nodded. "Yes, ma'am. Uh, thank you."

Mrs. Purcell waved him away. "Boy," she said to Jak, who stood at the counter waiting for hot pizza, "when you're through eating, you go to the bathroom and throw your pants out. I'll give them a good dry and find a new shirt for you."

Gulping, Jak nodded.

In the end, the boys stayed with Mandy and her mother until after sunset. Derek and Danny also had to pass Mrs. Purcell's medical review.

Everyone gasped when Danny struggled out of his shirt and revealed a bright red stomach and chafed armpits. After the pond swim, his shirt rubbed his skin raw. Otherwise he and Derek suffered mostly from bug bites and sore fingers from digging in the hard dirt. Mrs. Purcell sent Danny to the second bathroom with lotion and powder.

After a satisfying meal of pizza and milk, finished off with cookies, Mrs. Purcell finally let them go. Jak left with dry pants and a very unpleasant face. He wore an old baby blue softball shirt with the team name "Little Ponies" printed on it, a castoff from Mandy (she didn't seem too sorry to see it going). Thad left the house last, thanking Mrs. Purcell again for everything, especially for not being too nosy. The only downer, Mandy couldn't go.

"It's too late for you, Mandy," her mother told her when the boys got set to leave. "Say goodbye and come right back in. You're not camping out tonight, remember."

"Yeah, Mom," Mandy said.

She walked with them to the edge of her yard and showed them the deer path back to the tour road.

"I'll meet you tomorrow, early," she promised when handing Derek and Thad flashlights. "I want these back."

"And your shirt back," Jak said sourly.

Surprisingly, Derek gave her a quick, very awkward hug. "Thanks, Mandy," he said uncomfortably. "You, uh, helped … a lot."

"Don't you mean Beast?" she said, whacking him on the back. "Just don't do anything stupid."

Derek quickly returned to his usual self. "Hey, I'm the leader, remember?" he said cockily.

Mandy turned to Thad. "Thad, make sure he doesn't do anything stupid."

Thad chuckled. "He's the leader. We'll be fine."

"That's what I'm afraid of," Mandy said. "Remember, you promised to come by tomorrow. Y'all can have breakfast at my place."

"We'll be there," Danny said, sounding as if he meant it. "And thanks for the pizza."

"But not for this shirt," muttered Jak sulkily.

200

Mandy ignored the smaller boy. She gave a final wave. "Just hurry up and go before you miss everything!"

Chapter 25

The walk back went fast. Guided by a full moon, the boys didn't need the flashlights until looking for the turnoff for the pond. Derek urged them onward and refused to allow rest breaks. To him, the mission was personal. He meant to save Billy from the likes of Charlie, and at the same time, get revenge. Thad was more curious about what was going on. What had been in the shed that had to be locked away, and who was the mysterious boss that met with high school players in the middle of the woods?

It took some doing, but they found their old trail and all their backpacks where they'd left them. Relieved that Charlie hadn't come by and ruined them, they continued to the stream. Thad did stop long enough to retrieve Jak's first aid kit—just in case. He hadn't called all the parents, but did send a text message to Mr. Tranner saying everything was fine and they'd be back tomorrow—would he let their parents know? Thanks! He'd ignored the five new messages left on the phone.

When they reached the stream, Derek ordered the flashlights off and for everyone to be quiet. Climbing carefully back to the hill, they were rewarded when they made out a faint glow from the houses.

"They're still there!" he hissed in triumph.

"Do we *really* want to go back there?" Danny said.

"You don't have to," Derek whispered back. "You can stay here."

"Right," muttered Danny. "I'll stay by myself in the dark woods on a night with a full moon."

Derek slapped the back of his head. "Then be quiet and let's go!"

Going down to the road, they crossed over and stealthily made their way up toward the glow through the trees and bushes. At first they heard only murmurs and then words started to carry.

"Billy!" cried a voice sharply. "This is your future we're talking about! This isn't a game!"

Derek looked back. His eyes gleamed in the moonlight. "He's here," he hissed.

"Get closer," Thad whispered. "So we can see and hear!"

The boys got to their bellies and crawled through the brush. The leaves and plants were wet from the storm and muffled most of their movements. Finally, after several painstaking moments, they'd reached the brush near where the brown mutt had appeared that afternoon. Derek found a gap in the brush and the other boys crowded around.

A small fire flickered from a pile of logs in the middle of the old road between the houses. Lawn chairs were set around the fire and occupied by three figures. Derek whispered the one in the middle was Billy.

Thad saw a large youth with a dark brown face staring unhappily into the fire. Slouching, he refused to look at the other two men. Thad thought one of the men looked and sounded vaguely familiar, but he couldn't place him. Large and compact, he had a rosy, fleshy face and stabbed a finger at Billy.

"Think about it, Billy," boomed the voice. "I followed through on my end of the bargain. I got you here and we brought the stuff. It's your turn now."

The other man held up a hand in a calming motion. He sat with his back to the boys. Tall and broad shouldered, he had a shaved head covered by a fitted ball cap and a blue windbreaker. His voice sounded intelligent but nasal and bored.

"Come now, let's take this slowly. Billy, what's wrong?" he asked.

Billy mumbled something and the large man threw up his hands.

Billy said louder, "I told you already! I want to talk to him first!"

"He'll be here tomorrow!" boomed the large man. "I know you want to talk to him, but you already did by phone!"

Billy shook his head.

They were interrupted when Charlie appeared noisily from the white house and belched loudly.

"Yo, Coach," he said. "You may want to tone it down a bit."

"Stay out of this, Charlie," the large man snarled. "Go make sure the blasted dogs stay away from us."

"I ain't worried about the dogs," Charlie said disdainfully.

"Why?" asked the coach. "Did you get them finally?"

"No," the teen said, "but we sure scared them! I'm more worried about those little clowns."

The large coach scoffed. "They're far from here by now," he said scathingly. "In bed with their mommies, Charlie. Get real. I can't believe you blockheads locked them in a shed and lit it on fire."

"It wasn't on purpose," whined Charlie. "And besides, they got out."

"Yeah," muttered the coach, "but only because of the fire-repellent paint I made you use. Really, Charlie. Can you imagine if you burned that thing down with the stuff inside?"

"It wasn't me, it was dumb Ed!" Charlie said defensively.

The coach barked back, "You're the captain, act like it! Mistakes all lead to you!"

"Gentlemen," the tall man said calmly. "That's enough. Charles, have Edward and David walk around the perimeter just in case. They can take Eric with them. Make sure we're not disturbed by anything or anyone."

Charlie bobbed his head and immediately stood straighter. "Yes, sir. But, um, Ed lost his rifle ... he put it down to take a leak and can't find it now." He looked over where the boys hid and gestured helplessly. "It's somewhere over there."

The large coach looked ready to explode.

"Charles," said the calmer man. "He shouldn't have stopped looking for it. This is why I didn't give you the dart guns. They're too expensive to risk on stupidity. Now go."

Swallowing, Charlie nodded and disappeared inside the house.

"See why we need you?" the coach said to Billy, gesturing back toward the house. "This team is hungry for real leadership! The boys need you!"

"And might I remind you," said the other man slowly, "Charlie weighed barely a hundred pounds soaking wet when I first met him. He had nothing and that was just a few short years ago. Now the big schools are interested in him. You follow my instructions and we can increase your strength, size, and power in no time flat. Colleges from across the country will be begging you to play for them. Think about that."

Billy grunted and shifted uncomfortably. "What about tests?" he asked dully.

"Never been caught," the man said smoothly. "I've had a lot of practice."

"Billy, come on," growled the coach. "Think of your little sister. Your family needs the money and this is the surest shot to the pros."

"I am thinking about my sister," Billy said tightly. "And my brother."

"I can always arrange for your brother to get some ... extra help too," the tall man said.

Billy sat up straighter and stared at the stranger with fury. "You stay away from Kevin."

The man held up two shadowy hands. "Of course, whatever you say."

Billy snorted. "If that was true, you'll have a shot to cure my sister."

"She's intellectually disabled, or whatever they call it, Billy," the tall man said flatly. "The best you can do for her is to pay her bills and find a nice place for her to live. We can offer you that path."

The coach reached down and picked up a square package laying on the ground. "Right here, ready for you, Billy. Just say the word and sign the paper. You'll join my team and we'll start the program." From his lap, he took a sheet of paper and laid it on top of the box. "Let's do this."

"Ah, man, I don't know …" Billy seemed to be weakening. "I'd hate to leave my team."

The tall man coughed lightly. "I only work with one coach, Billy. You know that. Besides, he has all the connections to the big colleges. He can guarantee you can play as captain on his team this fall without any problem."

Billy squirmed. "Yeah, but my coach now trusts me!" he said.

"He'll get over it!" barked the coach. "Sign the paper!"

Derek had gripped the dirt in front of him hard. Now he crawled backwards and tapped Thad and Danny to follow.

"What do we do?" he hissed when they'd scooted several yards from their hiding place. "This is worse than I thought!"

"What are they doing?" Danny whispered hoarsely. "They sound serious."

"They are," Thad said. He bit his lip. "I bet there are steroids in that box."

Derek's shadowy head nodded. "They're trying to juice Billy and steal him from the team so he plays at Lincoln!"

It all made sense. The two men obviously had done this before. They took high school players to an isolated spot nobody knew about and offered dreams and steroids, all for the price of betrayal … or worse. Thad could imagine the two creeps blackmailing an athlete that found success through their twisted system. They would ask for money to keep the steroid use a secret.

"So, uh," Danny asked, fearing the answer, "what do we do then?"

"I can't use the cell phone," Thad said, "and it would probably be too late for Billy even if I could."

"We still need to stop them!" Derek hissed.

"Will this help?" whispered a voice from behind them. "I, um, smelled where Ed must have gone and found this." Jak crawled to them carrying a loaded pellet gun.

206

The boys returned to their hiding place with a rough plan in mind.

"I don't like this," whispered Danny. "I don't like this!"

"Just stay here and get ready to run," Thad told him, patting his shoulder. "We're just going to scare them and leave."

That was the plan. Derek would use the pellet gun to cause a distraction while Jak and Thad screamed like banshees. It wasn't much and probably useless. But, they hoped, if nothing else, it would spook Billy and stop him from signing. Then they would run, with Derek covering the retreat. If they struck fast enough, it should work.

"I just wish we could get that box," Derek mumbled. "Then we'd have proof to stop this from ever happening again."

Jak heard him and smiled.

Charlie had just left the house leading a sullen Ed and Dave when he heard the soft pop of a pellet gun.

"Ow!" the tall man in the chair jumped and slapped at the back of his head.

"Yeah," groaned the coach. "The bugs are nasty tonight." Then he also jerked. Swearing loudly, he clutched at his left arm.

"What's going on?" yelled Charlie. "Who's shooting—" Another soft report sounded and Charlie shrieked, crumpling to the ground while covering up his stomach.

Chapter 26

Derek stepped from the bushes and pumped another pellet into action. "Now!" he yelled. Jak and Thad shook the branches behind him and started screeching. Derek aimed and fired another pellet in the direction of Charlie. "Run, Billy!" he shouted. "It's a trap! They're all lying!"

"What's happening!" roared the coach, kicking wildly. The other man crouched behind his chair and continued to rub at his head.

Neither one saw the small boy dart from the bushes and race their way. Caught by surprise, Thad could only watch in momentary horror. Then he gave chase.

Eyes wide, Billy Boston sat in shock as chaos exploded around him.

Charlie crawled back for the house and yelled for the others to take cover.

The coach struggled to rise from his seat. Before he could, a dark shape appeared from the shadows and charged.

"Help!" he yelled, ducking back in the seat, hugging the box close. Then the box went flying up as his arms went windmilling back. The shadow had bent low and tilted the chair back. The coach and chair fell with a crash.

"The box!" the coach yelped.

"No!" cried the other man, stumbling to his feet. "It's just a kid. Get him!"

Twisting in his chair, the coach saw the box near him and dove for it.

Jak hurdled over his form and slid feet first, knocking the box away. Recovering quickly, he got to his feet and gave the box another kick toward the darkness.

"You brat!" screamed the coach in fury. "Give me the box." He moved to his feet, but groaned slightly. Shaking his head, he eyed the boy and smiled when seeing his size.

"Come and get it!" taunted Jak, turning to face him.

"With pleasure!" the coach said through gritted teeth.

The coach lunged and went to make a tackle, but fell only on air. Jak feinted right, but then, as if dribbling a soccer ball, cut left with the box at his feet.

"Next time break down, Coach!" yelled Ed from the house. He ducked when a pellet bounced by his nose. Nobody left the house to help the coach and his shadowy companion. They were too afraid of being hit by a pellet.

"I'll break you down!" roared the coach. Rising, he turned furiously to Jak. "You'd better run, brat, because I'm going to tear you apart!"

"Just get the box!" shouted the other man. "I have him blocked this way. Don't let him get by you."

Jak's eyes danced nervously as the two men advanced with him in the middle. Then he grinned suddenly as Thad stopped just beyond the glow of the fire, watching in terror. Fiery mischief danced in his eyes. Using his feet he knocked the box toward the fire.

"No!" screamed the tall man. "That's over two thousand bucks!"

Both men charged the boy. Before they reached him, Jak booted the box past the tall man and sent it skittering to Thad.

Both men's eyes followed the box's flight and they ended up colliding. They crashed to the cracked pavement painfully.

Jak by then was scooting to the woods.

Thad, gathering up the box, quickly followed.

"After them!" howled the man from the seat of his pants. "If they get away, we go to jail and lose everything!"

"I think I just lost a tooth," groaned the coach, rubbing his face.

The man shot to his feet and screamed in fury. "Charles! David!" he yelled. "Get out of the house and get after them! Edward, get your brother and go too! I'll give five hundred dollars in cash to whoever brings me back that box!"

At the edge of the woods, Derek saw Thad run by with the box. Then three teenagers charged out of the house with pellet guns firing. Gulping, Derek threw down his gun and dove into the bushes. "Run!" he yelled at Danny. "They're coming!"

Billy Boston still hadn't moved. His trembling legs finally settled and he slowly stood.

"Where're you going?" spat the man, just regaining his feet. "You're walking out on us?"

"No," Billy said calmly. "I'm going to get myself a box. I want that five hundred bucks."

The rest of the night passed in terror for Thad. He'd managed to keep up with Jak and together they plunged blindly through the woods. Branches whipped their faces and thorns tugged at their arms and caught at their jeans. Reaching the stream, they'd turned right and kept running. Behind them, the roar and calls of the teenagers followed until finally fading.

Thad desperately hoped Derek and Danny had made it.

After a time, they found a place where the stream narrowed and jumped across.

"I think we lost them," Thad said tiredly. He still carried the box and was about to put it down to rest when a beam of light shot out from only twenty feet behind him.

"Got you, you pansies!" crowed Eric's voice. "Hey, Charlie, over here!" He stepped forward when all at once he dropped the light and fell back. "Ouch!"

Jak fired another mud clod at him for good measure.

"Leave it!" Thad yelled. "Just run!"

They raced up a ravine with Eric shouting after them. The chase resumed. Charlie and Eric flashed their lights, refusing to back down.

Finally, after two more minutes of nonstop running, Thad felt too tired to breathe. More than once he had the urge to throw the box down, but grimly kept it under his arm. Behind them, beams of light continued to flash. Grabbing Jak's shoulder, he abruptly pulled him down into a thicket of bushes. Rolling, they entered a thick brush and went still. "Try not to breathe," Thad gasped, desperately following his own advice. "They can't see us in the dark."

Time went by and a beam traveled just outside their hiding place.

"Any sign?" snapped Charlie's voice.

"No," groaned Eric's voice. "I got mud in my eye. I can barely see anything, man."

"You'll be getting a lot worse if we don't find those clowns; they could be anywhere."

"I don't care, man," whined Eric. "I'm going back. Where's Ed?"

Charlie's voice grew ugly. "How am I supposed to know? Are you really quitting?"

"Like you said, they could be anywhere," Eric said sullenly.

At that moment a long howl rose from the darkness. It sounded nearby and not friendly.

Instantly the voices went silent. Then there came a shuffle of leaves and Charlie's voice said, "Ah … I forgot about the dogs. Fine, let's go."

Thad let go a huge sigh of relief as the beams retreated and dark silence took over.

"Thad?" whispered Jak's voice at his side.

"Yeah?"

"I think I'm bleeding again." The boy sounded more excited than nervous.

"Is it bad?" Thad asked tiredly. Suddenly it felt as if his body couldn't move. All the nervous energy drained with the departure of their pursuers.

"I don't think so …" Jak trailed off with a yawn.

"We'll look at it tomorrow … If it's okay with you, I'm not getting up until I see the sun." Both of Mandy's flashlights were dropped back at the old house. He hoped she wouldn't mind not getting them back tomorrow.

"Okay, Thad." Jak squirmed in the darkness and pressed against Thad's back. After a moment he went still and started breathing steadily.

The long, miserable night passed slowly for Thad. His eyes kept open wide and every noise sounded like a big, angry dog hunting for food … or worse, a big, angry coach hunting for children.

Thad finally managed to doze sometime just before dawn. Between the bugs, fear, and scratchy leaves, real sleep proved impossible. The chirping of birds caused him to crack an eye.

Jak stirred next to him and rolled to his side.

The crack of breaking leaves sent both boys shooting up, whacking their faces in a clump of ferns.

A startled deer bounded from its hiding place.

"Well," whispered Thad hoarsely. "We survived our camping trip. I hope Danny and Derek made it."

They crawled out stiffly, Thad dragging the box with him. It was just after dawn of the new day and the boys were tired, sore, hungry, and lost.

After finding separate trees to do their morning business, they met at the ferns and decided what to do.

"Do you think they're still looking for us?" Jak asked, his voice trembling slightly. The boy shivered, either from the morning coolness or from the thought of being found by the thugs.

Thad glanced down at the box now resting at their feet. Cardboard and weighing a few pounds, it had a sticker addressed to a Dr. Sandy Shelk in Annapolis, Maryland, with no return address. Heavily taped, it looked to have never been opened.

"There's a good chance," he sighed. "They want this stupid box. Let's see if we can find that stream again and follow it to the pond."

Jak wiped his nose, smudging dirt over his face. "Sure."

212

Thad grinned at him. "You look like a mess," he teased. "Maybe we can go to Mandy's for breakfast and get cleaned up."

Immediately Jak made a face. "Uh, no way. Not if her mom does first aid again." He shuddered. "This shirt is killing me."

Thad lifted his eyebrows at him. After all that happened, all Jak could think about was his stupid shirt? Didn't the kid understand the danger?

"You should have left the box, Jak," he said accusingly. "It was too dangerous taking it."

"But I thought you wanted it—"

"Jak, you have to think about the consequences too. Those guys are dangerous. They might have even hurt Derek and Danny."

Jak's face fell. "Oh ..." Then he brightened. "But we got the box, right? I mean, we still won."

Thad rolled his eyes. "Yeah, I guess. Here, before we go, let's look at your cuts."

Jak frowned impatiently as Thad took out the now slightly torn first aid kit from the back of his pants. "The bleeding stopped," he muttered.

"Good, then it'll be easy."

Sighing, Jak lifted his shirt and bounced on his feet as Thad cleaned and rebandaged the worst of the scrapes. Most of Jak's skinny chest resembled a brown board that a child had scribbled on with a red crayon and then decorated with Band-Aids. Once that was finished, they started their journey back ... hopefully.

Both boys were tired, rumpled, filthy, and looked as if they had gotten in a fight with a tree and lost. Jak's hair was a wild mess with rotting leaves sticking from it. Dirt smudged his cheeks and upper lip so it appeared as if he had sprouted false facial hair. Thad imagine he looked the same. He couldn't wait to find a hot shower and a real bed.

An hour later, they still hadn't found a stream. The sun continued to rise but lay hidden behind a canopy of green. Knowing which way was east proved difficult. For all Thad knew, they were going in circles.

"I'm tired," Jak groaned at last. The boy kept close to Thad's side the entire time.

Thad blinked and rubbed his eyes with the back of his free hand. His other hand gripped the cardboard box. "Yeah, me too." They had just climbed a ravine and stood on a knoll where two giant oak trees stood in the midst of several skinny pines. Thad brushed down a thin pine branch and looked down on the other side. His eyes widened.

"Look, Jak. I think there's a path down there. Come on!"

The smaller boy had just started to slump down against one of the oaks but obediently got to his feet and followed Thad. Down a little ways, just past the clump of young pines, they came to a sharp drop-off with a well-worn path beneath. Opposite the path rose a hill with more forest, but Thad only had eyes for the path. About four feet in width of packed gray dirt, the path had no vegetation growing on it, aside from a few exposed roots. Thad could tell people used it a lot. Civilization couldn't be far away.

"How do we get down?" Jak asked doubtfully, moving to the edge. The steep ridge, over thirteen feet high, traveled along the path in both directions.

"Climb, I guess. I wish we had your rope. Look around. I'm sure there's a deer path somewhere that goes down there."

After walking a little way along the steep ridge, they finally found a rough opening heading down, but it also proved steep.

Thad eyed the opening. He tugged at his cowlick, now wet with sweat and slick with grime. "We'll go together, Jak," he said finally. "You go first and I'll be right behind you. Be careful. The last thing we need is a sprained ankle."

Nodding, Jak crouched and stuck a foot over the edge. Thad was pleased to see the boy stop there and wait for Thad. Jak either was too tired to be reckless or may have finally learned to be cautious.

Thad tossed the cardboard box down to the path and crouched to help. "Grab my hand and I'll lower you. When you find a foothold let me know and I'll follow."

Jak reached up and grabbed Thad's hand. Jabbing down his leg, he searched for a foothold.

A sudden whistle parted the air and it ended in a soft thud.

"Ow!" Jak yelped. His eyes widened and his body jerked as if shocked.

"Hey!" Thad shouted as he was nearly pulled over the side. "What's wrong? Jak!"

"Something stung me in the leg! Ow, it hurts bad!" Tears entered the boy's eyes and he started to whimper.

Thad blinked rapidly. They may have climbed down right on top of a beehive. "Okay," he said quickly. "Just get back up here."

"Thad. I … I …" Staring up with pain and confusion, Jak all at once closed his eyes and went limp. His head rolled to his shoulder and hung listlessly.

Holding on to his wrist, Thad nearly went over the edge again as he struggled to keep Jak from dropping.

"Jak!" he yelled.

Then a terrible sharp pain pieced his left arm, just below his armpit. Falling to his backside, he let go of Jak and blinked. "What the—"

A small tube in the shape of a hypodermic needle found in a doctor's office stuck from his arm. Panicking, Thad yanked it out and threw it away. As he did so, he rolled to his side, lost his balance, and pitched over the edge.

He landed on his back with a solid thump on the hard path, his breath completely knocked from his body.

For a long time, or maybe a short time, he stayed this way. Swallowing hard, he managed to lift his head to see Jak's body sprawled face-first on the path a couple of feet from him. A similar-looking dart stuck out from the back of his thigh.

They'd been shot … shot … and he was very tired. Keeping his eyes open became a real struggle.

Deep voices approached and Thad recognized them.

"I can't tell you how long I've wanted to do that," laughed a man pleasantly. "We were looking out for dogs and got a couple of pups. Every classroom should have one of these babies."

Another man grunted. "I can only imagine what you were aiming at. Nice shot."

"You too," said the first voice. "Come on. Go check yours for a cell phone. Last thing we need is a GPS tracker to nail us."

"It doesn't really matter," said the second. "I have the box back."

"Oh, yeah?" asked the first. "What if the cops come right now?"

"Right," grunted the second.

Thad struggled to keep his eyes open. He knew those voices … especially the first one. With extreme effort, he rose to a sitting position and turned. "Mr. Freeman?" he croaked. "What are you doing here?"

Chapter 27

His fifth-grade teacher knelt beside Jak's senseless body and was in the process of rolling it over with the dart in his hands. At hearing Thad's voice, he froze as if zapped with ice.

"Th-Thad," he said thickly after a moment. The dart dropped from his fingers. "You're awake."

Another man, the man Thad guessed to be Dr. Sandy Shelk, groaned from behind Mr. Freeman. He still wore the blue cap and windbreaker from the night before. In his hands he carried an odd-looking gun with a long, rounded black tube attached to a strange-looking stock. It looked like a paintball gun crossed with a Star Wars blaster. A similar gun lay beside Mr. Freeman.

Thad blinked in confusion. His shoulder throbbed and even thinking hurt.

"I think we have one option," Dr. Shelk said after a moment. His voice sounded flat and hard. His right hand went into his pocket.

Mr. Freeman blinked rapidly. "No, you can't be serious!"

Dr. Shelk removed a pair of glasses and cleaned them with his shirt.

Mr. Freeman sighed but still looked nervous.

Dr. Shelk kept his eyes on his glasses as he said, "Why that moronic Mr. Boston wanted you there, I'll never know. But the fact of the matter is, he wouldn't sign without speaking to you face to face."

The teacher licked his lips. "I told you already, I taught him in the fifth grade, Sandy. I went to all his games then. He knows me and he trusts me."

"And I trusted you too!" snarled the doctor, losing his temper. He glared at Mr. Freeman. "I trusted you to get his signature. Instead your classroom of rejects comes and louses everything up!" He walked over to the box and picked it up as if it was his lost child. "I'm not going to jail because of your stupidity."

Mr. Freeman flinched. "I just needed the extra money ..."

"I hope it's worth it! Now what are we doing with this kid?" He gestured toward Thad.

Swallowing, Mr. Freeman avoided eye contact with Thad. "I don't mind knocking them out, but that's as far as it goes! Look, I'm still a teacher here!"

"Not if that boy walks out of here, you're not! We'll both be in jail!"

"Wh-what do you propose to do?" Mr. Freeman asked. He sounded like a student caught cheating on one of his tests.

Thad swallowed. They were discussing his life as if discussing a pawn in a chess game. Only pure adrenaline mixed with fear kept him awake. With great effort, he scooted back. Everything made sense now. The large coach ... he'd been the man he'd seen coming out of the library that time when he was hiding behind the trash can ... but why?

The doctor's hard voice brought Thad's consciousness back to the present. "Whatever is necessary. What do *you* propose to do?"

"Not hurt any kid any more than I already have."

"You're the one who wanted to tranquilize him in the first place, I may remind you."

"Yes, but—"

"You're in this just as deep as me. If you're a coward, then leave it to me. After all, I'm a doctor." The tall doctor walked slowly toward Thad. Mr. Freeman watched helplessly but made no effort to interfere.

"This will only hurt for a moment," soothed the doctor to Thad. "Close your eyes—"

A low growl from the ledge above Thad stopped the doctor's advance. A brown snout emerged.

"No way—Shoot it!" screamed Dr. Shelk. He fumbled to bring his dart gun up.

"We can't!" yelled Mr. Freeman. "We used the darts on the kids!"

Snarling ferociously, the mutt searched for a way down.

"This is your fault!" roared the doctor. He fumbled in his back pocket for another dart. "You can't do anything right!"

Then the dog, seeing no easy way down, leapt. She was the leader of the pack and she was not happy.

Screaming, the teacher and doctor dropped their useless guns. Mr. Freeman dove away as the large animal landed just in front of Jak's prone form. Baring her teeth, she barked ferociously. She eyed the two men, as if sizing them up.

"Run!" Mr. Freeman screamed. He started to flee from the scene.

The doctor tried to back away while pulling out a dart, but the dog settled her gaze on him. Snarling, she charged.

Panicking, the doctor only had time to flinch before the animal reached him.

"Get back!" he screamed uselessly.

Teeth flashing, the mutt tore at Doctor Shelk's pants as the man tried to loosen another dart. The muzzle came away with a piece of the windbreaker.

Screeching, the doctor took off after Mr. Freeman, running as if the path burned fire.

The brown mutt slowed her pursuit and stood in the middle of the trail, watching. After the men were about a hundred yards down the path, a line of snarls and barks burst from the ledge over their heads. The men only had time to duck before four other dogs descended from above with a fury.

Swallowing, Thad could only stare in dazed wonder. The brown dog whined softly and turned from the carnage. Behind her, screams rose and fell as the men disentangled themselves and got away bloody, but upright. With snapping dogs at their heels, they continued their flight.

Trotting to Jak's side, the mutt whined again. Her brown nose sniffed and licked his face. Caught in a deep sleep, the boy didn't stir.

"Uh, he's okay," Thad said sluggishly. With great effort, he pushed himself to his knees. "Th-thanks for helping us." Then he pitched over and took a few moments of rest. His eyes slid shut and all went dark.

Thad woke up with his cheek burning. For a moment he thought the dog was biting off his face.

He let off a startled yell and flung out his arms, but then he froze. A pair of green eyes stared anxiously down at him. They belonged to a human.

"M-Mandy," he croaked, "is that you?" Then his eyes started to slide shut again.

Immediately a new fiery sting burst across his cheek.

"Ouch!" he yelled, opening his eyes again.

Mandy stared down at him with a concerned look. Her bangs, dark with sweat, were swept aside and Thad saw tears in her eyes. Her hand was opened and poised above his face.

"Hey, M-Mandy …" he said blearily. "What are you doing?"

"Thad! Oh, you're finally awake!" She sat back with relief. "Man, I thought you'd never get up!"

"Wh-what happened?" He sat up blearily and found himself lying on the path where he'd fallen. Jak remained sprawled on his stomach, still unconscious. The large brown mutt sat over him with her tongue hanging out. Staring at Thad, she whined sorrowfully.

"That's what I want to know," Mandy said. "I've been looking for you for hours!" Her voice shook slightly and Thad, even though still groggy, could tell the girl was scared. She explained how she got up early that day and went to find the boys. When finding the camp area a scattered mess and no boys around, she got scared and started hunting for them.

"Then after wandering around for, like, hours, out of nowhere this giant dog jumps out and barks at me. I thought I was a goner, but then it runs off. Next thing I know, it's back. Finally, I follow and it brings me straight to you two guys lying asleep like …" She swallowed. "I thought you guys were dead at first," she admitted. "Then I saw the dart guns and darts and heard you breathing, so I figured y'all were okay. When you didn't wake up, I, uh, kind of slapped you."

Thad leaned his head between his knees and tried desperately to clear his thoughts. "How long have I've been asleep?"

"I don't know, man. It's close to noon, you know."

Thad groaned and lifted his head. "What about Danny and Derek? Have you seen them?"

The girl shook her head. "No, but there sure were a lot of people looking for them. I had to hide from Charlie and his bunch twice. What happened?"

He groaned. "I'll tell you later. I have a headache. Um, did you happen to find a box near the dart guns?"

"Yeah, I wasn't sure what it was doing there, so I put it in the woods with the dart guns. I mean, just in case it was something dangerous."

"Mandy, you're a lifesaver. Really." He rubbed his temples.

Mandy ducked her head. "Yeah, whatever," she said. "I'm just glad this big old dog didn't eat me."

"Well, let's wake Jak and go home."

Mandy now bit her lip. "Uh, I don't know about that. I'm kind of lost."

"What!"

"Hey, I just followed the dog … I didn't know where I was going!"

Thad's headache only grew when the brown dog started barking and wagging her tail.

"Fine, whatever. We'll just follow the path. I'm sure it leads somewhere. After all, Mr. Freeman went that way for a reason, I'm sure."

Mandy blinked and stared at him like he was crazy. "Mr. Freeman?" she asked.

"Uh, yeah. He's the one who shot Jak." Thad got slowly to his feet and nearly fell on his face. Mandy quickly rose and put a hand on his shoulder.

"Are you okay, man?" she asked. "You're not sounding right."

Thad took several deep breaths and said, "Let's get Jak and I'll explain. Uh, at least try to explain."

The small boy had received a direct hit from the sleeping dart and remained dead to the world. He never stirred when Mandy and Thad rolled him onto his back. Aside from the effects of the dart, he also sported a fresh scrape on his chin from the fall, but otherwise appeared okay. The large dog had at first bared her teeth when they'd approached the boy, but then backed away when Mandy crouched down and said firmly they were only helping Jak. The dog lay down and watched carefully as Mandy shook the boy's shoulder to no affect.

Thad eyed the dog and then rubbed his cheek, which still stung a little. "If I were you," he said ruefully, "I wouldn't slap Jak like you slapped me."

Mandy grunted and refused to look at him. "You deserved it," she muttered. Louder she said, "We'll just have to carry him, then."

Thad groaned. "Great. I'm glad he's small."

Mandy, after staring at the dog pointedly, slid an arm under Jak's shoulders and lifted him to a sitting position. She pulled one of his lean arms over her shoulder and started lifting him up. Thad took the boy's other arm and copied her so they had the boy supported between them. Jak never stirred.

"So," grunted Thad, "do we drag him the whole way? We don't even know where this path goes."

"Use your free hand to grab under his knee," Mandy said. "We'll carry him that way."

"Wait!" Thad said. "We need the box. The one you said you found near the dart guns. How do we bring that?"

"Easy," Mandy told him. "We put it on his lap. Hold the kid and I'll get it."

Soon the two were carrying the sleeping boy between them as they started down the path. The box rested on Jak's knees and appeared secure. The dog followed behind them, keeping a watchful eye on their progress. While Jak was small, he still weighed over eighty pounds. After a few moments, Thad felt his arms straining. He gritted his teeth and refused to be the first to ask for a rest. Mandy, her eyes pointed forward, did not seem to be even breathing hard. To keep his mind off the effort, Thad started telling her what had happened, starting with leaving her house the night before.

The path was well shaded by the arching tree branches on either side, and was spared from the worst of the hot sun. Birds flew overhead and a low hum of insects sounded in the distance, mostly drowned out by Thad's voice. If it weren't for the grim circumstances, Thad might have thought it pleasant to be walking and talking to Mandy. His head still felt groggy and the hum of insects seemed to grow louder.

Their progress was slowed by Jak's weight, but they were spurred on when reaching a section of the path flanked by an old, rickety-looking split-rail fence. Running for about ten feet just in front of the base of a wooded hill, the fence stood about three feet high in a patch of cut grass. The wood appeared dark and lined with age. It zigzagged four times before abruptly ending. It at least served as a sign pointing toward civilization. They were on the right path.

For her part, Mandy listened with grim disbelief to Thad's story. They'd reached a curve in the path about twenty feet from the split-rail fence. Suddenly, when hearing about their old teacher and his part, she all at once dropped Jak's side and stood straight up with a gasp.

"Hey!" Thad protested as he was thrown off balance. He dropped to a knee and managed to support the unconscious boy before he fell. The cardboard box hit the ground and rolled to Mandy's sneaker. Jak ended up draped over Thad's raised knee.

For a moment Thad thought about giving the kid the spanking he deserved but a low growl behind him ceased such thoughts instantly. "What are you doing?" he demanded instead.

"You said those guys ran down this path?" Mandy asked him, her eyes staring ahead. "Mr. Freeman and that doctor guy, right?"

"Yeah, the dogs were chasing them like they were breakfast," Thad said, instantly regretting it. Just thinking of food made his stomach growl. "So what?"

Mandy stared at him with a mixture of anger and horror. "What if they decide to come back?"

Thad frowned and he shook his head. "Uh, why would they do that?" he asked stupidly.

"To finish the job, man!" Mandy nearly yelled at him. "Can't you hear that? It's a motor and it's coming our way!"

Thad's eyes widened. No insects were biting them and the hum was quickly growing louder as it neared. Either every mosquito in the state had banded together to form an army or Mandy was right. Something with a motor was fast approaching.

The dog growled again, louder this time. She wasn't looking at him but down the path toward the sound.

Thad paled. "What do we do?" he asked.

"Run!" Mandy shouted.

All morning Thad's mind had felt like it was full of molasses. Now an electric shock coursed down his back. He sprang to his feet as Mandy grabbed Jak's shoulder and pulled him back up. Together they took hold of the still-sleeping boy and retreated up the path where they'd come from. Thad had a grip on the back of Jak's shirt and waistband with one hand while the other held the boy's wrist over his shoulder. Mandy just pulled Jak's other wrist over her shoulder with a hand. Her other hand cradled the box she'd scooped from the path. Together they stumbled and nearly fell twice as they desperately tried to put as much distance as they could from the rumbling pursuit. The dog barked in front of them, urging them on.

Now the motor was clearly heard. A loud whine and shriek filled the air. The motorized thing had reached the turn and had skidded to a stop. It was just behind them.

"What now?" Thad cried desperately. "We have to hide!"

"Just keep going!" Mandy spluttered between deep breaths next to him. "I have an idea!"

The dog barked furiously. Whoever it was behind them had to hear her.

The motor roared louder and started going forward. It moved slower now, but would still be in sight at any moment.

Thad risked a glance back and gulped.

Around the curve came a large, black four-wheeler driven by a man in torn, bloody clothes. Even with his head hidden by a masked helmet Thad still recognized him as Dr. Shelk.

"I think we're spotted," he gasped.

"Just move it!" Mandy shouted.

Dr. Shelk yelled in triumph as he saw them. Instantly the four-wheeler roared louder.

The dog sprang past the kids to face the four-wheeler, but she yelped in fear at the roar of the motor. She whined piteously as she looked back at where Thad and Mandy struggled to drag Jak.

"Keep going!" Mandy yelled. "We're almost there!"

"Almost where?" cried Thad in return. The steep ridge blocked their way on the left and the heavy wooded hill impeded their right. Trying to go in either direction with Jak between them was next to impossible.

Mandy jutted her chin toward the old split-rail fence just ahead on the right. "Get behind the fence! Hurry up!"

"That fence wouldn't stop a sneeze!" Thad protested. But the roar of the motor behind him cut off any more arguing. The four-wheeler threw caution to the wind. Dr. Shelk seemed determined to run them all over, starting with the dog.

The mutt tried to keep her ground, but she leapt aside in terror just as the large front wheels clipped her side. Crashing against the side of the ridge, she fell on her flank and struggled to rise. The four-wheeler barely slowed. It aimed at the children and quickly sped up.

All at once the rickety old fence looked like the Great Wall of China to Thad. As the roar neared his backside, he ran with all his might for the rails. Mandy at his side helped him drag Jak. They were still several feet away and the four-wheeler screamed with fury almost on top of them. The sound of the motor seemed to be everywhere around them. They weren't going to make it ... Suddenly, Thad burst forward, dragging Jak and Mandy with him. Both he and Mandy were screaming in terror. They just reached the fence with the four-wheeler still speeding up. Barely slowing, Thad heaved Jak forward, pitching the limp boy across the fence. Then shoved the small boy's backside up and over, jumping after. Mandy leapt just behind and just in time.

The three fell in a pile of limbs just as the four-wheeler reached them. Lying on top of Jak's back, with Mandy across his legs, Thad shoved his face in the dirt and squeezed his eyes shut. The whole world exploded right after.

Anger, pain, frustration, fear, and ultimately hatred controlled the doctor's actions. It all went away in a single moment. In his grim intent to run over the kids responsible for his trouble, he failed to see the fence. Or, more likely, he thought he could just plow right through it. In any case, thinking or not thinking, he did a very stupid thing. The old fence was not built horse high, but it was four-wheeler high. And it was pig tight. Not only that, but it wasn't made of wood. The rails were solid concrete sculpted to resemble rotting wood. They were meant to last a lot longer than a four-wheeler driven by a maniac.

A tremendous bang shook the ground under Thad, and at first he thought they'd been hit, but then he opened his eyes.

At the sudden impact, the fence barely budged. Instead the front of the four-wheeler exploded against it. The front tires blasted in two different directions as the frame crunched and flattened. Shards of broken, twisted metal flew all over. Among the flying carnage was Dr. Shelk. He sailed up and way over the fence, striking into the wooded hill beyond. Luckily he managed to miss any trees, but still thumped solidly into hard ground on his back. After the sudden violence, everything went still.

As the ringing in his head died down, Thad rose to his knees and stared around in wonder. Mandy sat up next to him and she brushed back her hair. The two looked at each other and blinked. The fence had managed to shield them from any shrapnel. All they suffered were a few scrapes and bruises gotten in their efforts of climbing over. On the other side, the four-wheeler was not so lucky. It looked like a toy model after being smashed by a hammer. Smoke and steam rose from the ruins. The motor would never sound again.

"Mr. Freeman was right," Mandy said dully. "These fences really are strong."

226

Just then Dr. Shelk's body jerked and a groan came from behind his cracked face shield. Amazingly, he started to sit up.

Mandy swallowed. "I'm going to say he'll be okay," she said with a glance at him. "But I don't know if we will be if we don't scram."

Thad nodded. "Uh, yeah. Let's go."

Amazingly, Jak remained blissfully unaware of the danger. This time, with Mandy's help, Thad boosted him up on his back and carried him piggyback style. Mandy walked behind, carrying the now pretty battered cardboard box. Carrying all Jak's limp weight, Thad had to walk hunched forward. Still, with the smoking ruins and evil doctor behind, he went uphill into the woods at a brisk trot. They would avoid the path—better to be lost than hunted by the likes of a crazy doctor. And Mr. Freeman was still out there. The brown mutt joined them as they left the wreckage and appeared uninjured. After several minutes of walking, they dipped down in a ravine and Thad stumbled to a halt. Sweat ran down his red face and his back and shoulders ached terribly. Without a word he let Jak slide off just before he went down. Both boys sprawled on their bellies onto rotting leaves.

"Hey," Mandy said. "What are you guys doing?" she demanded. "We still need to get out of here."

"Then you carry us," mumbled Thad thickly. "I think I've had enough ..." Mandy said something else, but his eyes were already sliding closed. Thad was barely aware of the dog settling between him and Jak before he drifted away.

It didn't take long for Mandy to be the only conscious one left. Sighing in exasperation, she settled against a tree and stared at the slumbering trio. The dog lay against Jak's head and rested her own against her paws. She wondered what it felt like to have a friend like that. Then she looked at Thad's sleeping form and wondered if she did. Her face grew warm and she decided to close her eyes for only a moment ...

Jak woke up with a big brown snout licking his face. Blinking, he rolled over and sat up with a groan that ended in a moan. "Wh-where am I?" he muttered sluggishly. He was on a slight incline in the middle of the woods and everything hurt. Cuts and bruises burned and ached all over his body.

Thad sat next to him and immediately put a finger to his lips. "Don't worry," he whispered. "We're safe now." He pointed up where just over their head Mandy slept against the roots of a thick oak tree. Hurriedly, as Jak petted the dog, Thad told him what had happened. This proved to be a mistake because as soon as he mentioned the four-wheeler crash Jak sprang to his feet, startling the dog so she barked sharply.

"I missed that?" he cried.

"You're just lucky it missed you," Thad said sourly. "Now keep it down!"

It was too late. Mandy blinked at them and shook her head. "About time you two woke up," she said. "I've been sitting here guarding you two sleepyheads."

Thad snorted. He made to say something smart when he noticed Jak looking slightly sick and bent over in pain from his sudden movement. That's when he remembered his own hurts. Groaning, he fished out the first aid kit again.

"Okay, Jak," he said, "you know the routine."

Jak rolled his eyes but nodded glumly. Under his shirt, along with many other scratches and cuts, he revealed a long, dark, ugly bruise forming across his ribs just next to the gouge he'd gotten the day before. Thad winced when seeing it and remembered how he shoved the boy into the fence.

"Could be worse," Thad said.

Jak grunted. He didn't mention the sore spot on the back of his thigh.

By the time Thad finished bandaging Jak's and his own wounds, the kit had nothing left. "It's that kind of day," he muttered hoarsely.

Jak only sighed in relief when stuffing the empty pouch in his pocket. "No matter what happens," he said with feeling, "you can never stick another thing on me again."

"Then don't do anything stupid," Thad said shortly, glaring at him.

After resting for a few more moments, the trio of lost kids forced themselves to their feet and tried to figure out which way to go. The trees suddenly all looked the same.

The brown mutt proved to be the savior again. As Thad and Mandy started to argue over which direction to take, the large dog barked sharply. Immediately a chorus of barks answered and a pack of four dogs appeared in the distance. The leader of the dogs started for them and Jak of course followed.

"Hey!" Mandy called. "Where are you going? Come back!"

"She's showing us where to go!" Jak shot over his shoulder. He limped slightly and clearly had a host of hurts but put all that behind him as he rushed to keep up with the dog. Mandy and Thad, holding the cardboard box, had no choice but to follow.

Amazingly, the dog did seem to be leading them somewhere. After greeting the four dogs, she headed into the woods. With Jak at her side, she went up and down ravines, crossed a narrow stream, and passed several deer trails. The other dogs trailed at a distance and never strayed too close. Thad had no clue where they were headed, but he decided to trust the dog. That was one thing he'd learned that day. You couldn't truly trust a person, or animal, until you saw how he or she reacted in times of trouble. And at his side he knew he could trust Mandy ... mostly.

After about fifteen minutes of walking, Mandy gasped. "I recognize this place! I know where we are."

"You said that twice already," Thad told her.

She glared. "This time I mean it!"

Jak half ran, half limped back to them with the brown mutt close at his heels. "Thad," he hissed excitedly. "I heard voices!"

"Oh, great," groaned Thad. "Here we go again!"

"Just get behind a tree!" Mandy hissed, tugging at his sleeve. She nodded at Jak. "You too, man!"

Chapter 28

"**A**re we there yet?" whined Danny's voice. "We've been walking, like, for days!"

"Does this look like you're home?" replied Derek's voice snidely. "I mean, really? Do you live in trees now?"

"Settle down, guys." Sounding tired, Billy Boston trudged into view with four backpacks and a tent bag drooped on his back. Derek and Danny trooped close behind. "You guys fight more than opposing linebackers."

Barking loudly, the brown mutt stepped from behind a tree and wagged her tail. She stood on a deer path several feet above them.

"Whoa!" hissed Billy. He held up a hand. Derek and Danny both froze in their tracks and huddled close together. "Just back up slowly," Billy told them. "Don't show her any fear."

"Too late," Danny squeaked.

Thad cradled the box in his lap as he kept out of sight behind a tree near the dog. He couldn't help but smile. Taking a breath, he deepened his voice and called out. "Who goes there?"

Billy gave a start. "Did that dog just talk to me?"

Danny and Derek stared at each other, both wearing faces of horror.

The dog barked again.

"Yes, now bring me food!" Thad said, but his voice broke into fits of laughter.

Derek suddenly yelled. "Man! Thad, is that you!"

Sinking to the ground, Danny took a huge deep breath. "I almost lost it!" he said. "I mean, I nearly wet my pants. Get out here, you idiot!"

Billy wiped his brow when seeing Thad, grinning, come out from behind the tree.

"Man, you dudes are enough to kill a quarterback," he said seriously. "Who else is with you?" Seeing Jak and Mandy appear, he shook his head. "I'll never be afraid of the dark again … just afraid of kids."

Derek ran at Thad and pretended to punch him. "Where were you guys? We've been wandering all over!"

"Us too!" Thad told him. "Mandy and the dog found us. What happened to you?"

Danny followed after Derek wearily and shook his head. "You wouldn't believe it."

The party gathered together and took a break to eat chocolate and granola bars and drink the rest of the water. The brown mutt settled with the other dogs and only went forward close enough to snatch a chunk of granola thrown by Jak.

First Thad and Mandy told their story. Billy shook his head throughout and interrupted many times with questions of "Are you kidding me?" and "You're not serious, man?"

Finally, when the story ended he rubbed the back of his head. "I know I need to thank y'all, but man, y'all are crazy!"

"Come on, Billy," Derek said, biting off a big chunk of granola. "You saved us, man!"

"Yeah," Danny said with a slight smile. "Now that's crazy." He paused to guzzle water from Jak's extra bottle. Then he said to Thad, "We were running last night, and—"

"You mean I was running," Derek interrupted. "I found you back at the camp hiding behind our backpacks!"

"What?" said Danny in a pained voice. "I thought that's where we were supposed to meet! Besides, you were almost crying when you came. All you cared about was your stupid tent."

"Yeah, well, it's my dad's tent. If I lose it, he'll kill me." Derek grunted. "So, uh, thanks for holding it." Derek grinned. "I found Danny hugging it like a teddy bear."

"I meant to throw it if one of those guys attacked," Danny said hotly.

"Just tell the story," Thad pleaded.

"We are." Derek took another bite. "So I find this guy hiding—"

"Waiting, you mean," muttered Danny.

Derek continued. "When all of a sudden Ed comes crashing through, waving a flashlight and yelling he was going to kill us. We ran, but he just about reached us when Billy jumped from nowhere and smashed into Ed."

Danny nodded furiously. "Took him right to the ground—it was awesome."

Derek stared at Danny with scorn. "What do you know? You were crying so bad you didn't see anything! But he did wallop him hard. Ed could barely run away after that. I think he's still in last week."

Sitting with his back against a tree, Billy took a drink from Derek's water bottle and smiled. "Yeah, well, I've hit Ed harder on the field."

"Then you told us not to worry, you'd stay with us," Danny said.

"He told me that," Derek said. "You were still running. I had to call you back."

"How come you did that?" Danny asked Billy, ignoring Derek's latest jab. "I mean, you didn't have to help. You even stood guard when we slept."

Billy snorted. "Let's see, I just about made the dumbest mistake in my life, when out of nowhere you little dudes pop up and nearly scared the living, uh, stuff out of me. You guys saved me, man. Anyway, once I saw it was just dumb kids taking down those losers, I couldn't be afraid of the dark. You guys risked a lot going in there." He looked down as if ashamed. "You guys did it for me, too. So when they started hunting you down, I knew what I had to do. I promise every single one of you, right now." Now his gaze went up and to each one of the kids before settling on Thad last. "I ain't never going to take no junk to get to the pros. Even if I fail, I'll at least have my respect."

"We know, Billy," Derek said.

"Good." He nodded at Thad. "Keep that box away from me, 'cause it already caused enough trouble."

Revived, the group gathered up the trash and got ready to keep moving.

"Do you guys know where you're going?" Billy asked Thad as he hefted all the packs and tent on his back. "We're lost."

"I told you," Danny said to Derek.

"Shut up!" Derek snarled back. "We're just taking the long way back.

"Actually, we've been following the dog," Thad confessed. He shrugged. "It's been working so far."

Billy threw back his head. "Ah, great. I'll follow from a distance. Tell her to lead on." While his fear of the dark was conquered, he still had some ways to go with his fear of large, hairy animals.

Woofing, the brown mutt traveled obediently to the front with Jak firmly at her side.

They'd been walking for about twenty more minutes when Thad started feeling as if he knew the place.

"Hey, guys! I think we're near the pond!"

"Better yet," Mandy said, "the tour road is just up ahead. We can get to my house easy from here."

"Let's," gasped Danny, "just make the road."

"Suits me," Billy said, mopping his brow. "This is worse than two-a-day practices."

Just over the next hill, they looked down and finally truly relaxed. As Mandy predicted, the tour road lay below them.

Derek suddenly called out. "Wait, what's that car doing parked there?"

From that point, Jak all at once broke into a limping sprint. "Daddy!" he cried.

The others rushed to keep up.

Barking, the brown mutt stopped near the edge and watched them go.

Thad broke free from the woods to see Jak run full speed into the arms of Mr. Tranner.

"Jakavos! I can't believe it!" cried Mr. Tranner. Tears glistened in his eyes as the large man swept up his son, holding him tight.

Jak hugged his neck fiercely. Then he leaned back, smiling. "How did you find us?"

"I want to know the same thing, buddy boy." He lightly slapped the seat of Jak's pants. "I've been searching for you since last night! Your sisters were about to start World War III when I left. Finally, I called Father Alexander early this morning and he told me not to worry. Just to show up at this spot in the afternoon and wait. I've been waiting since ten this morning!" He hugged and pulled Jak close again. "Some priest we got, huh? A real miracle!"

Thad coughed. He decided not to say that when Father Alexander had given him a blessing for the trip he'd asked specifically where they would be headed. Too afraid to mislead a priest, Thad had ended up telling everything, including crossing the tour road.

The others stood by Thad and watched sheepishly, suddenly a little afraid of what Mr. Tranner might say to them.

Looking at them, Mr. Tranner cleared his throat. He balanced Jak on his side and stared down the line until finding Thad.

"Well, I'm glad I found you," he said finally. "Do you all realize how worried your parents are?"

Before anybody could reply a loud voice called out. "Hey! You kids! Billy! I found you!"

Rounding a bend on the tour road, the large coach appeared at a staggering run. He looked as if he'd been up all night and sweat soaked his clothes.

"I got you, you little mag—" Seeing Mr. Tranner, he stumbled to a stop. "J-John, what are you doing here?"

"Getting these children to their parents," Mr. Tranner answered mildly. "What are you doing, Coach Marshall? And why is Billy Boston here?"

Coach Marshall's eyes bugged. Then he saw the crumpled box in Thad's hands. Gulping twice, he struggled to clear his throat. "I-I—"

"He tried to steal Billy," Jak said. "And he tried to kill some dogs!"

Mr. Tranner looked at his son and then at Coach Marshall. "What's this?"

Now the coach looked ready to cry. "I-I can explain—I, I—these children were trespassing on government land!"

"So were you!" Mandy cried. "You nearly got us all killed!"

"What's this, Coach?" Mr. Tranner no longer looked gentle. His eyes burned.

Letting off a squeal and grunt at the same time, Coach Marshall turned and started running back. "Charlie!" he yelled. "Get the car!"

Mr. Tranner lifted his eyebrows. "Okay … Somebody better start explaining."

Everyone started talking at once, except for Jak. Sliding down from his father, he ran past the mass confusion and to the forest.

By this time, Mr. Tranner had backed up to his car and put up both hands in surrender. Billy, Thad, Danny, Derek, and Mandy pressed near him trying to explain everything at once.

Kneeling at the edge of the woods, Jak held out his hand. "Okay, girl! Come out here!"

The brown mutt stepped daintily down from the brush and sniffed the hand. The mutt leaned against the boy. After having her ears scratched, she licked his chin. Whining, she woofed quietly and looked behind her. Four other dogs sat still, waiting.

Jak scratched her head. "It's okay … get back to your family. I'll go back to mine, too."

Wagging her tail, the dog gave his hand a final lick and went to be wild.

Chapter 29

It took a while, but finally some semblance of order was restored. Mr. Tranner took Billy into his car to have a long talk. In the meantime, he gave his cell phone to be passed around for the boys to call their homes. Thad meekly returned the borrowed phone, complete with a dead battery.

Calling home was not easy. Apparently, during the storm, Mr. Tranner had called Derek's house to check on the boys. He'd nearly panicked when Derek's mom answered and had no idea about any camping trip. Calling around only served to upset the other parents. Donald had stayed with his aunt and his parents were so busy packing that they'd never answered their phones. Thad's late text had arrived, so the police were never called. However, the parents were all very worried, especially when their sons never returned in the morning.

Thad's mother answered when he'd called and she nearly sobbed with relief. His father was now on his way and he was to wait without moving a muscle. Or else.

After his talk with Billy, before the first parents arrived, Mr. Tranner walked from the car scratching his jaw. He looked very serious.

"Boys, and, uh, Mandy, I can't say I approve of your methods … but thank you." He sighed. "I just wish we could get those men who are responsible for everything that happened."

Thad spoke up. "Just check the local hospital for two men with dog bites. One of them is pretty badly banged up from a crash." Sure, one was called a doctor, but Thad knew he wasn't any medical doctor. A medical doctor only helped people. They didn't try to kill kids and pump athletes with drugs.

"Okay," Mr. Tranner said slowly, "maybe I will." His gaze slid to his son and then he blinked. "Eh, Jak, when did you start playing softball?"

Unfortunately, no arrests were ever made. True, two men were found in an emergency room with multiple dog bites and deep scratches, including a Mr. Freeman, but little evidence existed of any wrongdoing. Coach Marshall had a few friends in the Park Service—one, a father of a football player. By the end of that day, no dart guns were found and the remains of any wreck had vanished. All that remained was a gouge in the middle of a split-rail fence. Also the shed back in the woods was totally demolished as part of park maintenance. And for the great, terrible box so many people had risked so much for? It contained a pile of old CDs bought off eBay. Dr. Sandy Shelk had brought the wrong box from his home. Mistakes do happen.

All that Mr. Tranner had left for evidence were testimonies given by the kids and Billy, who would have to admit to trespassing and being part of a steroid plot. Worse, already one judge called him to say he had no case. Too many good old boys in the county supported Coach Marshall—he'd been one of the most successful coaches in the history of the school.

This did not stop Mr. Tranner from writing two letters of resignation that night—one for Coach Marshall and one for Mr. Freeman. Hopefully they would sign. Unfortunately, Dr. Shelk remained free and Coach Marshall could always go somewhere else. Justice sometimes had a hard time being served.

Early the next morning, Thad took his bike and pedaled hard to Jak's house. The smaller boy, though slightly battered and bruised, happily snuck out his side window to join Thad. Apparently he was grounded and the front door was alarmed while his parents slept. He wore black soccer shorts and a blue football jersey as he hopped down on top of a clump of flowers. Thad didn't ask about the "Little Ponies" softball shirt. He suspected it hadn't survived the night. The boys silently moved to the front of the house.

As Thad patiently waited for Jak to get his bike, he happened to glance up only to see a face staring down at him from a top-story window.

Immediately his body froze. Then suddenly his face burned. Michelle, Jak's sister, lifted a hand and waved. Even in the early morning, Thad could see her grinning widely.

Smiling sheepishly, he lifted his own hand and made a shy wave in return. Next school year they would be attending the same school ...

"What are you doing?" hissed Jak, wheeling his bike from the side of the garage.

Thad hastily climbed on his bike. "Nothing," he mumbled.

Michelle, he was sure, was laughing.

Not long after, Jak and Thad coasted their bikes to the road and started pedaling furiously. They had a lot to do before they got in trouble again. The two raced neck and neck to Derek's house. The sun had just finished dawn's early light as they arrived in time for the first meeting of the Pond Scum Gang.

They walked their bikes to the back and added them to the pile already there. Then they followed the voices to the shed.

In Derek's shed, they found Donald, Derek, and Mandy already sitting around the table eating donuts. Danny, as usual, was late.

"Sorry, guys," he gushed, finally showing up minutes later.

"About time you showed up," Derek said. "Let me guess— you stopped to go swimming?"

"No, I tried pumping up my bike's tire and accidentally let the air out." His voice fell. "I had to take my sister's bike."

"Good job, idiot," Derek said without much malice.

Thad grinned as he reached for his second glazed donut. The day before, while driving home from being picked up, his father told him not to be too hard on Derek. After Mr. Tranner's phone call, Thad's father had driven to Derek's home. He'd found Derek's mom drunk and in no condition to do much of anything. After some phone calls he'd arranged it so Derek's aunt would stay at the house until his father returned. In the meantime, his mom would be getting help. It didn't hurt that Billy proclaimed Derek a hero. While the news could never be public, his brothers knew the particulars and promptly gave him the back shed to use as he wished. The first rule Derek made: no locks allowed.

"Let's just get this meeting started," Donald pleaded. "Since it's my first and last meeting I want it to go smoothly. Besides, guys, I'm leaving tomorrow."

"Hold on," Thad said, putting down his donut. "You might be leaving tomorrow, but this isn't your last meeting. We'll include you somehow."

"Yeah," Danny said, grabbing a cream-filled donut. "After all, you're the one who showed us the trail to the pond scum in the first place!"

"Sure," Donald said dryly. "Blame it all on me. I thought you guys would be searching for an old house, not saving quarterbacks and fighting criminals." He grinned. "But I'll definitely miss the excitement in California; just not the bugs."

"Why call it the Pond Scum Gang?" Mandy wondered. Everybody looked at her.

The day before, she'd been dropped off at her house by Mr. Tranner. But, true to his word, after much begging and pleading, Thad had convinced his parents to drive him to her house that evening. He'd just gotten the call from Derek about the morning's meeting. Mandy and Mrs. Purcell had been shocked to see him at the door. They were doubly shocked when he formally invited Mandy to the inaugural meeting of the new club. It had been first suggested by Derek.

Thad finally shrugged at her. "Derek named it."

"Who made him the boss?" Danny wanted to know.

"Hey," Derek reminded them hotly, "it's my shed we're in and you're eating my donuts! Of course I'm in charge!"

"No way!" Danny said.

"Then give me back my donut!" Derek ordered.

"You want it? Come and take it!" Danny stuffed the rest of his pastry in his mouth.

Mandy threw up her hands. "Guys, can't y'all just answer my question?"

Jak put his head down on his arms and closed his eyes. He started to snore softly behind a half-eaten donut. Only so much excitement could fill a small kid.

Tomorrow most of them would start a long period of grounding—they'd only been allowed this day free to say goodbye to Donald. They would spend it well.

Just then one of Derek's older brothers yelled angrily from outside the shed. "Mr. Tranner just called and woke us up! He's looking for his son and will call the cops if nobody finds him, pronto!"

Donald and Thad looked across the table at each other and grinned. Some things never changed.

And the summer had only just begun.

THE END

About the Author

Gregory Saur is the author of several novels for young readers, including *Panterror! The Epic Babysitting Adventures of Rachel Pugsley* and *Royal Pains and Angels in the Outhouse*. Born in Virginia, he continues to live there and explore new worlds. When not writing or reading, he enjoys being outside. This is how he discovered the pond scum back in the woods that led to this story.

www.ingramcontent.com/pod-product-compliance
Lightning Source LLC
Chambersburg PA
CBHW050351190726
48284CB00007BB/2235